Robertina

A Portrait of Courage and Hope

Bo HARRIS

Copyright © Bo Harris 2023

Bo Harris has asserted her right under the Copyright, Designs and Patents Act 1988 to be identified as the author of this work.

All rights reserved. No part of this publication may be reproduced, stored in a retrieval system or transmitted in any form or by any means without prior permission of the author.

Revised November 2024

ISBN 9798859380725

	Contents	**Page**
Part One	A Child is Born, Caithness Scotland	11
Part Two	Life in the Orkney Isles	39
Part Three	Journey to the New World	67
Part Four	A New Beginning in Dunedin, New Zealand	109
Part Five	Settlers in Moonlight, Otago	155
Part Six	Jane Harcus Finds Love	189
Explanatory Notes		215
Acknowledgements		219

For my mother, Jean Law.
She was the best story teller I have known.

Introduction

As a child in New Zealand, I used to gaze at a portrait on my bedroom wall of a woman with a lovely face and dark haunting eyes. I always wanted to learn more about her. Discovering the story of Robertina, who was my Great Grandmother, was inspired by her picture.

Whilst I have used as many facts and dates as I could ascertain, some details and descriptions in the 19th century timeframe of the book are a work of my imagination. Please accept apologies if any characters have been misrepresented or you have further information to share about them.

Bo Harris Great Grandmother* Line of Descent
b. born, GM Grandmother, GF Grandfather

22 January 1841 Dunnet, Caithness, Scotland
Margaret Sutherland - 3x Grandmother married David Stephen (b. Caithness)

27 January 1843 Greenland, Caithness, Scotland
Margaret Stephen born - 2x Grandmother
Siblings Ann, Elizabeth, George *tbc*

6 May 1868 Caithness, Scotland
Margaret Stephen 2x GM gave birth to an illegitimate daughter - Great GM*

29 October 1868 Caithness, Scotland
Margaret Stephen - 2x Grandmother married Robert Harcus (b. Orkney Isles)
Siblings born Eday, Orkney: Ann, William, Robert
Siblings born NZ: John, David, Margaret, Mary, James

7 September 1885 Palmerston, New Zealand
Jane Reid Harcus - Great GM* married Frederick Davis (b. Finmere, England)

18 September 1895 Macraes Flat, Otago, New Zealand
Margaret Harcus Davis born – Grandmother
Siblings: Frederick, Robert, George, Thomas

23 April 1919 Oamaru, New Zealand
Margaret Harcus Davis - GM married James McBeath GF (b. Herbert, NZ)

2 April 1929 Dunedin, New Zealand
Jean McBeath born – Mother
Siblings Margaret, Thomas Lennox

8 March 1952 Dunedin, New Zealand
Jean McBeath – Mother married Thomas Knox Law (b. Dunedin, NZ)

25 September 1956 Dunedin, New Zealand
(Bo HARRIS) **Sharon Margaret Law born – Daughter** *Married John Harris 1997, UK*
Sibling Maxwell James
Further information can be found at www.rootsroutes.com

Part One

1.

A Child is Born, Caithness Scotland

*Know now a county bleak and bare
With blooming heather
Cheerless and cold it looks, yet fair
To us. Together have we explored it
And how rare is Caithness*
Alexander Miller

Parish of Olrig

May 1868

Margaret longed to be near the crumbled remains of the watchtower on Olrig Hill when she felt troubled. She always found comfort in this elevated spot, as the Gaelic name for Caithness, *Gallaibh*, means 'among the strangers' and she sensed this here. It was liberating and she could dream of ways to escape the land which had brought her only sorrow and despair.

She had spent all her life in this cold, damp, climate in the far north east of Scotland. The county was mainly flat farmland and moorland but possessed ancient treasures including Viking graves, Pictish stones, ruined forts and medieval castles which reminded her of earlier dwellers, such as the Celts, Picts and Norse. She lived about three miles to the east of the watchtower in the Parish of Olrig; named after the *son of Erick*, a Norwegian chieftain, who settled there after invading the northern coast in the ninth Century.

In older times, the watchtower on Olrig Hill, the highest point in the Parish, provided advance warning of invaders due to the dramatic views of the coastlines. On a clear day, Margaret could see the bays of Thurso and Dunnet and the Dunnet Head lighthouse which stands on a rocky precipice overlooking the sea. Today, beyond the hazardous waters of the Pentland Firth, which divides Caithness from the Orkney Isles, she could just make out some of these tiny islands, the closest only ten miles away from the coast. Her thoughts lingered in that direction for a moment as she recalled her encounter with Robert Harcus, a fisherman from the island of Eday, who had come to Caithness for the herring the previous summer.

Margaret's waist had expanded so much since they met that it was difficult moving quickly these days. Her father practically disowned her when he finally noticed the thickening of her girth under her apron. She was probably six months gone by then and had only noticed herself after three months as she had few symptoms of pregnancy apart from a slight gain in weight.

She was well aware however, that she had disgraced her family and soon her child would come as a reminder of her wrongdoing. Of course, there had been no punishment for her blunder, but she tortured herself daily for her mistake and often cried herself to sleep at night. The last woman to be publicly hanged in Scotland was in April 1862 and she often thought to herself what a quick release from suffering this must have been. Now, as each day passed and her confinement to the farmhouse, on the borders of Olrig, Bower and Dunnet parishes crept closer, she was becoming more terrified about giving birth and her future prospects as an unmarried woman.

But this afternoon, she had left her domestic drudgery at the Castletown Inn earlier than anticipated and had taken herself off for her favourite walk on the way home to Tain as she craved more time alone. She had had to find domestic servant work after she left school, many years ago, to help with payment of her father's land rental. It was always such a struggle to pay the annual amount in order to keep the land and their farmhouse. But at least she wasn't toiling in the dusty, dry quarry of Mr Traill, removing the slate for paving like some of the young lads were forced to do after they left school.

Margaret felt overburdened however due to her many responsibilities. She had become acting surrogate mother to her younger sisters, a house maid to all at home and was needed for the harvest and other daily chores on the farm. It was a hard life for a young woman and no wonder her hands were as rough as sandpaper and she was exhausted most of the time.

Before she left Tain on this May morning, Margaret had mentioned to her father and sisters that she would be home later than usual in the afternoon due to an important visiting party to the Inn from the House of Rattar. They nodded and told her to be careful as she scurried away from the farmhouse. She was secretly overjoyed, as she knew that the visitors had cancelled their trip due to an outbreak of tuberculosis in their household, so it was a rare opportunity to use the extra time to do something she loved. She decided to finish work at her usual time and return home a few hours later.

It was late spring and Margaret noticed how the freshly blooming flowers and heather added so much more colour to the normally dull landscape which made her unconsciously begin to smile and her eyes glisten as she walked away from the Castletown Inn towards Olrig Hill. She spotted the blue heart shaped leaves of the common dog-violet which abounded and was engulfed by the beauty of the tiny Scottish primrose. The sun was visible, she could still feel its warmth but it was beginning to edge closer to the horizon and shadows were becoming longer. The hour was much later than she had realised but she felt at ease and tossed back her hair to let the breeze softly caress it.

Once passed the grand Olrig House owned by the Sinclairs, Margaret began to slowly climb the path to the watchtower on Olrig Hill. Due to the extra weight she was carrying and a persistent headwind that had sprung up, it took all her strength to climb the last steep portion and she arrived at the top breathless. An eerie chill had also descended but Margaret hardly noticed and gazed out to sea at her favourite view.

She continued to dream of finding a way to leave this land to start a new life when a sudden stabbing pain in her lower abdomen made her nearly keel over. She cried out like a frightened animal and thought she was going to die, but after what seemed two minutes holding her breath, she gasped and refilled her lungs with fresh air which helped to ease the pain. Her feet were also strangely wet but she could see that the ground around her was still dry and wondered if the mystical Pictish gods were playing tricks on her?

Her mind was immediately thrown back a generation to her mother, who died giving birth when Margaret was only seven years old. The child was stillborn due to a terrible prolonged labour and her mother, exhausted and in shock, died hours later. The midwife who arrived at the very end of her labour, said that perhaps the baby was the wrong way round and that her mother must have had an infection of her womb to have died so quickly. Even now she can remember the disbelief, and tears still filled her eyes every time she thought of her mother's suffering and the fact that no one could help her.

She recalled her mother's screams of agony but when she was finally allowed to see her, she lay silent and very still on the bed, her face white like porcelain and her eyes staring at the ceiling as though she had seen a ghost up there. She had loved her with every bone in her little body and when her father said they were going to take her away, she went to a vase in the bedroom full of Caithness flowers and placed two of the prettiest stems in her mother's hands that lay crossed on her chest.

"Never forget me mother," she said. "I will always remember and love you."

Tears had slowly tumbled down her pink cheeks onto the sheet as she watched the men carry her mother's body away. There were no words to describe her sense of abandonment and loss and this pain had remained with her. Margaret could not help but think it may be her turn to be carried away this very day.

Margaret was the eldest daughter, now 23 years old, and had been born in Dunnet, Caithness, close to where she now lived. She had two younger sisters, Ann and Elizabeth also born in Dunnet: Elizabeth was only eighteen months old when their mother died. No one was allowed to speak of their brother, it was too sad. Her father's sister came to live with them for a while after their mother's death, as she was 50 years old and unmarried, but it was never the same as the three girls desperately missed the love and kindness of their mother.

Margaret's family had always lived in Caithness as far as she knew. Her mother, Margaret Sutherland and father, David Stephen, were born in Dunnet and were married in the Dunnet Free Church of Scotland in 1841. Her father never travelled far and lived in Greenland, Dunnet before moving to Tain, in the Parish of Olrig after he married. He was a lucky man to have married her mother who was the kindest person you could ever meet.

David was an agricultural labourer before he married in 1841 but was now a tenant farmer and worked tirelessly tending the fields and animals on his 20-acre croft in the district of Tain. The land belonged to George Traill, Esq. of Rattar, to whom he paid an annual rent in the region of £5 5s. The Traill's were a notable family in Caithness and David considered himself fortunate but it took every ounce of energy he had to keep the farmhouse and land and make enough surplus money to pay the rental.

David was a good farmer and a strict father to his three daughters. He made the girls work hard at home, particularly in the summer, when there was no school due to the herring season. His daughters sensed he had changed since their mother died as he was no fun anymore, rarely smiled and they dreaded his temper if something went wrong. They would have to run and hide and pretend to be feeding the chickens or gathering wood for the fire. Their childhood was not like that of other children their age who had a mother and a father as they were so busy looking after themselves as best they could and doing chores. A rare treat was to be taken to the county fairs in Olrig or Bower three times a year if they were lucky so their father could inspect the animals and occasionally buy a new horse or cow.

For their entertainment, he insisted on telling them scary stories about Caithness and the Norsemen who came many centuries before to occupy their county. He loved warfare and would recall the famous battle of Mort Hill, the 'field of death' and how the native Scots were victorious over the Danes. It was as though he had actually been there fighting and had driven the invaders back himself! The Scots 'cleared the den' and destroyed the invaders near Murkle Bay and the place to this day, is still called Clairden. Murkle is a small settlement on the western boundary of Olrig and was originally known as Mort Hill. A story Margaret really liked was about St Coomb's church which was situated on the border of Olrig and Dunnet parishes. On a very dark, stormy night, the church and adjoining manse were suddenly overwhelmed by wind and sand and became invisible. No trace of any structures could ever be found, just sand dunes. This area is now called the Links of Old Tain and everyone is very cautious walking there in case they are made to vanish in the masses of sand. Margaret often thought as the size of her belly grew that, if only she could vanish and live somewhere far away from Tain, she might find happiness.

As their father liked ancient history and legends, sometimes he allowed his daughters to go for walks in the countryside with him. His favourite walk was to the monolith Stone Ludd on Lord Caithness's property in Bower Parish. It stands tall at nearly ten feet high and is supposed to be a memorial of another battle fought and gained by the Scots but some legends say it is the gravestone of Ljot Thorfinnsson, a 10th century earl of Orkney. Occasionally he also took them to the Druidic circles and tumuli in Bower and they would play hide and seek at the cairn of Heather Cow as it is surrounded by circles of large stones. It was very easy to make their father angry however as one of the girls would always go missing for far too long.

David did not want his family to forget Caithness history as he was proud of the land he lived in and also proud of his small farm and the acres he rented. The soil in Tain was adequate for cultivation but in certain areas it was heavy clay and the chief crops tended to be oats, beans, turnips and potatoes. He usually managed to grow enough produce to sell at the markets and keep enough back for them to survive on. Sometimes the girls were short of their daily mutchin of milk but they seemed healthy enough to him. Leicester sheep also thrived here but he could not afford a flock as yet but hoped to acquire some in the future if he could increase his yields. In the summer months before harvest he would also lend his hand at herring or salmon fishing as the extra money meant he could put some of the meagre income towards his annual rental to Mr Traill and also put aside more food for the winter months. Many small farmers were also fisherman to supplement their incomes.

An Illegitimate Birth

By now, from Olrig Hill, Margaret could see that the weather and the light were changing rapidly. The strong southerly wind started swirling around her and she was forced to sink to the ground by the crumbling wall of the watchtower unable to breathe; the pain was like no other she had ever experienced and she felt the mass in her belly stirring and kicking. She had no water and only a thin cape with a hood which she pulled up over her head. How will anyone ever find me here she moaned. "Please God, help me …" Another wave of pain overcame her and she nearly passed out but it eased off again long enough for her to sit up against the stone wall. She cried out but the wind took her words and she was left alone and distraught. "I am not ready to die, mother, please send me an angel or someone who can help me …" Margaret lay sprawled on the grass for what seemed hours; it was dark but the night was clear and the large moon shone light on the watchtower. She had tried to get up and walk but the pain was too great and her legs could not carry her, so she slid down the wall again on to the ground.

She was fighting the urge to push this unwanted mass in her belly out and screamed in agony.

Although Margaret was the eldest daughter and could take care of herself, her father David had become worried that she had not returned home that evening and was contemplating what to do next. Her sisters were also milling around the farm house unable to think clearly and trying not to imagine the worst, such as that Margaret had been abducted. It was a long walk home and now very late and dark. David, their father, suddenly announced he was going out to look for her. He grabbed an oil lamp and extra blanket and went out to the barn to rig up the old horse and wagon.

He headed for the Inn in Castletown where Margaret worked and quickly established that she had left hours before and had not worked late at all that night. His anger grew but he sensed danger and tried to plan what his next move should be. He was about to set off but went back inside to find Isobella, a bar maid Margaret sometimes spoke of, to see if she knew where his daughter may have gone. After many questions, she admitted Margaret may have taken the long route home as she wanted to see her 'favourite view'. David tried to think; she loved Murkle Bay but that wasn't on the way home. She also loved to watch for Risso's dolphins, porpoises and grey seals from the North Sea come in to Dunnet Bay to feed and play but that was too far away in the other direction. The only other place that sprang to mind was Olrig Hill, so he set off towards it.

The time must have been around 1.30 a.m. on the 5th of May, but he had to try and search for her as he would never be able to forgive himself if something tragic had happened.

He reached the path at the bottom of the hill and tethered the horse there as he would be quicker on foot in the moonlight. There had been no sign of anyone since the outskirts of Castletown, just an occasional drunk who had lost his way home.

He continued on the path towards the watchtower and wondered whether Margaret could be there. As he trudged on he hoped she hadn't fallen and broken a leg or injured herself in some way. Then suddenly he heard a horrible scream. It sounded like a wounded animal caught in a trap and he tentatively walked in the direction of the scream. A few seconds later, when he reached the top of the hill and could make out the watchtower, he thought he heard another cry this time sounding more like that of a child. As he approached he saw something move, covered in a green cape with a hood, by the wall at the base of the tower. He stumbled closer and saw it was a woman and there by her feet on the grass, was a bairn, whimpering. The woman turned her head towards him and to his horror he saw it was Margaret - his Margaret. His heart nearly stopped beating.

Luckily adrenalin soon kicked in and as he could see that the child was newly born, he had to try and cut the cord. He had experience of helping cows and horses give birth but the task ahead filled him with fear. Instinctively he reached into his pockets and found some twine which he often carried then pulled out his knife from the sheath anchored to his belt. It wasn't particularly clean so he wiped it on the damp grass and then dried it on his trousers. Carefully by the light of the moon and his oil lamp he tied the umbilical cord first, then cut it. He could see the child was a girl and she had a blue tinge to her lips and fingers due to the cold of the night. He tore a strip from Margaret's apron to clean her face and body as best he could then wrapped her in the blanket he had brought and gave her to Margaret.

"Welcome to this cruel world, my beautiful, unfortunate child," she said with tears rolling down her cheeks. She did not know what their fate would be - the future looked bleak, as her life could never be the same again.

It was still well before dawn and David's oil lamp was burning low. The child desperately needed more warmth otherwise it would not survive, so they had to get moving. He did not like the thought of burying his first granddaughter as his next mission in life. He had no idea what was to become of her and could not allow his daughter to keep this child as an unmarried woman. The shame on him and his family would be intolerable but he would do all he could to keep them both alive.

Margaret lay exhausted but was cringing with pain and discomfort once again. He knelt down beside her on the damp ground and tried to reassure her but he was deeply worried about another frightening situation over which he had no control. But nature was taking its course, and once his daughter delivered the placenta, he left her to rest and she seemed calm and in much less distress. The child was restless however but there was little he could do to help it, so he forced Margaret to cradle her. The first signs of dawn were now appearing and David thought it must have been about 4.30 a.m. The clouds were changing form and the sky had a faint tinge of pink near the horizon. He could hear the shrill sound of a blackbird close by and they were startled by the white underbelly and glaring eyes of a barn owl as it slowly ascended with wings arched from the nearby thorny hedge. It was hungry and this would be a last hunt for prey before it would disappear again until night fall.

"It's time to leave," David insisted.

Gently, he placed his hands under Margaret's armpits and, together with all the strength she could summon, she rose to her feet holding the child. It was cold, damp and slippery underfoot and the May mist was swirling far below at the bottom of the hill. It was a terrifying thought for her but she had to get down the path to safety and find warmth for the child. Her father helped her and very slowly they edged their way down the steepest part of the path towards the horse and wagon. But she stumbled and collapsed due to exhaustion half way down. At this point and without hesitation, her father picked her up in his strong arms and carried her and the child the rest of the way. For the first time in her life Margaret was overwhelmed by love and gratitude toward him. She knew that without his help, she and her new born daughter may not have survived. Although she didn't want this illegitimate child, she owed him everything.

The journey home was not easy; every rock and bump they went over rattled her bones and caused pain but the thought of returning to the heat of the fire in the farmhouse kept her going. Her sisters would also be frantic not knowing what had become of her. It was getting lighter by the minute and soon, to her relief, she could just make out the outline of the farm house in Tain.

Her father carried her off the wagon and into the farm house. Her sisters stood quivering, their mouths wide open when they saw she was holding a baby. They were like bees round a honey pot. Ann went and got blankets and hot water, Elizabeth cleared out a drawer from the smallest kitchen dresser and placed some bedding in it so the child had somewhere to sleep. They fetched tea and bread for Margaret and David. They also said Margaret must try and feed the child with her breast milk and although Margaret was very reluctant, her first attempts seemed successful and the child was soothed and fell asleep near the fire. However the child still had tinges of blue around its lips and David thought it may have caught a chill as they were outside for so long during the night. He would probably have to get the local doctor to call in and see if there would be any lasting, detrimental effects but, when he thought about the expense of such a visit, he decided to wait until after he had had some sleep before sending a message.

David also needed to discuss with Margaret *who* the father was and would do this when he could think straight. The stress of the last few hours was hard to deal with and David never wanted to experience this feeling again as it brought back memories of the tragic night he lost his wife.

Later that day, the doctor was summoned and he was able to call at the Tain farm house before nightfall. He gave a positive report after his examination of mother and child which was a welcome relief to all. But as soon as the doctor departed, David came in to speak to Margaret about the father of his bastard granddaughter. With reluctance, Margaret admitted that she had met the dashing Robert Harcus, an Orkney fisherman from the island of Eday she thought, in Wick during the herring season late the previous summer.

Her father had asked her to accompany him to Wick for the herring season and she had been loath to go and work in this stinking, smelly industry. She had heard about the conditions in Wick during the herring season and had read the account given by Robert Louis Stevenson in the *John O'Groat Journal*. He had stayed there while his uncle was overseeing construction of the Noss Head Lighthouse. He had said that Wick possessed no beauty due to grey houses, grey shores, grim grey sea and no green trees. The climate was also horrid, it was always breezy and the streets were often full of half-witted, drunk, lazy men as there were too many public houses serving whisky. The quays were crowded with fishermen waiting on wind and tide and those involved with fish-curing could be knee-high in brine, mud, and herring guts. It was no place for the faint-hearted and Margaret did not like the idea of going there.

She knew that migrant workers often lived in primitive, unhygienic accommodation and many were crammed into cellars, garrets, lofts and barns due to the housing shortage in Wick. It was also not uncommon to see suffers of diseases like smallpox and diphtheria and she had also heard of cases of cholera.

But last year, David had desperately needed her income from the herring season to help pay his land rental and as it was only about 15 miles to travel to Wick from Tain, Margaret agreed to accompany him. So while he crewed in the open boats, she and many other women gutted or packed the herring into barrels. It was common practice in the summer for many migrant workers to make extra income in the fishing season before it was time to harvest the crops. Over 900 boats could be in operation and hundreds of barrels of herring were cured with nearly two thirds of the catch exported to Ireland and Scandinavia. The herring season began about the middle of July, first in Thurso, then Wick, the largest market town in Caithness, and lasted until the end of September. Some also fished for cod, ling and lobster afterwards. Caithness men and women would go to Wick or Thurso and fishermen from neighbouring highlands and islands such as the Orkney Isles, often came in five-man boats for the herring to earn extra money while the season lasted. She had met Robert towards the end of the season in September and unfortunately had never seen him again since. He did not know she had been carrying his child.

Their first encounter was when Robert helped her fend off some drunken fishermen who were trying to steal her purse on the street. He took her to safety at a nearby hotel where he helped calm her nerves and they began to learn more about each other. She loved talking with Robert, he was so different from other men she had met and had such a wonderful sense of humour. They arranged to meet again the following day after his boat came in with the herring catch. Margaret thought she could slip away from her work unnoticed as the quays were so crowded and busy with the returning boats and fishermen.

The next day could not arrive soon enough for Margaret and she could hardly contain her excitement of meeting Robert again. She could hear the herring boats coming in from late morning onwards and kept looking out for Robert's tall frame on the quay. Sure enough he finally appeared, smiling and looking straight towards her. He took her hand and they quickly walked away from the outer harbour and headed south from Pulteney town. The views from the cliffs over Wick Bay in this area were much more pleasing than the centre of town and the weather was also fair.

They were enjoying their walk and fresh air and decided to stop and rest along the cliff by a stone wall which had a view of The Cove below. Robert removed his oil skin jacket and untucked his woollen smock shirt as he was now feeling the heat and beckoned Margaret to come and sit down beside him. After their shoulders touched, he could not help himself and began to gently stroke her hair. She felt a powerful attraction and when he leaned closer to kiss her, she made no resistance and returned his kiss without hesitation. It did not take long before her whole body was tingling with intense excitement and although she knew she should have controlled herself, she gave herself to Robert in an unforgettable wave of pleasure.

She had never experienced such feelings and he too admitted how special this moment had been. They straightened their clothing and hastily headed back to town and the quay; Margaret needed to finish her day's work before meeting her father and Robert had to get back to his boat.

They parted on the quay and, to Margaret's dismay, it was a final farewell as Robert told her he had to leave for Orkney the following day. She had felt so alive and happy but was suddenly overcome by sadness as she was unlikely to meet him again.

The local people of Wick thought it a huge relief and were glad to see the back of the visiting fishermen when the time came for them to return home. They watched the boats leave Wick, carried away by the cold southerly wind, however Margaret did not agree, she missed Robert and always wondered about his life in Orkney.

Robert Harcus Receives Unwelcome News

After Margaret's confession, her father gave a huge sigh and scratched his head. He had come to the conclusion there was no point in continuing to be so angry. He gritted his teeth and told her that he planned to send word to Robert Harcus. If he consented to marry her, Margaret could keep her daughter, but if he refused then the child would be sent away for adoption. Margaret sat still and quivered with fear. Her maternal instincts were now so intense that the thought of not being a mother to her daughter was not an option. She swore to herself she would find a way out of this terrifying predicament.

David's first problem was how to contact the fisherman Robert Harcus in Eday. Luckily, there had been a regular ferry service across the Pentland Firth to the Orkney Islands to carry the mail for some time and people were grateful to John Stanger for making this possible. Since 1856, the *Royal Mail* boat which was built locally, left daily from the deepwater harbour in Scrabster, near Thurso for Stromness on mainland Orkney. It was the 'long sea route' but helped reduce delivery times overall as fewer transfers on the rough Orkney roads were needed. Mail could also be quickly off loaded at Stromness to smaller boats for inter-island deliveries. There were other shorter routes to Orkney from the North coast of Caithness and boats set off from Gills Bay and Huna near John O'Groats to South Ronaldsay and Hoy, but they were not as convenient on this occasion. He remembered when Orkney had been acquired from Norway by King James IV of Scotland that the first small ferry to cross the Firth, from Huna to the 'subservient fiefdom of Orkney,' was run by the 15th century Dutchman Jan de Groot.

David then considered how he would get his letter to the *Mail Boat* in Scrabster and opted to post it in Castletown as he was busy on the farm and did not have time to travel any further. The letter would go via Thurso which was further east along the coast and known in those days as the Post Town and a busy port for fishing boats. In Thurso it would be sorted and the mail bags for Orkney sent to the ferry waiting in Scrabster harbour.

So that night he sat down at the table with paper and pen and wrote to Robert Harcus in Eday telling him about the birth of his illegitimate child and asking whether he would be honourable and marry his daughter. He also demanded a response by the end of May at the latest but knew it could take a long time to get mail to the required Orkney island and an equally long time to get a reply, so his timeframe was optimistic to say the least. David made Margaret aware of this deadline which caused her deep concern as she also knew that Robert was a fisherman and could be away from his home for days on end.

As planned, her father arose early the next morning for Castletown to post the letter so it would have a chance to be on the first sailing of the daily *Mail Boat* to Stromness. If it missed the *Mail Boat* sailing, he remembered there were other vessels that now ran a service between Caithness and Orkney so it would be sent on either the *Earl of Caithness* or the *Prince Consort*.

David recalled part of the route the boat would take as he had been to Stromness once on a fishing trip when he was younger. He settled on being a farmer, but most young men needed to learn how to fish to supplement their incomes. He remembered passing the giant red sandstone Old Man of Hoy, on the west coast of the Orkney Island, Hoy, as it was a massive sea stack perched on the eroded cliff edge. Further north on this coast he also recalled spotting the dramatic red and yellow vertical sea cliffs called St John's Head before they crossed Hoy Sound and headed to Stromness on the Orkney mainland. He hoped that one day he would see these wonders again but knew, deep down, he was too busy farming and fishing to spare the time. If Margaret did go to Eday, he would also struggle to find the money to visit her using the long sea route from Scrabster.

He was also aware that all too often, due to the immense strength of its tides, boats large or small could come to grief in the Pentland Firth which had to be crossed between Caithness and Orkney. The powerful force of the tides can give rise to overfalls and tidal races and lead to the formation of huge waves, eddies and other hazardous currents. If there were gale force winds at the same time, the sea could become so violent that boats or ships could be easily blown off course or sunk.

The shorter sea routes from the northern coastline had tidal hazards to overcome around Stroma, the closest Orkney island, and the Pentland Skerries in the Firth, but David thought the letter should be delivered safely as the *Mail Boat* and larger vessels from Scrabster were robust enough to tackle any tidal dangers on the passage to Stromness.

It was now a waiting game for Margaret and every night she feared closing her eyes because she constantly dreamt her child was suddenly taken from her. Although she wasn't sure she believed in God anymore – from the time she returned from the watchtower, she knelt and prayed by her bed every night in the hope there would be a way out of this nightmare.

On Monday, 2 June, over three and a half weeks later, a letter finally arrived addressed to David Stephen from Robert Harcus in Orkney. Margaret had nearly given up all hope of a response but her prayers were answered. It was just past her father's deadline, so it was both terrifying and exhilarating when Margaret and her sisters saw the Post Carriage arrive at their farmhouse late that afternoon. They ran to find their father waving the letter. He came slowly into the kitchen and they all stood rigid while he opened the envelope.

David showed no emotion and then moved his head up to look directly at Margaret.

"It seems Robert Harcus is an honourable man. He has confirmed that he met you last summer in Wick and would be prepared to marry you but you would have to leave Caithness and live with him in Eday. He also wishes to see you and the child before arrangements for the marriage can take place and could come to Caithness at the beginning of July when the herring season begins in Thurso and would then go on to Wick."

David was not pleased with the delay and walked out of the room.

Margaret also needed time to think, she was unsure if this was the right path for her. Then after a discussion with her sisters, she decided that this was a way to find a new life and to live some of her dreams at least. She reminded herself that when they met, she had strong feelings for Robert and hoped they would find a deeper love as time went on. But her concern was that she had never seen where he lived or met his family and it would be a strange leap in the dark. She would be among many strangers. She knew however she must trust her instincts. She had the fortitude and was prepared to take the risk and work hard at a new life. It had to be the best plan? It was her chance!

Reluctantly, David Stephen responded to Robert and accepted his terms. The marriage could take place after Robert's visit to Caithness in July. In the meantime Margaret and the child were confined to the farm house and his land. She could no longer work in Castletown, go for any walks in the Parish or make visits to other villages. The shame of her being spotted with the child was too much for David to bear.

1868 was not a good year for Robert Harcus - yields from fishing were low, his nets needed repair and the weather had been so atrocious that the cultivation of crops had proved difficult. The peat which was used to generate fire and heat in the cottage also took longer to dry out. He had always lived with his mother, Jane, whom he loved dearly, and they had shared his current address in Parkhead, Eday. He had lost his father, William, many years before which was a sadness he always carried with him as his death was never fully explained or his body recovered. He was a fisherman and just disappeared one day, most likely lost at sea. Robert's only brother called William, who was a farm servant at Greentoft, Eday, had left Orkney years previously therefore he took on all his father's responsibilities and the care of his mother.

On 18 March 1868, his mother had died of dropsy to the lower part of her body, aged 60 years. Her death came as a huge blow to him as she had always been such a strong woman which had given him strength to battle on and earn enough for them to live on. Life had now changed totally - he felt orphaned and longed to resume the closeness he once shared with her. Jane was buried in the Old Kirkyard at Skaill in Eday alongside other members of her 'Reid' family. To commemorate her death and his love for her, Robert had a headstone erected on her grave which stood close to the shoreline, overlooking the sea. It was the most beautiful, peaceful, final resting place you could wish for.

While he was grieving for the loss of his mother, the letter arrived from Margaret's father telling him that his daughter had had a child by him on the 5th May and demanded to know his intentions. Robert was now in total shock with the thought of having to marry the mother of his child and start a new life with her. He remembered Margaret well and decided to do the honourable thing and stand by her, but was worried it could turn out to be the worst decision he had ever made. He had sent his response quickly so he could have no second thoughts, but he could not conceal his doubts. His life was now on hold until he received a reply from Margaret's father so he kept himself distracted by repairing nets, tidying the croft, digging up peat and tending the ground for vegetables.

A return letter eventually arrived in the second week of June confirming that David Stephen had accepted his terms and stating that the marriage should take place as soon as possible at the Free Church of Scotland in Dunnet. Robert replied immediately and started planning his visit and fishing trip to Caithness in July. He did not want the wedding until after the herring season as this would severely affect his income for the year. He decided to make Margaret's father aware of this when he visited Tain to see Margaret and the child.

When Margaret heard that her intended husband, Robert, was coming to visit, her mind went into a complete spin. She could not believe this was really happening or contain her sense of anticipation. What if he changed his mind, she thought, what would become of her ... Margaret had suffered a tragic loss two years before when her first fiancé, a local fisherman, had been washed overboard on a fishing trip near Dunnet Head. His friend had tried to save him by holding on to his hair but the power of the wind and force of the tide in the Pentland Firth was too great and he lost his grip, so her 'love' descended into a watery grave, never to be seen again. From that moment, she despised the sea and the way it had cruelly taken her future. She did not want to ever suffer in this way again.

It worried her that Robert Harcus was taking on huge responsibilities by marrying her and becoming the legitimate father of their daughter. As he was an Orkney fisherman, which was a dangerous occupation, she would also have to live in fear every time he went to sea and pray that he would return safely.

She hoped fate would not intervene on this occasion and all would go to plan for their wedding as she was in her early twenties and knew it was probably her last chance of escaping Caithness and changing her life. She tried to be positive and concentrated on the new duties of motherhood. She was often deprived of sleep as the child required feeding or changing during the night and as her energy levels were always low, she could barely drag herself outdoors to complete her daily chores on the farm, let alone manage baking bread, cooking and cleaning. It proved to be a difficult, demanding time for her but she often told herself that everything would change for the better soon.

Eleven months after they first met in Wick, Margaret was finally reunited with Robert. He walked into their farm house in Tain to see her and the child and to have important discussions with her father. She was hesitant and subdued at first but watched his every move and secretly admired his muscular frame and strength of character. When she placed the child in his arms, she noticed how tender and loving he seemed which gave her every hope that he would make a good father. He did not ask too many questions, nor did she, and it was agreed with David that the wedding would go ahead after Banns and after the herring season was over. Their Wedding Banns would have to be proclaimed before their congregations on three successive Sundays in case there was any impediment to the marriage. As the bride and groom lived in different parishes, Banns had to be proclaimed in Robert's church, the United Presbyterian Church in Eday and in the Free Church in Dunnet where they were to be wed. As the herring season was likely to finish at the end of September, a marriage date was needed in October and David suggested that Margaret and Robert meet with the minister of the Free Church in Dunnet the following day to discuss and confirm a date for their wedding. To make sure this happened, David offered to let them borrow his horse and wagon for a few hours and Robert thanked him for his kindness. Margaret's sisters also offered to look after the child so there was a plan and Margaret was excited. How she longed for freedom, to be among strangers in a new land and to have a husband she could respect and love.

The Long Awaited Wedding Day

The day of her wedding finally arrived and Margaret could not wait for the hour to come. She was frantically dressing and packing at the same time as she was to leave with Robert for Orkney later that afternoon. Her father's attitude had changed towards her over the last few weeks and she could only assume it was because he would lose her help on the farm. She could have 'done away with him' several times and remembered there was an old tradition that if you committed a murder on a Sunday morning and then fled to Orkney, you would escape punishment. The problem was, she was not escaping to Orkney until today, Thursday, so she quickly had to abandon the idea. It did make her think about the death of Margaret Wallace however, the daughter of William Wallace, who is buried in the churchyard in Barrock where she and Robert were to be married. The inscription on her gravestone tells how she was callously murdered in Dunnet by Alexander Calder in 1635 as he could not have her in marriage. He was said to have escaped unpunished to Orkney as her murder was committed on a Sunday morning. A very unlucky woman, she thought and just hoped her future and that of her six-month-old daughter would be full of better fortune and happiness.

Robert and Margaret were finally married on 29 October 1868 in the Free Church of Dunnet, Barrock. Her cousins, David and Robert Sutherland, were witnesses. Although Queen Victoria began a new trend when she married Prince Albert in a white wedding gown in 1840, this was not the case for Margaret. She was able to discard her normal blue home-made dress and to her amazement, wore a long sleeve, full length, fine, cream wool gown. It was their mother's favourite dress and her sisters had secretly modified it for her which was the nicest surprise she had ever had. The bodice had a stand up collar and square shaped yolk and her sisters had acquired some lace from Thurso to trim the sleeve cuffs and belt. Ann and Elizabeth said that it was their wedding present to her and Margaret could not have been more grateful to them.

On the wedding day, Margaret carried a small bouquet of shepherds purse wild flowers tied with a white ribbon. She had carefully picked the stems with clusters of tiny, open white flowers the day before. Folklore said it was a hardy and vigorous plant which had meaning for her and she also knew that flowers signified new beginnings and she was desperately seeking something.

The non-conformist stone church where they were married was a plain oblong building with a tower at the west end. It was ancient. Another large aisle had been added to increase capacity so most of the congregation, who lived within four miles, could worship together. Once inside, Margaret felt dwarfed due to the size of the church but kept herself focused and only looked straight ahead towards Robert, who was waiting at the altar. David, her father, had stood rigid at the entrance to the church and seemed at a loss for words but, once she took his arm to begin their walk down the aisle, she sensed he was suffering from nerves and probably reliving the day he had married her mother. They slowly made their way to the altar. Margaret looked radiant and was full of hope about the next, new chapter in her life. The wedding service seemed like a dream but felt very real once they had exchanged vows and Robert placed the wedding ring on the third finger of her left hand. She had agreed to wear the wedding band of

Jane Reid, Robert's late mother and considered it an honour as Robert had so much affection for her and knew this would have pleased her.

After the service Robert took his new family to the Prince of Wales coaching Inn near Barrogill Castle in Mey as it was near the route to the ferry at Gills Bay to Orkney. After such a busy morning, he thought that a late lunch would be welcome and had managed to scrape together enough money to pay for them all. Barrogill Castle, built between 1566 and 1572 by George Sinclair, the 4th Earl of Caithness was a prominent landmark on the Northern Coast of Caithness with views all the way to the Orkney Isles on a clear day. Margaret wished they could have got closer but time was short and they couldn't deviate from the main route to John O'Groats and the ferry.

They were soon at the Inn and although the atmosphere was a little subdued, Margaret could see that her sisters, Ann and Elizabeth, found their meal and surroundings fun and exciting as they had never been to a celebration like this before. It was rare for them all to attend social events, particularly since their mother died, so Margaret was pleased she had brought them happiness on this her wedding day. David toasted his eldest daughter and husband and Robert stood up to toast his new bride and family. He was well aware of his changed circumstances and the responsibility of looking after his wife and daughter. He prayed to God their future together would be a happy union.

After the meal, they returned to the horse and wagon and proceeded directly towards Gills Bay which was three miles west of John O'Groats. Soon Margaret and Robert Harcus would depart for St Margaret's Hope on the Orkney Isle of South Ronaldsay and then make their way on smaller boats to Eday. It was the main setting off point from the Caithness mainland to the islands of Stroma, Swona and the Orkney Isles. This route, known as The Short Sea Crossing, was considered the quickest and safest across the Pentland Firth. Robert knew there was also a small boat from Huna to Brims in Hoy, Orkney. It was an important sheltered port from Norse times onwards but he decided the Gills Bay to St Margaret's Hope route was the better option and would save them time once they reached Orkney.

He just hoped that the treacherous tides in the Pentland Firth would not disrupt their journey. He was a fisherman, like his father before him, and well aware of the problems but Margaret had never crossed the Firth. He had sadly lost trusted fishermen friends who were never seen again after crossings to South Ronaldsay or Hoy from the north coast of Caithness. He also remembered a tragic accident many years earlier when heavy gales and seas blew up in the Firth which resulted in the loss of 30 herring boats and 37 fishermen drowned in their attempt to return to Wick harbour. He had every respect for the sea and would never relax when fishing on his own or in other boats, as this could prove fatal.

Soon enough, they could see Gills Bay up ahead and Margaret realised she was actually about to leave Caithness. Robert paid for their one-way sea passages and then went to fetch Margaret's two small trunks from the wagon. Her entire worldly belongings were in these trunks and she thought how sad it was that your life could be packed up so easily. They all then stood near the ship on the pier which would depart in less than half an hour and Margaret shuddered in horror at the thought of crossing the Firth in this rather small, rusty looking vessel. She clung to her child which began to scream, sensing her fear. This is it she thought, the last farewell …. She hugged her sisters tightly and wished them well – she had already said goodbye to her cousins after the wedding. She then turned to look directly at her father and took a deep breath.

As she stood riveted to the spot, she thanked him for saving her life at the watchtower and then as she lowered her head, slowly muttered, "goodbye father."

At that moment, he reached into his coat pocket and pulled out a small sketch of her mother and gave it to her. "Here, this is for you," he said quietly. Her eyes filled with tears as her shaking hand took the gift from him. Margaret kissed it and put it quickly away in her bag as it was a precious reminder of a woman who gave everything to protect and help her and she would always treasure her love and strength.

Her sisters were waving and wiping away their tears at the same time. Her father watched the ferry glide slowly away and knew in his bones it was unlikely he would ever see his granddaughter or Margaret again. He found it hard to express his emotions and, without delay, he walked away from the pier to return to his horse and wagon and begin the journey back to Tain.

Crossing the Pentland Firth to Orkney

On board the ferry, Margaret was already missing her sisters as they were the closest family she had known and wondered if they would ever be reunited. And as she looked back towards Caithness she realised that her old life was already becoming invisible and cradled her daughter more tightly in her arms as if to protect her, not only from the cool breeze, but from whatever the future had in store for them.

Margaret never uttered a word but turned toward Robert who, sensing her apprehension, placed his arm around her. She leaned into him and reminded herself that starting a new life was never going to be easy but she was on her way now and all the doubts and worries she had were being blown to the four winds as the steam ship ploughed on towards the Island of Stroma.

The route of the ferry was fascinating for Margaret as she had never experienced a sea journey before and loved the appearance of land and coastlines from the water. She felt very unsteady on the deck but slowly developed the confidence to look down into the depths of the water and was rewarded by the sight of a beautiful, Atlantic white-sided dolphin. To the west of the ship, she could just make out the 'Men of Mey' rocks on the Caithness coast but it was the dangerous tidal race also of the same name in the unpredictable Pentland Firth, which forms off St John's Point, that worried her. Danger was still everywhere she concluded even though Robert tried to reassure her that their route to Orkney would not involve passing through these waters. As the minutes passed she finally allowed herself to smile as the ship carried her onwards towards new hope and dreams of a better life.

Robert had been truthful but rather economical with all the facts and had deliberately not mentioned 'The Swelkie', off Swelkie Point which is the race at the north end of Stroma they would soon be passing. It can be particularly violent and extends in an easterly or westerly direction depending on the tide. "So far, so good," he whispered, as he looked towards Stroma. He was grateful for the relatively calm sea and weather conditions on their passage but, as he was an experienced fisherman, he knew how quickly things could change in these notorious waters.

His worst fear was realised within five minutes as the wind had quickened and the sea began churning. Something felt very wrong. When he turned around he suddenly saw an almighty wave looming on the starboard side of the ship. Within seconds they were thrown into it, the ship creaked and lurched with the force of the wind and sea and then 'all hell' broke out. The siren began blasting. Anything not tied down started rolling round the slippery deck. He then heard Margaret let out a bone-chilling scream as she was thrown with the child towards the open cabin door. Luckily Robert just managed to grab her and stop them falling 25 feet down the hatch. They had been in a calm eddy but it seemed a large swell wave had formed at the south end of Swona, the next Island, due to the fast moving tides. They were fortunate this incident was short – lived, although they were blown off course temporarily. Captain and crew resumed control within 30 minutes and reset their course to St Margaret's Hope, South Ronaldsay once all passengers and crew had been accounted for. There had been minor injuries to some passengers who needed medical attention and bandages but there were no broken bones. Nerves had been shattered however and Margaret had been shaken to her core just as she was beginning to relax and enjoy her new found freedom.

She prayed this passage would be over soon and was reassured again by Robert that they could now see the north coastline of South Ronaldsay as they were in the Sound of Hoxa and would be at the pier at St Margaret's Hope soon after passing by Needle Point.

Safe Landing in South Ronaldsay, Orkney

How grateful she was to step ashore and walk on dry land. It was a shaky start to her new life in Orkney which hopefully, could only get better. Robert decided to go by land and sea to Kirkwall on the main island. The roads would be rough but as many boats left for the islands from there, he was confident they would find one to take them to Eday the following day.

It was now early evening so that night he found lodgings in St Margaret's Hope at the Anchorage Inn. Margaret was too exhausted for any unpacking or change of clothes and after a light supper, fell instantly asleep with the child and did not stir until sunrise.

It was a slow journey to Kirkwall and after waiting patiently for two more hours, a fisherman friend of Robert's, who owned a small boat, ferried them across to Eday. It was a long crossing but the sea was mainly calm and the journey did not have the hazards of the Pentland Firth or other tidal races. Robert pointed out the Isles of Rousay and Stronsay as they departed Kirkwall and as Eday lay in the centre of the Northern Orkney Isles, Margaret also got to see some of the Isle of Sanday to the east, the southern end of Westray to the west and the smaller Isle of Pharay due north. When it seemed they were never to reach their destination, Robert pointed towards the Bay of Backaland on the south eastern side of Eday and soon the pier was in sight and the boat secured.

Considering the entire journey from Gills Bay in Caithness to Eday in the Orkney Isles was less than 60 miles, it had been the longest trip in her life time and she was exhausted. She craved rest and warm food and was beginning to wonder if they would ever get to Robert's cottage. He had been a gentleman and tried to keep her spirits up but he too was becoming impatient and wanted their travels to be over. It was not the sort of start a newly married couple should have been subjected to but the thought of their first night together in his croft filled him with a new sense of anticipation. He had waited a long time to be a respectable married man and to carry a new wife over the threshold. His only fear was that Margaret would not adjust to her new life on this very small island as she had no idea what was in store. He knew however that she was forced to take on many responsibilities after her mother died to help her father and sisters and had coped admirably. There was something about her he admired. She had a strong spirit, a good sense of humour which made him feel young and alive and were the reasons he was originally attracted to her when they first met in Wick.

Eventually, after their luggage was unloaded, they made their way to the district of West Side where Robert lived with his beloved mother for many years until she died in March. As they approached Robert's cottage, Margaret reminded herself that she wanted to be a good wife and mother and felt pleased to be the new mistress of the house.

Robert had said that his small croft had a bit more land to grow crops in West Side and told her that he had previously lived in the south east side of Eday. He chuckled when he said that nowhere was far away in Eday as it was such a small place. It was less than nine miles long and at its narrowest point about a third of a mile wide between the Sands of Doomy on the west and Bay of London on the east coast. He promised to give Margaret a tour of the island as soon as they were settled in.

Part Two

2.

Life in the Orkney Isles

Solitudes of land and sea assuage
my quenchless thirst for freedom unconfined;
with independent heart and mind
hold I my heritage.
Robert Rendall

Eday, a Northern Orkney Isle

October 1868

As the wagon lurched to a halt at Parkhead, Margaret looked in disbelief at the small cottage and its state of disrepair. How will I ever manage, she thought whilst fighting back tears. After months of waiting to see the island and where she would live, this was not what she had hoped for. But as it was late in the afternoon and she was weary after the long journey and the emotional turmoil of the last 36 hours, she pulled on every ounce of inner strength and told herself not to complain. She would try her best and make this marriage work. Very slowly she got off the wagon and followed Robert up the narrow path to the stone croft cottage.

As they approached the door, Robert opened it for her and with a smile, picked her up and carried her inside. Margaret laughed briefly. It was dark and gloomy inside and her eyes took some time to adjust. To her relief, the first thing she noticed was a large fireplace which seemed to take up a third of the room and immediately in front of it she spotted a child's crib which pleased her. Robert admitted that he had made it himself and that the linens were donated by his auntie, Barbara Reid. Margaret was grateful for his thoughtfulness and squeezed his hand in quiet acknowledgment. She continued to scan the dim interior but gave no reaction to what she saw. There were only two rooms and presumably an area beyond where a curtain was hanging. She realised how fortunate she had been to live in the farm house in Tain which was larger with more spacious rooms.

In winter it was bitterly cold however due to the drafts. The heat from the kitchen fire always escaped up the chimney so she had had to sit close. She just hoped that the chimney in this cottage would not allow all the heat to escape or let smoke fill the room as it would be horrid in such a small space. When she looked up she noticed there were charming 'strings of fish' hung up on the ceiling and Robert explained these were reserves of dried cuithes (coalfish) he had caught earlier in the year. Margaret was not a great lover of fish but knew from what Robert had said she may have to start getting used to the idea as fish would be important in their diet.

Once inside, Robert did not delay and quickly got the fire started from the dried peat and soon enough the kettle was boiling and a broth cooking in the pan. The smoke from the peat was mostly disappearing up the chimney which was an encouraging sign but Margaret could see a smoke haze in the room and the air stank of peat. She did not mention her displeasure as she quickly realised Robert was a capable cook and used to looking after himself. For now, her focus was to settle the child who thankfully, after taking her milk, had fallen asleep in her new crib the minute she was put down. Her little face looked pale as the journey had not been an easy one and Margaret hoped her rosy complexion would return the following day.

Margaret had no sooner noticed that Robert had disappeared when he suddenly stepped through the door clutching a special bottle of whisky which he said was a wedding present, given to him by his fisherman friends. He placed the bottle on the table and reached for the quaich which was sitting on the shelf above the fireplace. He told Margaret it was a special family 'loving cup' passed down from his mother's family which was used by the bride and groom for their first toast. By sharing the cup, it also sealed the bond between the bride and groom and their trust in one another. Without hesitation Robert filled the cup which wobbled as they each attempted to hold one of the handles. When it was level and the sea of whisky had stopped rolling they both said "slàinte mhath" and toasted their new beginning in Eday. As Margaret drank from the cup the rough liquid burnt her throat and smouldered like a fire in her belly. She succumbed to its power and felt its warmth radiate through her body. It was such a magic feeling she closed her eyes to make sure she would remember. The contents of her travel chests could wait to be unpacked in the daylight, she just wanted to relax and enjoy the moment.

It was late autumn and now dark outside but the light of the moon occasionally found its way to illuminate a corner of the croft cottage. On this night they were blessed by a light sprinkling of stars which sparkled in the huge sky above their dwelling. Margaret forgot to feel the chill and isolation of her new existence and embraced her new found sense of independence.

After some food and more whisky, Robert took the candle and walked toward the curtain which shielded the bed from the living area of the croft. He signalled with his hand for Margaret to follow him which she did, and he waited while she slowly undressed and removed her gown. He gazed at her and proceeded to remove the rest of her clothing while she quickly unbuttoned his shirt to feast on his strong chest and muscular arms. As it was cool in the croft, despite the fire still burning, without delay he scooped her up and placed her gently on the bed which creaked with their combined weight. He kicked off his boots and removed his trousers before their bodies finally made contact. She groaned and smiled in the candle light as his lips found hers and, as he held her safely in his arms, he began to explore the rest of her body.

She had never known such tenderness and felt the pain and anxieties of the last few months drift away, just like the clouds had drifted across the sky above Olrig Hill. As Robert caressed her and their passion intensified she knew she had made the right decision to marry him. She recognised that the spark she had felt the first time she met him was now a flame and she would love this Orkney man, now her saviour. For the first time in her life she felt she had a purpose and a future and, despite the many uncertainties, together she hoped they would overcome whatever lay in store.

The next day in the afternoon, Robert began to show Margaret and their six month old daughter the area where they lived. She could see Fersness Hill which was close by but rather than walk there for the view, they decided to take a gentle stroll to Sealskerry Bay where Robert said 'selkies' could be spotted. He was having fun with Margaret as folktales of the Northern Isles suggest these are mythical seals in the water which can assume human form on land by shedding their skin. Margaret was fascinated but had to make do with only spotting sea waders on the marshy shore near the dunes. They did find 'the mound' on this lovely beach, that is said to be the remains of a Norse castle, before turning back towards Parkhead.

Robert had always lived in the southern, flatter part of the island as it was generally better for farming but he knew every inch of Eday. The north had more ancient antiquities, he didn't know why, but promised to show Margaret the sights including the Red Head cliffs on the far north coast.

He explained that Eday was probably two islands before the wind and sand made it into one long, narrow piece of land joined at the waist (isthmus) by sand and that Eday's name actually meant *Isthmus Isle*. The centre was more rocky and hilly with farming land around the shores and Margaret had already noticed more crofts not far from the sea on their journey from Fersness and walk to Sealskerry. Robert also said that there were six smaller islands connected with Eday, which amazed Margaret, as she was still surprised by the small size of Eday. The largest of these included the Island of Pharay with its holms which protected the harbour at Fersness in the SW and the Calf of Eday in the NE which protected the harbour at Calf Sound.

He told her West Side, where they now lived had attracted more people from other islands once the Fersness Quarry began operating as they quarried the freestone, a type of sandstone, and didn't have to rely on farming so much. This fine-grained stone was said to have been used in the building of the spectacular St Magnus Cathedral in Kirkwall. The yellow and red sandstone found in Eday was also used in many other public and grand houses in Orkney. It made the island less fertile but fortunately there was more moss cover and peat found here than on other Northern Isles and the peat was a useful free fuel. Other neighbouring islands relied on Eday peat as well.

Exploring the Isle of Eday

As the next day was clear and the cooler, autumn weather was fast approaching, Robert decided to sacrifice a fishing trip to show Margaret more of the island. He was able to borrow a wagon so they set off with some food and water as they would be away from Parkhead for a few hours. They passed by Ward Hill to

Gutterhole, Robert's previous home and as they were not far from the south coast, Robert pointed out the Bay of Greentoft and Veness, known as the Holy Headland.

Next they headed north towards Backaland as Robert's Auntie Barbara lived there with her husband John Reid and family and Robert wanted them to meet Margaret and his daughter. After a brief visit and promises to meet again soon, they continued on to Banke near the east coast where Robert had lived with his parents, William and Jane Harcus and brother William junior. His father had been a fisherman and the bays of Backaland and Greentoft were good places to keep the small fishing boats. He then repeated the saying that an Orcadian is a 'farmer with a boat' due to the part-time nature of Orkney fishing, and for the first time Margaret laughed out loud. But it was true as she could already see that fishermen had to farm and grow other food for their families to live on. It was also similar in Caithness she thought, as farmers would go fishing in the herring season for the extra money.

He pointed out that his Auntie Barbara and her older sister Mary Reid had also lived in Banke when he was very young. In the 1840s Mary was a straw bonnet maker and Barbara was a straw plaiter whilst this industry survived. They continued north passing the school where Robert had attended before reaching the United Presbyterian Church which was erected in 1858. The original church, built in 1831 from stones quarried nearby, had soon fallen into ruins. Robert said he knew the Rev. James Ingram well as they had recently buried his mother, Jane Reid, in the Old Kirkyard at Skaill and that Margaret would meet him when they next went to church. Ministers normally preached in both Eday and Stronsay as they had been united parishes for years. It wasn't far to Skaill on the east coast but Robert said they would make a special visit another day as there was much more for Margaret to see.

They soon reached the narrow waist of Eday and Margaret could see the large Loch of Doomy on the left and Bay of London on the right. They decided to rest for a few minutes and were delighted to spot many colourful waders in the shallow water of the bay. It was also a good time to feed their daughter as they would soon be exploring more of the ancient sites.

Robert said that like Caithness, Eday was full of ancient reminders of the past and was even closer to Norway. He knew that there was evidence of dwellers here from as far back as Neolithic, Bronze and Iron Ages as well as the Picts and Vikings who came much later. Margaret suddenly thought of her father and hoped Robert would not bore her to death with his stories. She looked to the sky for some sort of sign, then took a deep breath. After passing the school in the north and the large Mill Loch, they were soon in close proximity to a huge, 17 foot, upright monolith which Robert said was the Stone of Setter. They walked up to get a better view as it was shaped like a giant hand and covered with a multitude of lichens. Robert proudly said that it was Orkney's most spectacular and biggest, single standing stone. As it was placed in a central point on the island, it was possible to see Calf Sound, the stretch of water between Eday and the small island, the Calf of Eday. They sat down and Robert began telling Margaret an old folklore story about how this stone had been put there by a laird. He said that the ground below had been dug and the stone was in place on an earth ramp ready to slide into the hole but the men helping were unable to move it. So the laird asked his wife, who had come to see how things were going and whom he did not like, to jump on the end of the stone to help it move into position. She was a large woman and, as she jumped on it, she lost her balance and fell into the hole just before the stone! "The laird's wife remains beneath it to this day," chuckled Robert, trying to hold back a grin. Margaret laughed at her new husband who was very amused by his own story.

He took her hand and said, "Follow me, we are going up the hill." On the way Margaret spotted two strange little structures in the field and asked if Robert knew what they were? He said that there were some people who believed these may have been defleshing chambers where dead bodies were placed for birds to pick clean before the human bones, necessary for the afterlife, were placed in the nearby tombs. Margaret had never heard of such bizarre practices and somehow wished she had not asked the question.

They could see Braeside Cairn which directly faced the Stone of Setter but decided to follow a path near the Stone and walked up the hill to a burial tomb which Robert said was the Vinquoy chambered cairn. It had been excavated about ten years before and caused some excitement on the island. Now it was at risk of deteriorating further due to the tomb's exposure to the harsh weather. Further on, Robert pointed out the unique, double storey burial chamber,

Huntersquoy cairn, and when Margaret entered cautiously and her eyes adjusted to the dark, she could see the many well preserved chambers.

Margaret was enjoying finding out about Eday and its history, there was a lot to understand about this island, but at the back of her mind she could not help but worry as to whether they would have enough food and provisions to live on and what would become of her daughter as she grew older. As a new mother she wanted a better life for her but was not sure this tiny island could offer that. She had noticed small communities working near the shore, looking for seaweed and shellfish and had seen crofters in the fields, but many of the men were also fishermen and away searching for cuithe or sillocks in their small boats. It concerned her how they could ever afford more supplies or a trip to Kirkwall as Robert had used most of his savings on their wedding and journey back to Eday. But she pushed these thoughts aside as she did not want to spoil the day worrying about their future and decided to run ahead to find the next view.

She was not disappointed. From a high point on the hill, she could see amazing red cliffs in the distance to the north. Robert told her that these were the impressive Red Head cliffs which, although not that high, were a bright red colour due to the Eday marl which also contained clay and silt. He said that the cliffs didn't erode and birds such as fulmers, puffins, razorbills, kittiwakes and shags could still find places to perch or nest there. Margaret had always loved birds and sea animals so this was of interest to her. Robert appeared to be quite an expert on birdlife as he had also spotted a pair of whimbrels, a hen harrier and even a rare merlin on the moors when they had passed the edge of Mill Loch on their way to the Stone of Setter. Margaret had pleaded for him to stop so she could get a better view.

Although they could see a large house in the distance and the Calf of Eday Robert suggested they return to the wagon and he could take them closer.

He knew the Calf of Eday, just across from Carrick Bay, had been unoccupied since the Iron Age apart from those who occasionally dug for peats. For such a tiny island, it had many standing stones, chambered cairns and burnt mounds from other settlements. Robert told Margaret that near the only sandy beach, is an area called The Graand where there is a little sheltered bay, the Norsemen were supposed to have pulled up their longships in winter. It made Margaret feel very close to the Norse presence that had been in Eday long ago and in her place of birth, Caithness.

Not far from the big house there was a public house, so they decided to take a break and quench their thirsts. Margaret had not seen any other Inns, so was very agreeable to go in. Once inside, a fishermen recognised Robert with his new wife and greeted them both. She thought she heard what he said but confessed later to Robert that she still had problems understanding the locals due to their Orcadian/Scottish dialect as it was different to that spoken in Caithness. Robert introduced him to Margaret as William Hercus. He said that William was born on Eday and they had been childhood friends but he now lived on the mainland. Robert said later that there were a number of people on Eday with the surname Harcus and that Hercus was a variant so he understood it could get confusing. He had heard that his Harcus ancestors had come to Eday, Orkney Isles in medieval times, circa 1500, from a place in South East Scotland and that his surname was special. He wished he knew more.

They sat down in the Inn and Robert went on to tell Margaret about the house and Carrick estate. He said the mansion dated back to the early 17th century and the whole estate was made a Scottish burgh of Carrick, in the time of Charles I. The mansion called Carrick House, sits in a fine position close to the northern coast, with a superb view across Calf Sound towards the Calf of Eday. It came into the possession of the Fea family and was the home of James Fea who in 1725, captured the notorious *Pirate Gow* in Sir Walter Scott's novel.

Margaret was intrigued as she had not heard this particular story and Robert promised to tell her more on their journey back to West Side. They finished their drinks and left the Inn and as Margaret craddled the child to sleep in her arms, Robert began the tale as they headed south.

"Sir Walter Scott first heard the story of Gow from an old woman in Stromness in Orkney, called Bessie Millie." He said, "She foretold the 'winds' to sailors by prayers and the steam of a kettle."

Margaret was immediately captivated and leaned closer as she wanted to hear every word.

"Calf Sound was described in the final act in this drama," said Robert.

"Oh, now I see," said Margaret. Robert then went on to tell the story.

"John Gow was born in Wick but grew up in Stromness where his father was a merchant. Like many Orcadians, the young Gow went to sea and in due course joined a ship called the *Caroline*. Due to bad food and conditions, Gow and other pirates murdered members of the crew and took over the ship, renaming it the *Revenge*. He became captain and Gow and his men were soon famous for their acts of piracy in the seas surrounding Spain, France and Portugal. Eventually they did not have enough provisions to cross the Atlantic and Gow decided to sail home to Stromness, Orkney. He changed the ship's name to the *George* on the way and also called himself Mr Smith. But the ship was spotted for what it really was by crew from another visiting ship and led to one of Gow's pirates surrendering to the law in Kirkwall. As the authorities were now alerted, ten more pirates deserted in the ship's longboat to the Scottish mainland.

Gow then decided to head for Eday in the *Revenge* (alias the *George*) to target and plunder Carrick House where his school friend, James Fea, lived. But dangerous currents off Eday's north coast carried the *Revenge* too near the Calf of Eday, and it was grounded opposite Carrick House. With no longboat, the ship could not be kedged off the sand by the crew, so they were stranded. Gow tried to get help from his friend James Fea but James was smart and, after many messages, he cleverly forced Gow and the pirates to surrender and claimed the reward."

"In the end," said Robert, "Pirate John Gow and seven of his men were hanged in London and Gow had to be hung twice as the rope broke on the first attempt. His body was left in the Thames for 'three tides' then tarred and hung in chains as a warning to others."

Margaret gave a huge sigh of relief and wrapped her shawl firmly around her shoulders. "What a great story," she admitted to Robert. "Our children are going to love it and there be a lesson to all," she said with a smile.

It had been such an enjoyable trip. She was so grateful for the time Robert had given to show her the island and did not want this day to end. However soon enough they turned right and could see the Sands of Doomy, then the Sands of Mussetter in Fersness Bay and once they passed the Quarry, it did not take long before they were in West Side and back at Parkhead.

She would never forget the beautiful views and spectacular sights she had seen on her day out. The sun had shone on Eday and she realised it was a hidden treasure, a gem in the Northern Isles. But as she stepped down from the wagon it occurred to her that there were few trees and the countryside was rather flat and windswept. So little shelter for animals or humans she thought and as winter was drawing near, she could feel the chill coming already. She decided that the people here were hardy souls and had grown used to this environment. She hoped, given time, her resistance to the elements would increase and she wouldn't notice things as much. She counted herself lucky to have such a loyal, hardworking husband who would always protect her.

Fishing and Farming to Survive

Over the coming weeks Margaret found life on Eday extremely testing. Robert was regularly away at sea, fishing, so her days were long and lonely. When he came home he was exhausted but there were always more chores to do whilst there was daylight and before he could rest. The first winter was the hardest and coldest she could ever recall and the wind chilled her to the bone. The bonus of rough seas meant that fishing was too dangerous for the small boats and Robert would be at home to help her, but the downside meant there was less money and food. He tried hard to keep her spirits up and after he returned home early from Fersness Bay one afternoon, as there was no sign of even a meagre catch, he said, "Remember the saying that an Orcadian is a farmer with a boat," and reached for the hoe to tend his turnip crop. Margaret managed a smile but prayed they would be rewarded with a good harvest.

Their main food was fish. The sillock or cuithe were a big part of their diet for three quarters of the year but herring had a short season of about 6-8 weeks from the end of July. Herring fishing was the most demanding time as Robert could be away for longer periods. Cod was important when in season and lobsters were caught for export in April, May, June but Robert didn't go to Scapa Flow in search of these leggy crustaceans. They rarely ate meat as it was expensive to raise the small Orkney breeds of sheep and cattle. Robert and other fisherman had to farm and grow other food such as turnips, oats and potatoes in order to maintain a subsistence living for their families. Margaret was so famished one day that when she closed her eyes, she was sure she smelt the heavenly aroma of lamb cooking. She woke up drooling with the thought of pouring lamb juices over the meat and potatoes but soon found herself choking from the acrid peat smoke which always tormented her inside the cottage.

Now it was spring and the longer, lighter days were slowly returning. A highlight of Margaret's week was a visit to the United Presbyterian Church for the Sunday service. She was happy to meet some of Robert's extended family and talk to other women with children as she had missed the closeness of her sisters for company since she arrived in Eday. Margaret was pleased the long winter months were over as it had been particularly grey and cold and they could now look forward to the onset of summer and enjoy warmer temperatures. Their daughter, Jane, was nearly one year old and it had been seven months since they had left Caithness. Her life revolved around the child, who was a joy to her but, as she was starting to walk, Margaret had to constantly watch out for all the dangers in the cottage, including the open fireplace, every waking minute of her day.

One morning Jane found a beautiful smooth stone in the cottage and loved to play with it. She was intrigued by this plaything. Margaret knew it was called a healing stone as she had seen one before in Caithness. In pagan times, in the north of Scotland, they were used as a charm to heal disease. Robert confirmed it had always been in the cottage and that his mother had loved it too. She had kept it close to her breast on several occasions when she thought she was seriously ill. Margaret was nearly at the point of trying this cure as she had not been feeling at all well lately. She knew their high fish diet did not particularly suit her as she much preferred meat but even when she stopped eating sillock or coalfish, she still felt nauseous and tired. For some reason, her mind flashed back to the moment she thought she was pregnant for the first time. She had very few symptoms, but did notice her belly becoming extended and a preference for certain foods. The horror and shame of her secret had overwhelmed her then but now she could separate her feelings and she was sure her physical symptoms were those of early pregnancy!

That night she mentioned this to Robert who beamed at the thought of another child and quickly took her into his arms. "We will visit the howdie wife who helps at births as soon as possible," he said, which comforted her briefly.

During the next week, they made a special trip to see this old woman, a type of midwife, who was now in her eighties. Her qualification was the fact that she had had eight children and helped with numerous pregnancies and births on the island. After a short examination, she confirmed that Margaret's instincts were correct and her child would arrive in December. They were delighted, but Margaret could not help from worrying about the limited space and extra food they would need, let alone the uncertainty of the child remaining healthy. She feared any problems as there was practically no one with any medical skill on the island and they would struggle to pay the fee if a doctor had to be called to Eday. But Robert soothed her and she was able to enjoy an uncomplicated pregnancy and carry on with most of her chores. She also had summer to look forward to and the warmer temperatures which always lifted her mood as the washing dried quicker, the wild flowers were in bloom and, hopefully, there would be fresh vegetables to harvest.

Occasionally, early on a summer's evening, Margaret and other families went to watch the fishing competition, which proved very entertaining. Robert was such a showman with his fly hooks as were some of his fishermen friends. Usually what was caught by bait or fly was small and they threw it back in the water, but, occasionally a fine sillock was reeled in and by the end of the evening there would be a winner based on the heaviest weight of a single fish. The suspense of revealing the winner was the highlight of the evening and everyone cheered as the hand-made, first prize medal was pinned to the chest of the elated winning fisherman. Once during the summer Robert won the competition and they were so overjoyed, they went right passed Parkhead on their journey home and had to turn round and go back which made them laugh even more.

Summer had always been Margaret's favourite time of year and now in the Orkney Isles, midsummer was unique as she had experienced 'simmer dim,' when it was never truly dark. The night long twilight filled her with hope and sometimes she would take a walk if Robert was home to care for Jane and observed dusk gradually turn to dawn. It was beautiful and Eday felt the best place to be on earth.

Violent Storm Brings in a Strange Bounty

But the daylight hours slowly shortened as the autumn came and Margaret could not believe another winter was fast approaching. About three weeks before Christmas the weather had turned foul, keeping them all indoors from the howling wind and rain which lashed the cottage. The sea was too rough and dangerous for Robert to go fishing which was a relief to Margaret as she needed more help these days. She could not walk far or fast due to the size of her belly and the extra weight she was carrying. On this cold, miserable afternoon to their surprise, someone was frantically banging on their door. When Robert opened the door a man clad in wet weather fisherman's clothing was yelling at Robert to follow him as a large pod of whales had come ashore and were stranded near Fersness. This was a rare event and Robert knew that if he became involved he would receive a share of the whale oil obtained from the blubber. This oil had so many uses, including for lighting and always commanded a good market price. Robert looked intensely at Margaret who flinched as she knew what acts of barbarism would follow. She loved sea animals and could not bear the thought of their butchery. But realising he could not let this opportunity slip by as it had been about 20 years since whales had come aground, he told his friend to come inside while he found more clothing and his flensing knife. In a few minutes he was back and turned to Margaret and said. "I will be away for some time, try and not worry." Both men walked to the door, letting in the gale force wind and rain which sucked them in like a magnet until they became invisible.

Margaret was distraught and held back her tears at the thought of the suffering soon to befall those beautiful creatures. Her daughter was awake, her eyes were sparkling with joy and love, so she picked her up and softly kissed her warm cheeks. "I hope you never hear the cry of the whales, my darling girl," she whispered and laid her gently back down. But as she did so, she felt a stabbing pain in her abdomen but shrugged it off. Jane was about eighteen months old now and heavy and she thought she could have over exerted herself. She sat down to rest and all was well but after another ten minutes the pain returned. Margaret then began to worry that something was not right. Was this her time? she thought. Perhaps this child wanted to make an entrance to the world today? It was the 5th of December 1869 and she was told it would come this month ....

Margaret sat very still. After about half an hour she stood up and suddenly noticed that her feet were wet. Oh no, she thought. Please God, I don't want to be alone to have this child. I have no mother or father, no husband, no sisters, no one to help me. She let out a spine-chilling cry for help, then dissolved into tears. Why is this happening to me again, why am I alone and here in this godforsaken place?

Margaret had no close neighbours and other women she knew, including the howdie wife, were miles away so could not help. She quickly realised just how vulnerable she was as she had no one to contact. She told herself to remain calm and tried to remember what the old woman had told her she would need before and after the birth. She was due to visit Parkhead soon to help her prepare for the birth but this child could not wait. Margaret's head was spinning but she was able to find some linen towelling, a blanket, the oil lamp and candles and put them down close to the chair she had been sitting on. Before she sat down, she added more peat to the fire to keep the water in the kettle hot and found a knife and some wool to tie the cord. She also found a wooden peg to put in her mouth to bite down on when the pain got too much. The room was slowly filling with more smoke which was choking her but she could not open the door due to the storm.

She was losing track of time. It was dark and the storm raged outside. In between contractions she managed to feed Jane some breast milk and find some dried bread for her to chew on. She prayed for a straight forward birth, she was not ready to die. "Oh mother," she pleaded. "Please send an angel to help me ..." After many hours her contractions were getting closer together and she was finding it hard to move. She resorted to lying on the floor so she could keep an eye on Jane at the same time. She could no longer get up and as she lay looking up at the rafters she became captivated by the strings of dried cuithe hanging high above her. As the candle light caught them they gave off a phosphorescent glow and seemed to be dancing on the ceiling. Then another surge of pain overcame her and she screamed in agony until the contraction abated. Her body was telling her she needed to push, but she was afraid. Little Jane sensed her fear and was becoming upset as she watched her mother struggle in labour.

Suddenly, with no warning, she felt a huge blast of cold air and rain in the cottage and Robert came hurtling in through the door. The storm had not subsided and he had come home for food and dry clothing. He was not prepared for what he witnessed as Margaret lay exhausted and whimpering. Their daughter, Jane, was now screaming but he knew he had to tend to Margaret first who had begun panting on the floor.

"Hey hen," he spluttered and knelt down by her and clasped her hand. Perspiration was pouring off her and her hair was soaked. He decided to check what was happening and then said to Margaret. "I can just see the head!" "Oh my God," she cried. He propped her up against the chair and held on to her. "I think a huge push may just see this bairn come into the world …." Margaret followed his instructions and gave an almighty push until she was breathless. When Robert looked down again, he signalled that she had delivered the head. "One more push should do it," he said excitedly. And sure enough, on the next push, the child slithered out into Robert's waiting hands. Huge tears ran down his face and onto the floor.

"You have done it Margaret, it's a bonnie wee lassie."

"You mean we have done it," she whispered. "We have done it."

After Margaret relaxed and took a few more breaths, she mentioned to Robert that he would have to cut the cord and told him what to do. He found the wool to tie it first and the knife, which was far cleaner than any of his own, and carefully severed the pulsating cord. He then wrapped the child in the linen towel and placed her on Margaret's chest.

"Welcome to my world, my beauty," she said and a rush of love overcame her. Robert was speechless momentarily as he gazed at his wife and new daughter. Thank you Lord for this gift of life, he thought and then went to put more peat on the fire as he was famished and needed to get a broth cooking. He remembered he still had a dram or two of whisky left and found the bottle on the top shelf and poured the contents into a small cup. "To our new daughter," he said and raised the cup and drank. He then handed it to Margaret who took a sip and smiled. "Yes a sister for Jane, shall we call her Ann?" Robert nodded and finished the whisky.

It had been such an eventful night and he had planned to go back to the grounded whales when it was daylight to continue carving off the blubber with the locals. It was not something he was looking forward to as he had witnessed the whales slowly dying and the blood and stench of the blubber was intolerable. As word of the whales' misfortune had got out, many men and boats had arrived from the south and other northern isles, so the share of the whale oil was diminishing by the hour.

"I will go back to the bay," he said. But he didn't go until he had done all he could for Margaret and the new bairn.

It took a few days for Margaret to regain her strength after her second daughter came into the world in the wild, stormy early hours of 6 December 1869. Jane was not sure what to make of her new sister as she was now sleeping in her old crib but gradually accepted her. Margaret hoped they would be the best of friends as they grew older as they were living in such a small space and, so far, Jane seemed mesmerised by her tiny sister. Margaret had so much love for them both but still remained troubled about their future on Eday due to the shortage of food and other supplies. There were small caring communities on the island as Orcadians worked hard on the land, sea and on the shore. Everyone helped each other, but it was a constant worry to have enough to survive on. Robert did not admit it but he was also concerned about providing sufficient food for his growing family. Sometimes he bought home fish, mainly the cuithe which could be dried or smoked but the children were not that fond of it and often pushed their plates away and the food would end up splattered all over the floor. But hopefully the harvest of turnips and potatoes would be better this year as they were useful vegetables for broths or stews.

Another Mouth to Feed

During the next year Margaret took pleasure in the views from the coast on clear days but found the wind often relentless as there was little shelter outdoors due to the lack of trees. The cold breeze seeped into her bones and made her body stiffen and ache and there were days when she could hardly bend over when she was out foraging or digging for vegetables. She had also developed a deep cough and her chest felt tight and painful some days. Robert had lost his mother back in March 1868, so there was no one in his family close by who could help her with their children. His nearest relatives, the elderly sisters of his mother, did not live in West Side. Robert had some cousins but they rarely saw them or got together. Margaret dearly wished her sisters were near but knew that her father would not allow them to visit her and, due to limited space, there would be nowhere for them to sleep. She thought however she would write to them soon when she had more time to spare.

In 1871, her life was gruelling and her health was beginning to suffer more than she cared to acknowledge. She had to admit that she had not been feeling at all well lately and really did not know what to do next. Her constant daily dilemma was caring for the children whilst trying to find food and then preparing it in a way they could eat it. She had no time to be unwell.

Ann was about eighteen months old when Margaret fell pregnant again. She had begun to recognise the symptoms early now and was sure she was with child which was one of the reasons she had felt ill. She cried herself to sleep with the worry of another child to feed and clothe. Robert as usual was elated by the news but secretly it made him anxious due to the additional responsibility and how he would provide for his growing family.

It was not an easy pregnancy this time for Margaret as she always seemed anxious and distracted. The wind and rough seas during the summer had also made fishing more difficult during the herring season and Robert and other Eday fisherman, who had a seat in the five-man herring boats, were also noticing a reduced catch. Of growing concern to everyone was the fact that other larger boats from the north were coming in and taking more of the herring, so their future in the smaller boats was not looking good. Lack of investment by the fisheries, the short herring season and part-time nature of Orkney fishing was also forcing some young fishermen to take up opportunities elsewhere. Landlords were dividing up their land into tiny crofts which were not sustainable for those trying to remain, so it was no surprise that the population in Eday and Orkney was starting to decline. Some went to ports on the Scottish mainland or England, while others took up work with the Hudson's Bay Company in Canada or whaling off the coast of Greenland as the wages were far better than being a casual labourer or fisherman. This new life provided adventure and could combine farming, fishing or whaling and travel. Unfortunately, some of them did not return to Eday and their families never saw them again. Many of their wives were left destitute and turned to straw plaiting, spinning linen, making bonnets or gathering kelp whilst these industries lasted. Some also took up casual labour salting or gutting the fish in the herring season.

Some of the young men looking for new opportunities were acquaintances of Robert and had told him there were adverts in the *Orkney Herald* and *Orcadian* newspapers regarding emigration schemes to America, Australia and New Zealand. He could not help but think this was a last resort, but he knew some of the more adventurous souls were taking this seriously and applying for passages to America. The *Orcadian* newspaper had been in print for about 20 years and the *Orkney Herald* had been first published in Kirkwall in 1860. They were such a life-line to Orcadians as they brought news of the Orkney Isles and the outside world. Robert also remembered seeing adverts for passages to the New World in the *John O'Groat Journal* some years before when he was in Wick for the herring. He was intrigued by news of the Gold Rush in New Zealand as many Scots, English and Irish were said to have gone there to make their fortunes. He had not given it another thought but recalled that many of them had gone to the South Island as the countryside was meant to be more like Scotland.

Somehow, they managed through the winter and Margaret gave birth to a son in the spring, on the 31 March 1872, at home in Parkhead. Jane was nearly four years old and excited to have a brother and knew that he would be next to sleep in her old crib. He was her parents' first son and was named William after Robert's father. He was a bonnie boy and her father, Robert, was particularly elated he had a son and heir at last.

The summer of 1872 was uneventful and they had a reasonable crop of vegetables but the returns from fishing had diminished even more and Robert was becoming depressed every time he came home after a fishing trip. He could not go further afield to Wick as he had done in the past due to their growing family but did get a seat in a five-man boat and went to Stronsay where the herring industry was developing. Once again it was noticeable that the larger boats from the north were taking more of the catch and, as these fishermen could also sleep in cabins on board their boats, they wasted no time in preparing for their next haul.

By May 1873 Margaret fell pregnant again and was distraught with worry. Her health was suffering and she looked and felt wretched most of the time.

The strain of bringing up the children in the small cottage single handed when Robert was away was becoming unbearable. She longed for Olrig Hill with the familiar view and to be on her own for just for a few minutes.

Unfortunately, that summer was fraught, with too much wind and rain and by the autumn they faced the huge problem of crop failure. They needed to grow their own food in order to survive but the shallow topsoil had become water logged over the summer months and most of the crops rotted in the ground. There was little they could do.

Margaret knew this meant they would have to be sustained by the wind dried or smoked cuithe which was the most unappealing prospect imaginable for her. During her last pregnancy, the smell of the fish cooking made her feel so nauseous she often had to run outside for air to avoid vomiting.

They both realised that something had to change and that their way of life could not sustain them and their growing family. They needed to be inventive and possibly take some risks if they were to survive.

New Hope of a Better Life in New Zealand

One night after the three children were settled, Robert and Margaret agreed to sit at the table to have a serious discussion about the future prospects for their family. As much as Robert hated to admit it, he was struggling to put food on the table. Margaret knew he was trying his best and worked all the hours possible but they had barely enough to live on. Their children were still small but it concerned them that as they grew older they would not manage to feed and clothe them. Robert said that he could apply for work with the Hudson's Bay Company and receive a steady wage which was a possibility but Margaret forbade it as she knew he would be away in Canada for several years and she would be left to cope on her own. She secretly knew from other women that some of the men who took up an adventurous life with the Hudson's Bay Company, never came back. Robert talked about fishing on the Scottish mainland or in England but once again Margaret was not keen on this as he would be gone for long periods.

They were not getting anywhere when suddenly Robert got up, found his coat and pulled out a copy of the *Orkney Herald* from the pocket. "What do you think to this idea," he said to Margaret and turned the pages until he could see the adverts on emigration. It had finally dawned on him that changing their life and going to the new world might be a possibility for them! They would be together and could carve out a new life in a place where there were more opportunities for all. In the dim light, Margaret leaned closer and saw several adverts for emigration to America and Australia. But on the edge of the page there was an advertisement with a circle around it. The advert had been placed by the Otago Home Agency offering assisted passages to Port Chalmers, Dunedin, New Zealand and requesting agricultural labourers, farmers, navvies, ploughman, and shepherds and those with families to apply. Robert knew he had farming skills and was married with a family which must be just the sort of credentials the New Zealand Government were looking for?

An area called Otago in the South Island needed immigrants to help develop and contribute to the prosperity of the new province. Gold had been found in Otago and on the west coast in the 1860s. Dunedin was the largest city and port in Otago and still a thriving place offering many opportunities if you were prepared to work hard. They also noted the advertisements stated the New Zealand Government was offering 'subsidised passages' so it seemed an excellent time to take such a huge leap of faith.

Robert told Margaret to think about this new development for their future over the next few days and they agreed to speak again at the end of the week. Margaret could barely think of anything else and found herself dreaming of days of sunshine and warmth in this new world where food was plentiful and the children were laughing and playing all day. The idea filled her with positivity as she knew she was prepared to take this chance. When she married Robert, she had trusted her instincts and taken the risk which had proved the right thing to do. She loved Robert more now than ever as he was such a good man and father. She would trust her instincts again and, as long as Robert was in agreement about emigration to New Zealand, they would take the biggest risk in their lives together and leave Eday for a new home in a new world.

Robert thought there were two ways to look at this opportunity - it could be the biggest mistake he would ever make or it could be the best thing that ever happened to him, apart from marrying Margaret. He could no longer see a future if they stayed on Eday. He knew he had the courage to take a risk. Every time he went fishing in dangerous seas was life threatening so he had been well conditioned over the years. He was an 'Orkney farmer with a boat,' and told himself he had the skills needed and could survive almost anything ….

As agreed, when Robert returned from fishing at the end of the week, they sat down together in the cottage after all the children were asleep. Margaret reached for Robert's hand and they looked intently into each other's eyes. No words were necessary, they knew what the answer was – aye, they would be prepared to sail to the other side of the world to improve their chance of a better life.

In the past, Robert would never have contemplated leaving Eday but things were different now. With a growing family, very limited space and food, they needed a plan to change their lives. They took deep breaths and began to talk about their plan. They did not want the same life style on Eday for their children, they wanted something better for them.

Many of Robert's fisherman friends were also talking about the possibilities of living elsewhere and some were going to America and Canada. Robert however was more drawn to New Zealand, particularly the southern part as it was more like Scotland and Margaret agreed with him. Otago and Dunedin sounded the ideal starting point for their adventure as there was plenty of land for cultivation and some of the settlers were prospecting and still finding gold in the Central Otago area.

The first step of the plan was to follow the instructions in the advert and send a letter explaining their situation and why Robert's skills would be so useful to the New Zealand Government and the colony. They wasted no time and, after finding a suitable piece of paper and pen, together they carefully drafted the application letter and Robert made sure it was posted the following day. Waiting for a response was excruciatingly difficult as they tried to not think ahead and get their hopes up. They tightened their belts and brains in order to stem the hunger and excitement for change.

It took weeks for a reply to their letter to arrive, they had nearly given up all hope but by late summer, Robert stood in the cottage with the response in his hand. He could feel his heart racing and Margaret could not move on the floor, her feet seemed glued to the spot as she stared at the envelope. Finally Robert turned over the letter and opened it. His eyes scanned the page until he got to the end and with no emotion, he lifted his head and smiled widely at Margaret who knew it was a favourable reply. She ripped the letter out of his hands to read it and Robert recalled not having seen Margaret so happy since their wedding day. She danced around the cottage holding the letter and Jane was so intrigued by her mother's jubilation that she reached for her hand to dance with her.

Having got through the initial screening, the next crucial stage of selection meant Robert would have to go for an interview in Kirkwall on the Orkney mainland. He needed to meet with a representative of the Otago Home Agency who was responsible for the recruitment of potential immigrants in the Northern Scottish Isles. He would assess Robert's character, skills and overall suitability for the scheme. They were careful to select only men with the best character and skills to be part of the new colony. Orkney people were often described as adaptable, hardy and used to turning their hand to a variety of trades so Robert hoped he would make an ideal candidate. For once he felt confident in his abilities. He now needed some luck to be offered the chance to prove himself and begin a new chapter in their lives in New Zealand.

A date for his interview was suggested before Christmas and Robert and Margaret responded agreeably to this request. It was definitely a better time of year for Robert as it was winter and he didn't go fishing as often. Margaret was also pleased as their fourth child was due in January and she wanted Robert home during that month. She couldn't face the situation she had been in when Jane and Ann were born. Giving birth alone again was her worst nightmare.

The thought of changing their lives gave them both new hope and they managed their low food supplies and growing family better than they had anticipated during the weeks before Robert's interview. Margaret was heavily pregnant but her strong resolve gave her 'fuel' that helped her in those dark times. Some days were harder when the weather prevented them spending more time outdoors as the smoke from the peat made her cough more and her chest ached.

Robert thought he would not be away for too long but they planned things as well as possible so Margaret could manage without him. Jane the eldest, was given chores to help her mother and could now fetch certain items which she enjoyed doing. She also amused her sister and brother William which was a help as the three of them could now play together for short periods.

Their father left two weeks before Christmas. The weather was dreich and as he dissolved into the mist and gloom Margaret continued to look for him long after he had disappeared. She did not like to be separated from her husband and was relieved when he returned safely the following day. He said that the interview seemed to go well and was told he was a likely candidate to be offered an 'assisted passage' together with his family. There were many people applying for passages to the New World and they would be in touch in the New Year with the outcome. Detailed information such as dates of sailings and destinations would most likely be sent to him. Margaret's eyes widened in astonishment as this was such positive news. Robert explained that although it was an assisted passage and the New Zealand Government would pay £47 5s for their fare, they would most likely need to pay £5 per adult in cash or agree to a promissory note for £10 to be paid once they were in New Zealand. He stressed that they would have to sell everything possible in Eday to scrape together further money. They had to travel a long distance to the port of Greenock near Glasgow to begin their journey and would need money when they arrived on the far-off shores of Dunedin, South Island.

Margaret gave birth to their second son at home in Parkhead on 24 January 1874 after a relatively swift labour. This time, Robert was able to fetch the howdie wife to help her while he looked after the other children and their son entered the world at 8 o'clock in the morning. They called him Robert (junior). His sister Jane, who was nearly six years old, was amazed she had another tiny brother and went to her old crib to make sure it was ready for him to sleep in. She wondered who would be next as this kept happening every eighteen months or so. The only thing she didn't like before she had a new brother or sister were the loud shrieks her mother made sometimes, as it sounded like she was going to die. This time during her mother's labour, she heard her cry out the name "Robertina" which puzzled her. It was not the first time Jane had heard the name mentioned by her parents but as they always quickly changed the subject, she never knew if the name belonged to a lost brother or sister in the family or if there was another reason. She found it strange but liked mystery stories and hoped one day she would discover the answer.

A New World in the Southern Hemisphere Awaits

By the end of January, they had a letter from the Agent of the Otago Home Agency confirming that Robert Harcus and family had been selected for the 'assisted immigration scheme' of the New Zealand Government and two dates for travel to the colony were given. The first date was too close to the birth of Robert. It would take time for their emigration arrangements to be made and as they needed extra money from the sale of their possessions, they opted for a sailing on the 1st of October 1874 from Greenock, Glasgow to Port Chalmers, Dunedin New Zealand.

Over the coming weeks they drew up a list of what belongings to sell and what essentials they would need to take to New Zealand which included clothing, utensils and tools. Their possessions seemed sparse. Some were of sentimental value only but it was difficult for them to make decisions as space was limited for steerage class passengers on board the sailing ship. Over the summer of 1874 they sold off as much as they could to other families or fishermen and said many tearful, final farewells.

In late September, Robert said he wanted to make a final visit to the grave of his mother, Jane Reid, in the Old Kirkyard at Skaill. There were also other members of the Reid and Harcus families buried there and Robert liked to remember his father in the Kirkyard as he hadn't had a proper burial as he was probably lost at sea.

The whole family set off the next day to Skaill and after exploring the many graves, Margaret was reduced to tears when she saw and read the headstone that Robert had erected in 'loving memory' of his mother in March 1868. Her grave was in the most beautiful spot, the closest to the shore and overlooking the sea. Robert then dropped to his knees and slowly ran his hands over the letters on the stone, pulling back the pale green lichen in some places in order to see better.

"Goodbye dearest mother," he said. "Please watch over us in New Zealand."

Jane, who was standing near him, sensed her father's grief and placed her hand on his shoulder.

"Don't worry father," she whispered. "I think she heard you."

Robert drew her closer to kiss her and then slowly rose to his feet to join Margaret. He grasped her hand and they stood motionless for several minutes staring out to sea, thinking and hoping they were making the right decision to leave Eday. Margaret admired his passion and strength and could also see these traits in her eldest daughter. She was aware their new adventure to New Zealand would test their love for each other and test the survival of their family in very unfamiliar surroundings. But her heart told her it was the best way to give hope to the next generation.

By the time they left Eday, Jane was six and a half years old, her sister Ann nearly four years, William two years, six months and her youngest little brother Robert junior only eight months old. Her mother, Margaret, was soon to discover that infant mortality was high on board sailing ships due to dehydration, mesenteric and contagious diseases like scarletina. If she had known more about the dangers to young children they may have reconsidered their plan for a new life. But it was too late now. They were soon to set sail.

Part Three

3.

Journey to the New World

"The ocean is an object of no small terror."
Edmund Burke

Greenock, Scotland

1 October 1874

Jane stood mesmerised as she looked up at the magnificent three masted clipper moored at the Greenock dock. "Is that the *Nelson?*" she beamed and turned towards her parents. They had talked about the ship so much over the last few weeks that she could not believe this day had finally arrived. "Aye, it is," Margaret reassured her. "We will be on our way in no time, I hope."

Jane was fizzing with anticipation but had no idea that she was about to start one of the longest and most dangerous sea voyages of over 12,000 miles. The *Nelson* would take them half way round the globe in order to reach Port Chalmers in the South Island of New Zealand.

It was all very exciting and overwhelming in equal measure for Jane but she could see that her mother was not feeling the same elation and looked more miserable as each minute passed. She noticed her father was also subdued and not in a good mood, which was strange.

The thought of sailing on this floating colossus, which lay quietly waiting for its maiden voyage to begin, now filled her mother with dread. She had become petrified about the journey as the wait to board the ship lengthened. Jane's parents had discussed the options for improving their future and chose to emigrate rather than find work in industrialising cities like Glasgow which was not for them. Now, the reality of leaving Scotland for an unknown land so far away had finally struck and uncovered deep feelings of regret and helplessness which were clouding their vision of the future. Margaret had an ache in her heart which made it difficult to breathe and she could only hope the pain would leave her soon.

Jane sensed her mother's grief and tried to comfort her by saying that she couldn't wait to begin the journey so they would finally see the wonders of New Zealand. Ever since she could walk, she had developed a love of birds and wildlife like her mother. She had been told there were fantails and other brilliantly coloured native species, as well as a small brown, long beaked bird that only came out at night. Her father told her that fish were so plentiful they could be scooped up straight from the rivers.

Margaret managed a smile and from that moment, felt more able to bring her emotions back under control. "You are a special child, my bonnie girl," she said as she stroked Jane's hair. It had been a tiring overland journey to the Greenock dock near Glasgow and they had been waiting too long to board the ship. It had become increasingly more difficult for passengers to keep track of their children, bags and possessions due to the crowded dockside. Confused people were pushing and shoving for no reason. This had all got too much for Margaret and, with four young children to keep safe, she needed food and rest. They were not alone in their frustration as there were many other families with children as well as single men and women waiting to board the *Nelson*.

But Robert heard there would be further delays from a fellow passenger, Archie, who had spoken to one of the crew returning to the ship. The good news was that the New Zealand provincial and central governments set even higher standards on the immigrant ships than the British, but the problem was they would have to wait until the inspection officers had finished checking the sea worthiness of the vessel, the ventilation in passenger accommodation and the amount of food on board for the voyage. Robert and Margaret were only just beginning to realise that poor rations and conditions could lead to deaths and disease and this sudden new fear terrified them. They could also see that a carpenter had been summoned and were told he was needed to secure several bunk beds in steerage class. So the inspections continued on the *Nelson* and they had no choice but to huddle together on the dock, cold, hungry and wishing this day would be over.

In other ports in England such as London, Plymouth and Liverpool, hoards of young single men, women and families also had to wait patiently for departures of immigrant ships. Free passages to New Zealand were offered after 1873 and this decade became New Zealand's largest immigration period. Demand was high and thousands of skilled workers, labourers and domestic servants were selected by agents to travel to the southern hemisphere to start a new colonial life.

Like Margaret and Robert Harcus, they were desperate for change and prepared to give up their homeland and a life they knew for the unknown in a new world. Full of hope and courage, they had seized a free assisted passage to New Zealand in search of the greatest adventure of their lives. Gold, first found by Gabriel Reid in Tuapeka in 1861 started the Gold Rush in Otago and the South Island was still booming. However New Zealand needed more single men, women and families to work and settle on the land to help the new colony continue to thrive.

In the 1870's the journey time to New Zealand on sailing ships took between 75 and 120 days depending on the weather conditions and many passengers, including the Harcus family, would not have been able to afford the passage if assisted emigration schemes had not existed. It was therefore out of reach for a large family who were already struggling to make ends meet. The cost for single women was free. Single men had to pay at least £8 before they sailed or £4 in cash and an £8 promissory note after they arrived in the colony. Some chose the shorter route across the Atlantic to America and Canada as it was much cheaper.

Departure Greenock Dock

As the minutes ticked away, Margaret wanted the waiting to be over and was tempted to leave the port but could see that her six year old eldest child, Jane, still seemed genuinely excited about the ship and their voyage. She was relentless in trying to keep the family's spirits up by singing and playing guessing games and, although Margaret did not acknowledge it, she was grateful to her.

Then, without warning, fierce pushing and shoving began as the crowd of people waiting surged forward towards the clipper. Margaret's heart leapt at the prospect of departing and nearly missed a beat as she suddenly hauled herself up. Robert had to cope with their luggage, including some bedding whilst Margaret tried to control all the four children. She carried the bairn, Robert, whilst holding onto William's hand who walked unsteadily. Ann was told to hold Jane's hand and the two sisters walked together sandwiched between their mother and father so they did not get lost or pushed out of the way by other impatient passengers. Very slowly they eased their way forward until it was their turn to stumble up the gangway on to the ship where they felt the hard wooden planks under their feet and a slight roll due to all the extra weight of emigrants hovering on the port side of the *Nelson*.

At the top of the gangway, on the ship's main deck, a handsome officer nodded and said he was Captain Anderson. Jane giggled as she liked the captain's cap and uniform but Margaret and Robert did not dally due to the pressure from people behind them and the need to find their quarters. A crew member near the captain asked their names. Margaret felt a huge lump in her throat and tried to speak but it was too difficult, so Robert answered and they were sent in the direction of the married couples' compartment. She checked to see if all the children were present and then nodded to Robert. They were desperate to get settled before this exodus to a new world began and struggled on with their possessions to look for their hatchway. Jane was ecstatic, it was the most exciting thing she had ever experienced and she wanted to race around the deck to see everything but found her sister, Ann was not as keen.

Margaret took tentative steps as the ship seemed low in the water and she shuddered at the thought of it ploughing through heavy seas. She found it hard to fathom how such a huge sailing ship kept afloat and feared the deep ocean, the high winds, storms and shipwreck. She had also begun to worry about seasickness and how her young children would cope. Her husband, Robert who was a fisherman, would have good sea-legs she thought, but this seemed rather unfair as the rest of the family would have to 'find' theirs.

They did not know exactly how long this voyage would take but knew they could be on the ship for up to four months. "Dearest God," Margaret uttered under her breath. "Please protect us and allow a safe passage to New Zealand." She swallowed her prayer and set about finding her way around the vessel that would be their home and children's playground for the rest of the year at least. They were unbelievably tired and hungry but found the married couples' section of the ship by following the swarm of other families. Some immigrants had paid for their fares and were in 'intermediate' cabins or cabins below the poop deck but the Harcuses had been paid for by the New Zealand Government, they were in steerage.

As they climbed down through the hatchway on the narrow stairs Margaret was aghast when she saw this low-ceilinged space beneath the main deck. Robert had difficultly carrying their luggage and had to stoop the whole time as headroom was limited. Her eyes took time to adjust to the dim interior but the smell was already overwhelming due to so many people crammed into this confined space. She could now understand why these ships were inspected for ventilation but immediately knew there was scarcely any. Unless you were on deck, or in a cabin, there was no chance of adequate fresh air in steerage. Tears filled her eyes as they limped on until they found their allocated tiers of bunks.

Young Jane loved the new sleeping arrangements and immediately chose a bunk and rushed over to bounce on it but the straw mattress was solid which was disappointing. Her father looked particularly worried as he could see how cramped they were and wondered whether he would be able to stretch out. They had brought very little bedding with them but could see they were unlikely to need much as it would be so hot and stuffy. Their entire living space consisted of the tiers of bunks with a table between and wooden forms either side to sit on. Their small cottage in Eday seemed cavernous by comparison. Margaret knew it was a newly built ship and meant to be well appointed, but from what she saw it was hard to believe. They were surrounded by many other families and their closest neighbours were friendly souls who immediately introduced themselves. The husband, Duncan, from Lanark told them that steerage was divided into three compartments with separate hatches. He said that like other immigrant ships, the single men and women were kept well apart; the young men occupied the forward area next to the crew's quarters, while the lassies were near the stern. All the married couples and children were in the middle with a main hatch to reach the deck. He also said, scathingly, that it was only the privileged cabin passengers who enjoyed more space, better food and privacy but forgot to mention that the cheapest cabin class fare was over three times that of steerage class so it was no surprise the majority of passengers were in the space below decks.

After half an hour, they heard the unfamiliar clattering sound of the anchor being hauled up and shouting going on above them. A steerage passenger then suddenly came rushing down from the hatchway to announce that the Union Jack had been raised and the ship was about to leave the dock. Feelings of excitement and fear were palpable and everyone rushed to the stairs leading to the hatchway so they could be on the deck to take their last view of bonnie Scotland.

The *Nelson* was finally loaded with passengers, emigrants and 1500 tons of cargo including 300 tons of railway iron for the colony and to help her on her way, due to a lack of notable breeze, this splendid clipper was being assisted from the dock by a small steam tug until the winds picked up to begin their journey.

As the ship was slowly pulled away from the dock by the tug and out into the Clyde, the emigrants who stood on the deck were crying and waving as they bid farewell to Glasgow and Scotland. But the festive air was tinged with doubt by many and the jubilation faded quickly. Margaret stood rigid, trying to ignore the gentle roll of the ship and the creaking of the rigging. She remained silent as she took her last fond look of her native shore and summoned every ounce of courage to drive away her fears. The hope of a better future was all that mattered now. She turned away from the dock and thought that tomorrow would be brighter, it had to be. Robert had no time to be downcast as he was dealing with the children and making sure Jane did not fall overboard due to her excitement.

To everyone's surprise the clipper was only pulled about half a mile out by the tug and then dropped anchor. This confounded most of those on board, as the scary anticipation then jubilation they felt when they left Greenock now seemed unfounded. They did not know the reason for the delay and would have to keep their emotions in check until this voyage was genuinely underway. Margaret let out a huge sigh and tried to remain composed although she could have easily screamed with frustration. There was nothing that could be done apart from wait. The children were tired and irritable so they would have to go below decks to steerage and hope they could be settled.

One of the benefits of having close neighbours in their compartment was the fact that news did not take long to circulate and within an hour, Margaret heard that an Emigration Officer had now boarded the ship and there would be a Health

Inspection of all passengers before the *Nelson* could be on her way. She was shocked to hear this after all they had been through but realised it was a requirement of the New Zealand Government before immigrant ships could sail. If anyone showed signs of contagious disease they would have to leave the clipper and be returned to land. New Zealand did not want immigrant ships bringing diseases into the new colony or deaths on board during the voyage if a disease took hold, such as scarlet fever or measles. There were terrible stories already of immigrant ships to New Zealand where many children and others had died during the voyage or when in quarantine on arrival, so the threat from disease was very real.

Everyone was summoned to the main deck and all the emigrants had to stand in a long snaking queue in order to be examined by the ship's Surgeon Superintendent, Dr John Harkness Macaffer and the Emigration Officer. It seemed the inspection was a brief affair due to the large number of people and Margaret could see that other families stood in front of the Doctor and Emigration Officer for only a few seconds.

While they were waiting in line, Margaret and Robert had plenty of time to talk to other passengers and found out there were about 360 souls on board, including single men, women, married couples and children. Most were Scottish but there were a small number of Irish. They also discovered that the paying passengers in cabin class had a special transfer to the *Nelson* from the Princes Pier in the *Flying Dutchman* tug and did not have to undergo all the inconveniences steerage were suffering. They would also soon discover that the smell emanating from the live animals and hens in the hold, below where they slept, was the fresh meat and eggs for the dinner plates of cabin class only and not for themselves.

Eventually, it was time for the Harcus family to give their names to Dr Macaffer and the Emigration Officer and be examined fully clothed. They were asked brief questions and once their names were checked on the passenger list, they were all deemed free of disease and told to move on.

When Robert was waiting for their health inspection, he saw Archie who he had met on the Greenock dock. They discussed the *Nelson's* current predicament and

Robert soon realised Archie was very knowledgeable about the ship. "This is her maiden voyage, you know," he said positively. "Yes," said Robert, who had been told by the Agent but had only shared the information with Margaret that morning to prevent her from dwelling on it over the past few months. "Robert Duncan, the ship builder, has produced a fine clipper and credit must go to the owner Patrick Henderson," Archie went on to say. "She now runs for the Albion Company on the New Zealand - Britain trading route with similar fine ships such as the Dunedin, Invercargill and Auckland. She has an iron hull unlike the older sailing ships whose wooden hulls suffered from the likes of ship worm and barnacles which slowed them down.

"Is that right," said Robert who knew a thing or two about sailing and boats but was not aware of the latest developments in ship building. "Clippers are designed for speed," Archie remarked proudly. "The first smaller ships were designed to clip over the waves rather than plough through them. The *Nelson* was designed to be fast, so we shall see how many knots she can make riding a trade wind or with the Roaring Forties westerlies behind her." Archie was prepared to have a bet there and then but Robert held back, he wanted to see how well she could harness the wind, fully rigged first.

Archie then admitted that, even as a boy, he had found sailing ships fascinating. He never had the urge to join a ship's crew but stuck to farming as he had read too many stories about sailors and ships who had been lost or wrecked navigating round Cape Horn at the bottom of South America. It was one of the most treacherous places in the world and he also knew about freak storms or icebergs that can arise in the Southern Ocean which had claimed many souls to the deep. Luckily the *Nelson* was returning via Cape Horn so they were spared that worry but the more Archie talked, the more concerned Robert became. He had not seen much of the ship yet and had no idea about its seaworthiness or how it would cope in rough seas. He hoped they had a capable captain and crew as everything was out of his hands. He had been in control of the smaller boats he sailed back in Orkney, so this new sea adventure began to deeply concern him. He looked up towards the three masts and Archie followed his eyes. "Some of these tall ships can have up to five masts you know Robbie," he said. It was obvious the middle, main mast was the tallest, the fore-mast nearest the bow was not quite as high and the aft mizzen-mast towards the rear of the ship was slightly lower than the fore-mast. Robert became intensely interested to see the ship with full canvas on the masts but would have to wait for now. Both men began to think about how long they thought this maiden, port to port, voyage would take with such heavy cargo and over 300 souls on board.

They were to meet many times on the journey to discuss the route and how well the *Nelson* harnessed the winds which gave them great comfort. Robert was already aware that the ship would follow a similar passage taken to transport convicts in the late 18th century to Australia. After heading out of the Clyde to the Irish Sea, the first part of the route would take them round the coast of England towards the Bay of Biscay, off France. On a southwest course in the North Atlantic Ocean, they would pass the coasts of Portugal, Spain and West Africa and continue on to cross the Equator in the latitude of northern Brazil. The *Nelson* would travel down the coast of South America and then sail in a south easterly direction and pass South Africa below the Cape of Good Hope. This second part of the journey would allow the ship to pick up the stronger westerly winds which should move her at good speed towards New Zealand. Robert was looking forward to the ride but he worried about sailing further south for stronger winds as Archie had said that there was always the risk of violent storms and icebergs in the Southern Ocean or the Tasman Sea between Australia and New Zealand. Archie had also read that daring captains of other clippers had encountered atrocious conditions or been ship wrecked when they travelled too far south in the ice zone. Robert frowned and stroked his beard. He knew they would be at the mercy of the winds and the sea and dearly hoped for everyone's sake, they could trust the navigation skills of Captain Anderson and his crew.

Margaret looked exhausted and, as all the family needed rest, they made their way towards the main hatch and their quarters. It had been 48 hours like no other due to the upheaval of leaving Eday and finding their way to Greenock to board the ship. Then, just as the younger children were falling asleep, they felt the tremble and grinding of the anchor being hauled up and a steerage passenger excitedly shout from the hatch that the tug had been cast off and sails were being hoisted. Some of the emigrants let out a cheer as this time their journey seemed certain to begin. Many scrambled up through the hatch in time to see the Gun being fired - the signal the *Nelson* had set sail.

Like children learning to walk, the majority of people lost their balance and stumbled around the main deck, but they were laughing and joking as the strong breeze caught the sails. They learnt quickly about the best places to hold on as the ship pitched and rolled. Robert made his way up to the main deck to experience, for the first time, the wind in the sails of the clipper and to check how slippery the wooden planks on the deck felt under his feet when the waves spurted over them. Protecting his family from injury on the deck was going to be a difficult job.

Below decks there was relief and a new excitement as families began to organise themselves as best they could as the *Nelson* rolled from side by side. They learnt about the ship board meal routines and discovered that they were expected to be up by 7.00 a.m., with the children washed, dressed and tidy before Breakfast at 8.00 a.m. At 9.00 a.m. the children would go to school and other emigrants were expected to begin their chores such as cleaning their berths, doing the washing on their designated day, scrubbing the decks or other areas of the ship. Dinner was at 1.00 p.m., Tea at 6.00 p.m. and lights out at 8.00 p.m. This night-time curfew was going to be tough and already emigrants were thinking of ways to keep on a low light in their section of the compartment. The main deck was also off limits to them at night to protect their safety and crew would be on watch duty. Margaret worried how they would cope with such long nights and the need for fresh air. She also found out it was very different for cabin class passengers who could do anything and go anywhere they pleased.

Food for steerage would be cooked in the central galley then divided for each 'mess' and the Harcus family found out they would share their allowance with another neighbouring family of three. The Albion shipping company was required to follow 'dietary scales' on emigrant vessels and Margaret and Robert hoped the ship owners would not skimp on rations as they were ravenous. When their tea arrived it was mainly salted meat, ship's biscuit and potatoes but, thankfully, there was a good quantity of it. They were so hungry they ate every morsel and washed it down with tea or coffee. Each person was allowed over three litres of fresh water a day but it was stored in barrels which worried them as it could quickly become undrinkable. It also had to be used for washing which was a problem so they decided, like other families, they would try and catch any fresh rainwater for drinking or washing.

As the *Nelson* was a brand new ship, it might have a condenser to distil sea water for drinking and one of the men said he would find out. Everyone knew it may not increase their ration but at least they would know fresh water could be provided. As time went on, they realised they needed to drink more water on board ship than they would normally need on land to stave off dehydration and gut problems.

Margaret was surprised by the military style of discipline on board but was relieved to hear that their afternoons would be free to do as they pleased and looked forward to the prospect of some spare time. That day she also became aware of the importance of their young Surgeon Superintendent, Dr Macaffer who was only 23 years old. He was said to be trustworthy, but he had only just qualified from Glasgow University and had never been on a long voyage on a sailing ship. Other passengers confirmed that sometimes the Surgeons appointed for these voyages could be very inexperienced and too fond of a drink! They had easy access to 'medical comforts' like sherry, gin, brandy and stout which were only meant to be for the sick or those with stomach complaints. Some were known to also take opium for their own ailments. They were paid very little for their services but hopefully this was not a problem for Dr Macaffer as he was emigrating to New Zealand on this voyage. They prayed he could cope and that they would be in safe hands if emergencies arose.

Margaret discovered that he was not only responsible for their health, but he had to keep order with the emigrants below decks. They found out that he had appointed a matron, who was charged with looking after the moral wellbeing of the single women and constables to ensure the single men behaved at the opposite end of the ship. He also helped organise the distribution of rations and gave the single, male steerage passengers other shipboard duties to keep them more occupied. Margaret and Robert were also pleased that he had appointed a schoolmaster to teach the children as Jane would enjoy going to school and mixing with other children her own age.

Leaving the Clyde

The rest of their first day was long, cold and exhausting. As they carefully headed out of the River Clyde towards the Isle of Bute, a southwesterly gale became relentless which forced the ship to constantly pitch and roll. The majority had never experienced the strange motion of a huge clipper under their feet before or felt the punishing wind and salt on their skin. So it was no surprise the bewildered emigrants staggered like drunks and screamed in fear when huge waves crashed over the deck in front of them. For many this was accompanied by nausea and other symptoms of seasickness.

One by one, the children became ill due to the rolling of the ship. William was violently sick, then Ann and the bairn, Robert. Margaret had felt nauseous for some time and eventually had to rush to the side to relinquish her last meal. She was not alone, as many others were retching and coughing on the deck around them. There seemed no escape from seasickness!

Robert tried to give sound advice to his family but knew that their bodies had to get accustomed to the motion of the sailing ship. He was not feeling great either but did not admit it and just hoped they would not suffer for too long. To his amazement Jane, although looking a little green in colour, had not been ill and stayed close to her father heeding his every word. She was also keeping herself busy trying to help the others by bringing water which was a useful distraction for her. Margaret was becoming more nauseous and stressed by the minute as the youngest children urgently needed fresh clothing and a change of napkins but she knew their other belongings including clothing were in the hold and not available to them as yet. They were all better off on deck rather than the poorly ventilated steerage quarters, but as the ship continued to roll and the southwesterly wind swirled like an ice blanket around them they were forced to retire below decks.

Margaret was desperate to lie down. Her emotions were in tatters. If the passage on the *Nelson* continued to be so wretched she would, most likely, not live to tell the tale. She had never felt so ill; her head throbbed, her stomach churned and her throat was so parched she could barely swallow.

They struggled to find their way to the main hatch in the wind and rain but found the steps and slowly descended to their compartment. Half way down, Margaret witnessed a scene, like a war zone, as bodies lay sprawled on bunks or on the floor and the pungent smell of human excrement and vomit made even the hardiest, feel nauseous. Due to inadequate toilet facilities and no privacy, it was difficult to find a dry patch on the floor to walk on.

Margaret's symptoms escalated further and, as well as nausea, she suffered clammy perspiration, vertigo, stomach cramps and seemed to be drifting into delirium. It was a dreadful, debilitating illness like nothing she had ever experienced and she lay helpless as her body was involuntarily still trying to remove the evil. Sometimes women suffered more from 'mal de mer' but it could effect anyone at any time on ships due to bad weather and rough seas.

Jane was standing by her mother's bunk trying to help when she heard her cry out. "Where is Robertina, is she safe?," before her eyes rolled upwards. Jane was rather dumbfounded, but replied. "Yes mother, all is well …" as she thought the reply might help. Robert told Jane, her mother did not know what she was saying and stepped closer to try and soothe his wife but by then, she lay limp. Suddenly when he turned away to try and think more clearly, she began choking which frightened him and he rushed back to turn her on her side. "Enough," he said. "I must call for the surgeon. "Jane please watch over your brothers and sisters while I am away." Fortunately, Jane was not overcome by seasickness and Robert junior, William and Ann were nearly asleep due to their exhaustion. Robert was worried that they might fall out of their bunks while he was away, as Margaret was on the bottom bunk, but he decided he had to take the risk. He made his way on the slippery floor towards the hatch to try and locate Dr Macaffer and was rewarded quickly as by the time he was up on deck, he could see the surgeon heading towards him. Robert pleaded for him to tend to Margaret as a matter of urgency and he told Robert he would do his best but there were many needy passengers in steerage in want of his medicine.

Robert could see Dr Macaffer was horrified when he saw the state of their compartment and watched him quickly cover his face with a handkerchief. He was summoned first to a small infant who looked gravely ill but within ten minutes he made his way to see Margaret. He checked her vital signs and declared she would not die but they must try to keep giving her water. "And more water for the children too," he said. "They must keep drinking." This was easier said than done but Robert and Jane would try their best.

Dr Macaffer confessed there was no cure as such for seasickness but often a dose of 'comforting liquor' was a useful medicine. As his medical bag was open it was no surprise they could see brandy, sherry and gin in his tool-kit. He suggested that Robert should try and give Margaret a tot of brandy when she awoke to help settle her stomach but Robert did not hold much hope she would be able to tolerate this hard liquor. Getting her to take water was his first concern.

He could hear passengers close by agreeing that a remedy containing alcohol, sugar and opium was the best cure for adults but Robert had never heard of it and was very wary of giving this to Margaret. He prayed that she would be strong enough to overcome her sickness soon.

Late that night, Dr Macaffer informed Captain Anderson of the distress many passengers were under and as there was no let-up in the severe southwesterly gales, the captain gave the order for the *Nelson* to take shelter in the bay near Rothersay, Isle of Bute. They were still in the inner sea off the west coast of Scotland but this pause came as a welcome relief to all and, as it transpired, the ship lay there for two more days awaiting a change in the weather.

Margaret could not move from her bunk during most of this time at anchor and Jane and Robert fed her spoonfuls of water on an hourly basis. They were lucky the *Nelson* was detained as it gave her and other passengers a chance to recover. She couldn't help clean up their compartment and was horrified at the sighting of the first rat. Many emigrants escaped on deck to shirk this horrid chore and the crew complained bitterly that they had to help. The smell lingered due to the poor ventilation and Robert felt physically sick every time he returned below decks.

Their Last Sight of Scotland

When the weather became more moderate they put to sea again and some emigrants, with an interest in the sport of curling, took delight when the granite rocky island of Ailsa Craig was spotted off the Ayrshire coast. The quality of the green granite used in curling stones from this small island was well known by players. As well as travelling far away from other family and life-long friends, it was another pastime many were leaving behind. Upper most in their minds however was coping with their new life and conditions on board ship which had already proved challenging.

The *Nelson* encountered more westerly gales in the Irish Sea but she cleverly weathered the winds and they continued onwards. They passed Rosslare, south of Wexford, Ireland and were now headed towards St George's Channel. The ship had not lost sight of land yet and this was proving a very difficult start to the journey unlike the ships *Araby Lady* and the *Florence* that preceded her. The following day she encountered a further heavy, southwesterly gale but battled her way through and proved herself an admirable sea-worthy ship as those in steerage only noticed a small amount of water had seeped through the planks from the main deck.

But just as Margaret was able to find the strength to get up and take short walks, the intense winds and rolling of the ship made her feel wretched once again. She was forced to remain in her quarters in a very sorry state. She had lost a lot of weight and looked grey and frail. Her hair was lank and her eyes had no sparkle. She needed a good wash but carrying out women's hygiene on board was difficult due to a lack of privacy and inadequate washing facilities. Robert asked Dr Macaffer to see her again as he was so concerned about her and he diagnosed that she was so dehydrated she was now constipated and supplied the necessary remedy. He also advised more tea and ship's biscuits as she was not eating. Swallowing food had become a problem due to suffering such discomfort from seasickness. "You must eat," he bellowed, "or your strength will never fully return." Margaret nodded, but the thought of food still made her retch.

Crossing the Bay of Biscay, France

Soon the *Nelson* entered the Bay of Biscay off the coast of western France but, unusually, she found herself in a 'calm' and endured the lack of winds for three more days. It was another setback and many emigrants got bored with yet another delay and the swell in the Bay triggered others to feel the misery of seasickness once again. Margaret felt nauseous but was not ill and Robert reassured her she was now finding her sea-legs. She hoped it was true as they had many weeks of travel to come and oceans to cross. The journey had begun badly for her as she had already experienced some of the dangers and misery of sailing ships.

There was a cheer when the *Nelson* set to sea again. They were now well clear of land and as they continued to travel further southwest their journey in the North Atlantic Ocean would be helped by the northeast trade winds for a faster passage towards the Equator. At last, at full sail in moderate winds, it became easier to move around on board and everyone including Margaret, spent more time on deck to experience the freshness of the breeze.

They thought they had lost sight of land but someone started pointing to a land mass in the ocean on the port side of the ship and the crew member on watch duty, shouted "Madeira." It was hard to believe how far they had travelled as they had passed Spain and were now off the coast of Morocco, Africa. That day there was also great excitement when porpoises started leaping out of the water and the first gigantic whale was spotted following the ship.

Unlike her mother, Jane realised she loved sailing ships and being on the sea. She lingered on deck whenever she could and became fascinated by how the many different sails captured the wind to allow the ship to travel at such speed. She looked up to the tallest, middle mast of the ship to focus on the crow's nest as she often watched seamen scampering up there on lookout duty. She promised herself that one day she would climb to that tiny platform, high above the ship, to feel what it was like. This voyage was such an adventure and, even as a young girl, she knew she would never forget the exhilaration of the wind on her face and in her hair and the anticipation of a new exciting life when they finally reached their destination. She held on and smiled to herself as the *Nelson* expertly carved her way through the ocean.

Margaret, her mother, then came rushing over and told her it may be best to go below decks as there was going to be a funeral. Margaret could hardly believe what she was saying but it had come to her attention that a family she had met in their compartment had lost their six month old son, Thomas, the previous night. He had died of a mesenteric disease and Margaret was deeply concerned as her youngest son, Robert, was only eight months old. Many of the women with young children were talking and crying due to the loss of a child so young and when Dr Macaffer appeared they all flocked round him. He was very sorry for the death of this child and had tried his best to save it but said that there was little he could do in the end. Very young children were particularly vulnerable to infections and the shipboard diet was not always adequate as it lacked preserved milk and other foods containing protein, like eggs and cheese that are good for mothers who are breast feeding. One woman cried out that it was very different in cabin class as they got fresh meat, fruit and milk. Margaret now understood that the stinking smell of animals that permeated steerage from time to time was the destined meat, main courses for the cabin classes. It made her angry when she thought of the class privileges but admitted to herself that no one was starving in steerage, the meals were just rather monotonous. Dr Macaffer also said that so far, there was no sign of infectious diseases such as scarlet fever, diphtheria, whooping cough or measles on board which were his worst fear.

He had been pleased with the cleanliness of the ship when the emigrants first boarded. It was her maiden voyage after all, and although ventilation was not good in steerage, which was often blamed for the spread of disease, no one had presented with any symptoms to make him suspicious. The Doctor thought they must be a good, strong class of emigrants as other ships he had heard of had suffered terrible losses if passengers brought infections on board with them. He recalled voyages of emigrant ships to New Zealand earlier in 1874 when 26 died on the *Scimitar* from Plymouth as some passengers boarded the ship already infected with scarlet fever or measles from their temporary barracks. On the *SS Atrato* 33 children had tragically died of croup, measles or diphtheria. He knew New Zealand quarantined ships on arrival if there was disease on board and hoped that the *Nelson's* voyage would be free of major infections and passengers would remain healthy.

The next thing that Margaret heard was the call for 'all hands' on deck and everyone stood speechless as they watched a man carrying a small body bound in a sail cloth and covered by the Union Jack. It was the father of the child who had died the previous night, the 26th of October. He was followed by his wife and their other children dressed in their Sunday best.

All passengers, officers and seamen were expected to attend and show respect by removing their hats. The family with the dead child walked towards the captain and doctor at the side of the ship where a boatswain was balancing a plank. The body was placed on the plank and the captain began reading the service. When it was time the captain gave a blessing and committed the child to God and the deep. The boatswain, holding the plank with the corpse in one hand and the Union Jack in the other, carefully lifted the plank upwards to allow the small bundle to gently slide over the side and enter the cold, watery grave of the North Atlantic Ocean. Everyone slowly recited the Lord's Prayer as the corpse sank further and further into the dark depths. Many just kept their heads lowered and there was hardly a dry eye to be seen. Once the prayer had ended, the captain signalled for a return to normal duties and the crowd quickly dispersed in all directions. Others offered words of comfort to the bereaved family. Margaret was feeling emotionally drained. After experiencing her first funeral on board, both herself and Robert were well aware this could have been one of their children. He gently guided her to their quarters for some tea and a drop of left over brandy which might just help to restore them. He had also overheard the father of the dead boy asking the captain for the exact latitude and longitude at the time of his death as he wanted to put the coordinates on a burial stone back in Scotland, in memory of his son. Margaret was comforted to hear this as the life of this small child should never be forgotten and it would help relatives at home come to terms with this tragic loss.

The next morning at breakfast, Margaret noticed her elder daughter, Jane, would not eat. They always had oatmeal porridge and dry biscuits which was not a favourite of the children but they had to make do as there were no alternatives. Some families had brought more food with them such as jam, sugar, cheese or ham but this was not the case for their family. They had eaten the meagre rations they had brought with them from Eday days ago. When Margaret questioned Jane why she would not eat Jane, still with her head down, said that they were going to burn a dead horse. Margaret looked at Robert in bewilderment? "Where did you hear this?" Margaret asked. "After we found the best place for our classroom on the deck yesterday, one of my friends told me." Margaret still looked confused as she was not aware there were any horses on board. She thought there were only sheep, pigs and hens. As Jane loved all animals, she could not bear the thought of what might be about to happen and overnight her feelings had intensified which explained why she had now completely lost her appetite. "Your father and I will find out what is going on," Margaret said to try and pacify her and quickly changed the subject.

Jane went off to school at 9 a.m. and, during their cleaning chores on the main deck, Robert asked the first mate who was standing close by, if he had heard about the burning of a dead horse? The young man smiled, and told him that it was a ceremony played out by the seamen, usually after dark, and was called throwing the 'dead horse overboard.' It happens on the last night of the month after leaving port as the seamen's pay then begins again. They were paid a month in advance before sailing, so on the 31 October all old scores were struck out and they get rid of their 'old horse.' It involved hauling a sack of rubbish from their berth onto the main deck and making fast a long line from it up to the foreyard. Then, whilst singing an outlandish song, amid cheers and cries from all on board they pulled the rope and the 'old horse' dropped into the waves, soon to be left far behind. Robert thanked the first mate. It was great news to tell Jane. She would be heartened to know it was just a ceremony and could begin eating again!

The *Nelson* stayed in the path of the northeast trade winds and the constant breeze was welcome. Robert had ventured up on deck in the afternoon as he liked to have a short time alone. He also loved to see the ship fully rigged and today he counted 30 sails which was spectacular; no wonder she was proving a fast goer. He spotted his friend Archie and the first mate on the starboard side of the ship enjoying this section of the voyage and walked over to greet them. Archie beckoned him to hurry as he was pointing at a speck of land in the distance. The first mate confirmed they were looking in the direction of the Cape Verde Islands off the coast of West Africa. He handed his telescope to Robert so he could take a closer look and said that the first small Cape Verde island in view would be San Antonio. Archie got very excited and said to Robert, who was trying to focus on this tiny land mass. "What can you see?" Robert held Archie in suspense for a moment and then said. "I can see a rocky island and a sign that says, this way to New Zealand!" The first mate smiled but Archie and Robert roared with laughter as they continued to gaze towards the islands.

From where they were standing, they could also see young ladies on the poop deck having fun. They were rolling up paper and then trying to stuff each piece into a bottle. The task seemed a difficult one and they were making a lot of noise due to failed attempts inserting the paper down the neck of each bottle. "What are they up to?" asked Robert. Other emigrants were also watching and a woman close by told Robert and Archie. "The girls are sending a message in a bottle." A minute later, amid much laughter, they saw them hurling the corked bottles into the sea. "Of course, they are sending messages home," said Archie. "Could take a few years ...." said Robert. They discovered it helped some of the passengers to put a message in a bottle saying 'all is well on board'. Many missed their friends and families back home dreadfully and it was a way of sending a message to tell them they were alive and all was well. Other passengers sent a message just for fun and to dream of where the bottle might be washed up.

Robert and Archie enjoyed each other's company and their friendship helped to pass the long days at sea. Archie liked being on board and told Robert that the *Nelson* was proving a splendid ship. "The crew have been very obliging to me as they know I like to ask questions," he went on to say. "I need to be careful though, as they will have me on a midnight watch before too long." He jested. "Better than stuck in steerage," Robert replied. He had to admit that, most nights, he was finding it hard to sleep. "Aye, what you need is a ration of brandy, that will help you sleep," Archie said. "I will see what I can do." Robert raised his eyebrows and smiled at his friend.

They talked again about the route of the ship and Archie reminded Robert that they were headed towards the Equator and should cross it close to the Saint Peter and Paul Rocks about 600 miles off the northeast coast of Brazil. They would then sail down the South Atlantic Ocean following the natural winds and currents and go close to the large island of Trindade before slowly curving southeast past Tristan da Cunha, the most remote group of inhabited islands in the world. On this course, the *Nelson* would pass well below the Cape of Good Hope, South Africa and head straight into the Roaring Forties, known for strong westerly winds which should speed up their journey towards New Zealand. "Remember that well before this, we will cross 'the line'," Archie said. "The line,"

Robert asked looking confused. "Do you mean the Equator, my friend?" "Yes indeed," Archie replied.

Sailing in the Tropics

They were well into the Tropics now and as they edged towards the Equator, the temperature soared, sometimes it was nearly 80 degrees in the shade. The sun slowly rose from the east about 6.00 a.m. like a glowing ball of fire and sank to its watery western bed like clockwork at 7.00 p.m. Many on board watched in wonderment as the sun cast its spell on them twice a day. It somehow settled them and filled them with hope and certainty.

Whilst in the equatorial belt, another child, aged five months had become desperately ill with chronic diarrhoea and had died on the 5th of November. A sombre mood befell those on board the *Nelson* once again. Margaret was aghast and her heart ached for the family of the little girl. She clung to Robert, her youngest child, and wouldn't let the others out of her sight. This was the second death within a month. It was apparent that a small child could become ill very quickly with no warning, and in such cases little could be done to save it which was horrifying for parents. This time the family wanted the funeral 'under the stars' and that night 'all hands' were called on deck once again. Margaret did not know the family concerned and was spared attending the service and the sight of the small bundle committed to the deep. But she lay awake in her bunk, unable to sleep, while the service was taking place above her on that still, hot night. She became so restless, she made her way up the stairs of the open hatch and sat there to try and listen to the service. She was fortunate to hear part of a poem recited by one of the family.

"There are no roses on the grave or wreaths upon the storm tossed waves. No heartbroken words carved on stone, just a little body floating alone. The only tributes when the seagulls sweep and a teardrop as a loved one weeps. May the lord watch over you and keep you safe as you rest in peace in this watery place." (Far From Home, author unknown).

Margaret was able to whisper the Lord's Prayer at the end of the service which soothed her briefly but her tears fell to the floor as she crept back to her bunk in the darkness. The sadness she felt was unbearable but she bore it alone and did not wake Robert who had unusually remained asleep. He would be awake soon enough as he never managed to sleep after about 4.00 a.m.

Reaching the Equator, near Brazil

The day after the second funeral the ship's normal routine resumed with morning cleaning taking place, inspections of steerage berths and chores such as scrubbing the decks with lime and soda while the children continued their schooling in the shade, under a tarpaulin. In the afternoon, a strange sense of excitement began to infect everyone on board as they would soon be crossing the Equator. Sure enough they crossed 'the line' at 30 degrees longitude on the 6th November.

The captain made a brief appearance on the main deck and announced they were now days out from Greenock. He had hoped for a faster journey but explained it was due to the unusual seven day delay around the British coast. He hoped to make up time in the cooler waters of the Southern Ocean with the westerly winds behind them. To everyone's surprise a handful of playful crew suddenly sprung up and began to hose people down, especially some of the men standing nearby. Robert was in close range and found himself drenched in seconds. It was a special moment as seamen always loved to celebrate crossing the 'imaginary line' to the southern hemisphere. Some shaved off their beards if they had never crossed the line before and were also known to seize other passengers and shave them, especially if they had big beards. The problem was the lather could be tar and the razor a broken blade of an oar!

The sun was high overhead and with the increasing heat, Margaret only wished she had been hosed down as she longed to feel cool and clean. It was so tiresome for women that they were not able to wash properly on board and sea water was unpleasant to use, even with the special soap. Her hair remained lank and dry throughout the voyage and her clothes felt damp and smelt of salt most days. The current weather should have helped dry the washing quicker, Margaret thought, but she found that the high humidity meant clothes remained damp for much longer.

It was a problem as the children's clothes needed to be washed regularly to keep any lice or other bugs at bay. It was another fear everyone faced as infected children could pass the lice on to others so easily in steerage. She had also seen the family who had just lost their daughter throw all her bedding and clothes overboard as this was a requirement on emigrant ships to try and reduce any further problems in the compartments. The women were rapidly realising how dangerous it was for young children in the poorly ventilated steerage class to pick up these infections, including diarrhoea, let alone their risk from dehydration.

The *Nelson* was soon to be stuck in the Equatorial doldrum belt for several more days due to headwinds from the southeast trades. An upset came when a sudden squall blew up in the night. Passengers began to feel sea sick again due to the severe gusts and the rolling of the ship. Accompanying torrents of fierce tropical rain caused flooding on the deck and the mizzen royal sail was partially shredded. 'All hands' were called during the night as the ship was in danger and the seamen frantically worked to reef down more sails.

The baking tropical sun returned the following morning and once again it became too stifling hot to remain below in steerage. The smell from the latrines and animals was sickening and worsened as the temperature continued to rise. Fresh water was limited to their normal rations but they all needed more to drink in the humid, hot environment. Some of the young men jumped overboard for a swim if they were brave enough and the children got very excited watching them. Jane wished she could join in but Robert held on to her dress ties just in case she made an attempt. Luckily, she occupied herself playing other games such as quoits with plaited rope and enjoyed skipping and singing with children her own age. She also loved to look out for 'flying fish' with her father. She thought he was telling tales as he liked to keep her guessing, but then one day when they were gazing out to sea, the most beautiful, torpedo shaped fish flew out of the warm water right in front of them. It had large, wing-like pectoral fins and an uneven forked tail and Robert said that the big fins helped it become airborne although the shape of the fish allowed it to travel fast underwater to gather speed before it propelled itself upwards. He didn't know much about these fish, a type of cod he thought, but he knew that sometimes fish did leap out of the water to escape predators. Jane was impressed and everyday rushed to the side of the ship in the hope she would see more. Other times, during their days at sea any boredom was rewarded by spotting porpoises, dolphins and whales. She adored sea life as did her father and became overjoyed if these amazing creatures ventured close enough to be seen clearly.

To relieve some of Robert's boredom, he started fishing off the stern of the ship. He was more inclined to try catching smaller fish on long lines but one day managed to bring in a barracuda which took all his strength to haul on board. He was the top fisherman that day and Margaret and the children were extremely proud of him. As it was such a large fish, he shared it with their 'mess' and they all enjoyed eating it that night. It was such a change to have fish and he thought it tasted a bit like mackerel. During their tea, he told those around him that there were other unruly souls at the back of the ship attempting to harpoon porpoises and sharks. "It was barbaric," said Robert. "I could not condone the hunting of these species just for entertainment." But he then laughed loudly and added that some of the men nearly went overboard due to their daring, unsuccessful attempts. It was a jolly evening, full of good cheer and laughter but the time for 'lights out' to retire for the night would soon be upon them. Their two youngest children were already asleep.

Margaret was sitting on the bench by the table and whispered in Robert's ear that she needed to go on deck. She had not eaten fish for weeks and hoped she would not suffer due to her delicate digestive system. "Of course," he said. "You must go, I will watch over the children."

Margaret got up and walked slowly towards the hatchway in the dim light, she needed air due to the heat in steerage and more space to breathe. She climbed the stairs to the deck and carefully made her way to the side of the ship. She found herself alone on this part of the deck and couldn't believe the magnificent moon and star-studded sky above and all around her. I have been waiting for this moment all my life she thought, as she tilted her head back to gaze into the sparkling depths of infinity before closing her eyes. The slight, soft breeze brushed over her like a warm blanket and it was wondrous to be on the sea where time didn't seem to matter. Her heart was nearly bursting with this heavenly sensation but gradually deflated to a more normal size due to her worries about the future.

After what seemed an age, she opened her eyes and the same question still came back - what had driven her to give up everything and take this path to a new life? Her rational side continued to torment her as to whether she had made the right decision. She prayed her children would not suffer more or die on this journey as already two bairns had been taken and their tiny bodies given to the deep. Her inner voice told her to be strong, she had made her choice and must live by it.

At that moment, Robert appeared as he too was finding it a hot, stifling night. "All the children are now asleep," he said, as he put his arm around Margaret's waist and pulled her towards him. He could sense her deepest fears and as usual he reassured her and whispered that together, they would survive and make a better life for their family. They turned to gaze at the glittering night sky above the bow and each made a wish. The *Nelson* was their path to a new world and she was steadily bringing them closer.

During their days near the Equator, although the temperature could be sweltering, Margaret was happy to remain on deck in the shade in the afternoon. She read, caught up on sewing and enjoyed writing notes in her diary whilst keeping an eye on the children. There was talk of a music concert in the coming week as some of the emigrants in steerage were going to play and sing to everyone and she hoped any change in the weather would not prevent it from happening. The single girls, who were only allowed on the poop deck, were also hoping to arrange a ball but Margaret didn't feel she had appropriate clothing to attend such a grand function.

She was looking forward to the church service the following day, Sunday. There were always two services to choose from. The first at 11.00 a.m. and a later service at 5.30 p.m. It was an impressive affair as the captain, who was the preacher, stood by a table covered with the Union Jack and spoke the gospel of peace. The Precentor, who led the singing or prayers, normally sat on a cannon in front of the Preacher so it made for a splendid shared service. For the first time, cabin class and steerage would be a mixed congregation which would be interesting Margaret thought, as steerage passengers were not allowed to mix with cabin class passengers under normal circumstances. Some emigrants got annoyed that the 'fancy folk' in cabin class had many more privileges than steerage, so it was best to keep them apart. They were also able to dine with the captain and first officer in the saloon and it was felt they were fortunate to have the ear of the Master and second in command. Margaret refused to get anxious about the class system on board. As far as she knew, there were only about 13 adult and two children cabin class passengers on this voyage which was a low number and hoped if she did meet any of them they would be of good nature.

There was great excitement for many on board the following afternoon and Jane rushed to tell her parents she had spotted another ship. It was not the first ship they had seen so far but this time the *Nelson* came close and they got a good view. It was a barque called *Fanny* and Captain Anderson allowed letters home to be sent on board. They danced around on deck knowing there were other people nearby, it was a happy occasion. The *Fanny* was bound for Valparaiso, in Chile and then would return to Sunderland. Many of the emigrants shuddered when they realised the *Fanny* would have to navigate the treacherous Cape Horn, at the bottom of South America on both her outward and return journey. They were grateful that the passage of the *Nelson* had been relatively free of such violent sea conditions and that they were not rounding the Horn.

After the excitement was over Robert met his friend Archie to discuss their voyage so far and to make a wager on the date when they would reach their destination. Archie thought they would arrive in New Zealand before the end of the year but Robert was not so sure due to the problems with the weather which had caused delays. Archie commented that he could see why new, steam powered ships were being built as they did not have to rely on the wind and were more reliable in terms of journey time. "Some of the shipping companies were also using the Suez Canal," he said. "It is a passage between the Mediterranean Sea and Red Sea and a more direct route between the North Atlantic and Northern Indian oceans, so it reduces the journey distance." But he told Robert that many of the shipping companies still preferred the clippers as they did not need stops for recoaling and the route of the *Nelson* with her return via Cape Horn, was still considered the fastest, if the winds prevailed.

The *Nelson* continued her journey in the Southern Atlantic Ocean in lighter winds for the next two weeks, and as no one in steerage had ever been to the southern hemisphere, many had become mesmerised by the sky at night. It was not at all like the sky in Eday and Margaret, Robert and their children loved to make a special visit to the deck before bedtime to try and spot new stars. They were told by a seaman to look in the Milky Way and find the brightest stars that form a cross, in order to see the constellation called the Southern Cross. Once they found it, by first spotting the two pointer stars, they were always struck by the beauty and brightness of the four main orbs. It felt so right when they found out that as well as the Union Jack, the four brightest stars of this crux were the basis of the national flag of New Zealand, their new home. There was also a faint fifth star in the Southern Cross which they discovered was on the Australian flag to distinguish it from the New Zealand ensign.

They were now well clear of the Tropics and although some days were beautiful and warm, they felt the temperature steadily decreasing as the *Nelson* headed in a more southeasterly direction towards the Cape of Good Hope. Once the ship crossed over the Tropic of Capricorn, passenger boxes were retrieved from the hold in order to have warmer clothing at hand for the cooler weather.

All was well on board until just before the westerly winds in the Roaring Forties found her later in November which bowled the ship along at greater speed. At a latitude of about 38 degrees south, Robert junior had become increasingly more unwell as were some of the other children in steerage. He was lethargic, would not eat and had persistent diarrhoea. Dr Macaffer diagnosed a mesenteric problem, which was obvious, but could do little to help such a small child. "He must take fluids." He insisted. But Margaret had been trying patiently with little success.

On the 29th of November there was the first birth on board, a girl, and everyone thanked God she had been delivered safely. That night however Robert junior took a turn for the worse and Margaret could not rouse him. She wept over his small body and prayed that it was not his time to be taken. "Please, please watch over and protect him dearest God," she prayed. She also asked for the Precentor to visit and say prayers and Dr Macaffer returned to check on him, but he just said that the next 24 hours would be crucial to see whether he could fight the infection.

The following morning, to Margaret's horror, she was told that a little boy of three years six months had died of mesenteric disease in their compartment. It was agonising for her to witness the grief of the dead child's parents as she knew them and found the situation impossible as Robert junior's life was hanging in the balance. She was living one of her worst fears and felt utterly helpless as there was nothing more that could be done for him. All she could do was keep him cool by bathing his tiny body and feeding him droplets of water. His temperature raged and he lay so still unable to move. By some extreme act of mercy, in the late afternoon, he opened his eyes. Margaret could not believe it. She told Jane to quickly go and find her father who was pacing up and down on the deck. When Robert returned to their bunks his son had now moved his head and had begun to whimper. Tears of joy rolled down their cheeks and they believed he must be over the worst. Dr Macaffer had been right, Robert junior had managed to fight off the infection which was unusual for a child so young. He could have easily died from dehydration alone.

The Greenwich Meridian

It was such an emotionally draining day for everyone concerned. The elation of a birth, the sorrow of a death, then the relief of Robert junior waking and showing signs of recovery. It was also the day that the *Nelson* crossed the Greenwich Meridian. Robert, whilst pacing on deck, had talked to the second mate who informed him that it was the imaginary line of zero degrees longitude that passes through Greenwich in London and ends at the North and South Poles. "It's how the ship's position can be calculated due to its degree of longitude east or west from this prime meridian together with the latitude, horizontal lines north or south of the equator," he said. Robert was pleased to be reminded of such things and to know the *Nelson* had crossed another line. He also thought Archie would be impressed with this information when he next saw him.

The funeral of the boy was now over and seeing that Robert junior continued to improve, Margaret could think about relaxing and begin to understand where she was on the wide ocean. Jane stayed close to her and was there to help in any way she could. She had not liked seeing her mother so distressed and was very intuitive for her age. "You are such a special child," said Margaret as she gently stroked her face. "What would I do without you?" She reminded herself that one day she would tell Jane a story so she would know she had always been a special child.

Sailing South of the Cape of Good Hope, South Africa

Margaret and Jane went up on deck to join Robert and the rest of their family. They enjoyed the fresh breeze and took a moment to steady themselves, as the westerly winds were behind the ship. It was a great feeling when the *Nelson* was in full sail, as they had both developed more balance and better sea legs when on the deck. The ship was making good progress. It was the beginning of December; the islands of Tristan da Cunha had been spotted and they were now south of the Cape of Good Hope and beginning the run in the colder waters of the southern passage towards Australia and New Zealand. It was an exciting part of the voyage as they saw whales spouting, porpoises leaping and were being chased by Cape Pigeons. A ten foot shark was also following them and on the hunt for any juicy morsels thrown overboard. No one knew exactly when they would reach their destination but it felt like they were on the homeward straight due to the speed they were sailing. One day they made 15 knots under reefed royal sails. It was exhilarating.

The temperature was dropping daily and Robert said they would be at the South Pole soon but he was only joking. Jane and her brothers and sisters loved his jokes which always made them shriek with laughter. The fact was the passage of the *Nelson* in the Roaring Forties was inside the ice zone of the Southern Ocean and as they hadn't been to the southern hemisphere before, they had not realised they would come this close to the bottom of the world. For safety the ship needed to keep to the northern edge of the ice zone due to the danger from fierce winds, huge waves and potential icebergs.

But after a cold day of good sailing in early December the weather suddenly changed in late afternoon and no one could stay on deck as the winds had whipped up so badly. The sea became enraged as though tormented by an invisible, underwater being and the ship began to pitch and roll. Its iron hull seemed trapped in the jaws of this monster as it battled to get free. The sky turned an ominous dark grey and soon sheeting rain fell in stair rods, hammering the deck and ricocheting off anything solid. As the ship continued to be squeezed by the forces of the unruly ocean and the size of the waves grew mountainous, all on board prayed they would not be drowned. Margaret started to feel seasick as did many others in steerage. She attempted to rush to the latrines but did not make it and was thrown to the floor, covered in her own vomit. All that could be heard was moaning, crying and children screaming as they were tossed about by the storm. But no one was expecting the sudden torrent of sea water that came hurtling down the hatch. It had been left open to let in some light, but due to the size of the waves crashing over the deck, the violent, foaming sea rushed down the stairs to find a way out and swamped all those in its path. Robert gathered the children on the top bunk and clung to them. Luckily Margaret had been out of the direct path of the water but was on the floor. She dragged herself up to try and return to their bunks but could see that the flow of water was creeping closer to her with every step and knew the entire floor in their compartment would quickly be covered.

To prevent a further deluge of water coming down the hatch a brave soul with a rope tied around his waist and secured by two other men, climbed the stairs in order to close the hatch cover. He nearly made it but was washed away on his first attempt by another wave crashing on the deck above. There were gasps as he fell to the floor then silence until he rose to his feet unscathed. With water swirling and circling over his boots on the floor boards, he took a deep breath and boldly attempted to climb the stairs again. This time he managed to reach the last step and closed the hatch. In the darkness, there was shouting and clapping, he was the hero of the hour and deservedly so. Some of the emigrants managed to light lamps but it was still eerily dim and wet. Steerage had endured the worst of the storm, particularly those with children in the middle of the ship. Families clung to each other on their bunks. No one could sleep and they prayed for the storm to subside and this nightmare to be over.

It was the only time Jane had felt afraid on the *Nelson* but she tried not to show her feelings for the sake of her younger brothers and sisters. She held their hands and tried singing to distract them. Margaret and Robert could see she would grow up to be a strong woman, as even now, she was coping with whatever life threw at her.

The hero of the hour, who had closed the hatch, was asked to open it the next morning and tentatively he climbed the stairs once again. A small flood of water greeted him, which splattered over his face and shoulders, but he carried on and opened the hatch to its full width. The rays of light that flooded into steerage were welcome but allowed everyone to see the mess caused by the storm. Clothing, utensils, food and human waste were scattered everywhere or floating in the thin layer of sea water. Margaret began to retch but she pinched her nose which seemed to help. "I need air, I must go up to the deck," she said with a thin voice. Robert understood but knew there needed to be a plan to get everyone on deck and out of this hell-hole.

A group of men gathered together quickly and decided that the women and children should go on deck first so they could begin to clear the carnage and mop up the water in their compartment. Two of the men went up through the hatch first however to make sure this was a good plan in case of any awaiting dangers. The crew had already begun the clear up on the main deck which was heartening, so slowly the women and children filed up the stairs of the hatch to fill their lungs with fresh air and feel the dawn of a new day. It was going to take days for steerage to dry out and for the smell to be tolerable but everyone was accounted for.

Captain Anderson told all on board that the *Nelson* had weathered the storm well as she did not take on that much water. Other passengers knew of people on emigrant ships who had been drowned in their bunks due to severe storms, so they had to count themselves lucky. The captain also told them that the ship had been trapped in what he called a 'boil', where conflicting currents met. That would explain things, thought Robert, hoping it would be the last time they would ever have to experience such treacherous conditions.

Margaret was able to find a change of clothing for the children by dinner time and as the weather was fair, although cold, they all remained on deck for as long as possible. Robert joined them briefly as he needed a break from making their compartment habitable once again. They now required good weather to air the bedding and dry their clothes. He had not been on deck long when Jane came running over to him full of excitement that he come and see a big bird. Sure enough, when they crossed to the port side of the *Nelson,* he spotted the largest bird he had ever seen in his life. It was soaring majestically over the water near to the ship and seemed to be following them. Others on deck had spotted it too and were watching in amazement at the ease this creature could fly considering its size and gigantic wing span.

Fortunately, an older seaman, called Jimmy, was looking through a telescope towards it. "Aye, it is a fine specimen," he muttered. Robert could not help himself asking, "What sort of bird is it, Jimmy?"

"It's an albatross, my friend. You only see them in certain parts of the world. They are a sign of a safe voyage. We have a lot of respect for them as legends say they are the *soul of sailors* and if we find people killing them, we will be cursed!" Jane stood stunned and grabbed her father's leg for support. She didn't say a word. Jimmy then knelt down by her and began to tell her more.

"There is a story called the *Rime of the Ancient Mariner*, a very long poem in fact bonnie lassie."

Other children nearby also gathered around them. Jane was already spellbound before he uttered the first word …

After Jimmy recited the poem he told them that the largest albatross had a wing span of about 12 feet, which was more than the length of two men and it could fly round the world in less than 50 days. Some thought of it as a holy symbol as it is a beautiful white bird but with piercing black eyes. He said that it didn't need to flap its wings very often, as it glides on the wind above the ocean and can survive so long without landing because it can drink sea water and spit the salt out of its nostrils. Everyone was totally hooked and eager for him to continue speaking.

"In the long poem, the albatross is a symbol of good fortune, of hope, but it is killed by the mariner from the ship with his crossbow for no reason. All the good fortune then leaves him and his shipmates; they have bad luck and horrible things happen as a consequence." Everyone leaned in closer …

"There is a simple message from the poem - we should always seek to respect and love nature in order to be a part of it … "

When Jimmy had finished they all looked out to sea again. Several albatrosses now soared on the wind currents alongside the clipper - it was an awesome spectacle and Jane could not believe it.

"We are lucky," he said. "They are watching over us which is a sign of a good voyage."

Normal ship–board routine resumed for all on board after the storm and the sighting of the albatrosses. Some days were beautiful but as they ploughed further east other days were so fearfully cold they had to wear as many layers of clothing as they could find and gloves when on deck. Jane was happy going to school and playing games with other children. Margaret seemed content and looked forward to the plays and concerts that were regularly organised as she had never been able to enjoy such entertainment before. But she was feeling rather lethargic now due to the lack of proper exercise and so much time in confined spaces. She longed to walk on dry land again but kept this thought to herself so as not to upset Robert or those around her.

Robert was currently on deck enjoying the ride along the 45th parallel in the southern hemisphere. The ship was at a latitude of 45 degrees south, the halfway point between the Equator and the South Pole. It was everything he had hoped it would be and he felt so 'alive' on the clipper surrounded by the vast ocean. As a fisherman, who only ever sailed in small boats in Orkney, this was the most exciting sailing he would ever experience. The *Nelson* was magnificent in these conditions with the westerlies behind her and in full sail, including the top royals, she proved the ship had been built for speed. The crew also proved they could master the wind and used every inch of canvas possible. Archie said that they had made it to south of the Cape of Good Hope about seven days later than other fast clippers but the next stage of the voyage would be far quicker. Robert secretly thought they would arrive in Port Chalmers early in the New Year and he would win their wager as at a minimum, they had about two weeks sailing to go. They both hoped there would be no further storms or threats from icebergs so the rest of the passage could be completed in good time.

On the 16th of December, there was an announcement of another birth on board, a girl. It pleased Margaret to learn Dr Macaffer had done a good job and that the mother and child were safe and well. A few days later some of the emigrants were bored and once again tried to shoot or harpoon porpoises and sharks behind the ship. They also tried to snare albatrosses by baiting hooks on long lines that trailed in the ship's wake. Robert discovered their evil sport and was mortified when he noticed an albatross seemed to have taken the bait and had plunged into the water where it would most certainly die. Remembering what Jimmy had told them, he shouted at the culprits. "Are you aware of the legend and how sacred these birds are?" "Our luck could turn, we may all be doomed." Robert stormed off and immediately reported the emigrants' barbaric antics to the first mate who was not far away. He agreed to reprimand the men but Robert did not stay around to watch, he was too annoyed.

Later, bad luck did befall the *Nelson*. A little girl called Grace, only two years old, died from diarrhoea on the 20th of December. 'All hands' were called on deck for the funeral at the end of the day. A very sombre mood swept the *Nelson* once again as the tiny bundle, wrapped in sail cloth, was lowered into the foaming sea. Her parents were inconsolable and Margaret felt their pain. She sobbed as she tried to recite the Lord's Prayer at the end of the service as she knew it could have been one of her children but they had been spared. She also found out that a cruel, arrogant man in steerage was to be court-martialled as he had tried to stab his wife. She was a handsome, younger woman and he had got jealous of the attention she was getting from other men. Such was the plight of those who could not control their anger and spent too long in the confined space below decks.

Passing Cape Leeuwin, Australia

On the same day, the 20th of December, Captain Anderson confirmed that they were in the same longitude as Cape Leeuwin, the most westerly headland of Australia. This was exciting news as once they were beyond Australia, their destination, New Zealand, lay waiting across the Tasman Sea. There was much talk about when they would land now, which could be in about ten days time, so a new sense of anticipation was felt by all.

To everyone's surprise they were shaken from their thoughts by the blast of the fire alarm. They had a weekly Boat drill, where the hoses and small boats were manned, but it wasn't a Saturday, so they were all confounded. The last thing anyone wanted was a fire on board so they knew to take this seriously. Eventually, they heard, "All's well," from the helm. There had been a minor fire in the galley when the baker had his bread in the oven but fortunately, the blaze had been dealt with quickly. A seaman had gone overboard however when refilling his bucket but luckily was saved from a watery end as he had a rope around his middle and was hauled to safety. It had been an eventful day.

The next Sunday afternoon they were told it was probably the last weekend Muster before their arrival in New Zealand. The entire ship's company, apart from cabin passengers, were inspected every week and had to be properly washed and dressed otherwise they would be sent back to their quarters to tidy themselves up further. Captain Anderson was in good spirits and pleased with the majority of souls on board. He and Dr Macaffer were also delighted that, so far, they did not have a single case of contagious disease to report. They were fortunate and the captain hoped the *Nelson* would be spared any form of quarantine when they arrived.

The captain also announced that the cook had been reprimanded for selling produce to young men on the ship and he was to pay all the money back. This was an attempt to dissuade others from trying to buy restricted rations. The matron was also reprimanded in front of the entire ship's company for her fondness for a drink and required to pay a fine for the extra bottles of Gin found in her berth. Everyone knew the matron had a difficult time trying to maintain order amongst the young women on board but it did not justify theft of the alcohol. Having been suitably embarrassed she scurried away and the emigrants also quickly dispersed to their separate compartments to await tea.

After another three days, they had passed southeast Australia and were soon just off Tasmania, previously named Van Diemen's Land, at a longitude of approximately 145 degrees east and latitude 47 degrees south. Margaret was told by an excited passenger that this remote island had the first penal colony where Britain transported convicts. She thought how they must have suffered when they were abandoned with only wild ocean around them and no way of escape.

They had been on the *Nelson* for around 80 days with over a week's sailing to go. The weather began to deteriorate once again and they could feel the ship pitch and roll due to powerful gales which had enraged the ocean. When a huge wave broke over the poop and the main deck, everything not tied down went flying and it was unsafe to walk on the slippery planks. It was also so bitterly cold, the captain granted an extra round of grog to the crew for inner warmth which they welcomed.

Due to the fierce gusts and threat from fog, which was unusual and dangerous, Captain Anderson gave the order of 'hove to' later that night. He was concerned that fog could be shielding ice in the cold Southern Ocean, his worst fear, so the *Nelson* would wait out the bad weather. His experienced, loyal crew reefed many of the sails including the topgallants and high royals at the very top of the masts. And, as he was an experienced master, the time the ship was 'parked' was not wasted as the crew began cleaning the clipper and polishing the brass in preparation for their arrival. Most passengers went below decks or to their cabins well before dark that evening to shelter from the ferocious conditions. Margaret was awoken by the wind during the night which made an eerie, moaning sound in the rigging, as though it was 'calling' them. It was frightening, and she reached for Robert who was lying with his eyes wide open.

The following morning, the *Nelson* resumed her course and headed into the Tasman Sea towards the southern end of New Zealand. During this passage, some of their trunks and boxes were brought up from the hold in preparation for arrival and they could see the single girls prancing on the poop deck as they couldn't wait to dress up in their feather hats and best clothes to go ashore. The Harcus's would remain in the clothing they always wore and would be clean and tidy.

Robert asked the second mate about when they were expected to land and was told they should make Port Chalmers in about four days. He realised Archie had a good chance of winning their wager but was still hopeful his bet was right, as there could be further delays. Everyone's excitement grew as each hour ticked past. Jane was beside herself and remained on deck as long as she could in the hope of being the first to see New Zealand, but as it was perishingly cold, they all had to go below to keep warm. Once back in steerage, some of the men were talking about how hard it would be to work again after all this time feeling idle on board ship. Margaret overheard others say that they were so desperate for freedom and dry land under their feet, they would head straight for any green countryside and just keep walking. Margaret also longed for her freedom and space for the children to run and play.

Approaching New Zealand – Sighting The Snares

In the final stage of their passage the captain and crew informed passengers to lookout for a landmark called 'The Snares' which the *Nelson* was soon to pass. Jane was particularly nervous about this as she had been told by a seaman that it was also called *Tini Heke* by the Māori people, who were the first native people to inhabit New Zealand. He also said that they called one of the larger islands, *Te Taniwha,* as it reminded them of The Sea-Monster. Jane's mouth had dropped open at the thought of seeing a giant sea-monster when they were nearly at their destination. Margaret tried to reassure her but knew Jane would not settle until they were well clear of these islands.

The next morning, the 30th of December, the *Nelson* was making good speed and the weather was clear. To Jane's delight those 'on watch' had caught site of The Snares at 10.30 p.m. the previous night. "We have all survived," she exclaimed and breathed a huge sigh of relief.

This small group of uninhabited islands, only 125 miles south of New Zealand's South Island, was a hazardous navigation point for Captain Anderson, so he was glad to be clear of it. The *Nelson* would go no further south in latitude as The Snares was 48 degrees south and getting close to the bottom of the world. Those on board could not believe the distance they had now travelled and how far away and isolated they felt on the other side of the world.

The anticipation of the next sighting of land helped to distract everyone and most passengers were now on deck eagerly waiting an announcement. They did not have to wait long and gave a loud cheer when the seaman on lookout shouted, "Land on the port bow." It was Stewart Island, New Zealand's third-largest island. When they realised it was only about 20 miles across the Foveaux Strait from the South Island, their arrival seemed imminent, but the captain confirmed they should make Port Chalmers the following day.

The ship rolled in the northeast winds but most emigrants could walk about the deck like 'old salts' now and even Margaret seemed impervious to seasickness. She would never have believed this at the start of their journey. Jane, who was standing close by her suddenly began jumping up and down while pointing in the direction of tiny far-off specks out to sea. "Look," she cried. "Is that New

Zealand?" No one was sure but waited for 'the lookout' who eventually shouted. "The Traps." These were two gigantic rocks 60 miles apart and Captain Anderson did well to avoid these hazards as the *Nelson* passed close to the lower Trap.

Robert spied a confident Archie on the deck as there was every chance he would win their bet if they arrived the following day. Archie knew there was still risk involved and decided to tell Robert the fate of the *Surat* which was shipwrecked off the nearby Catlin's coast of the South Island.

"On the 31st December last year, the clipper hit a rock when en route from Gravesend, England, to Port Chalmers. The hull was thought to be sound but overnight a section weakened and the crew had to frantically man the pumps. The captain, it is said, became intoxicated and refused help from a passing ship. He also threatened to shoot passengers if they defied him! As many feared for their lives, the ship was anchored and the captain allowed some of them to land at Jacks Bay. But it became clear the *Surat* was in danger of foundering, so he continued on and deliberately beached her in a sandy bay, now called Surat Bay, where all on board were safely landed and taken to Dunedin." Robert was speechless.

Archie paused and then said. "But the new settlers lost all their possessions as they had to be left in the wreck." Robert gasped and thought what a miserable way to begin life in a foreign land. It also made him realise how little they had brought with them that would be useful for their new life.

Stewart Island and The Traps had now faded into the distance and the *Nelson* continued to edge further up the East coast towards Port Chalmers, Dunedin. In steerage there was feverish activity cleaning and packing before lights out but no one slept that night due to the excitement of arriving in Port Chalmers the following day.

The next morning was beautiful, the wind had disappeared and most passengers were on the deck in the hope of sighting land. The *Nelson* looked magnificent as everything had been cleaned and polished. The Union Jack was flying at the fore mast, the ship owner's flag on the main mast, the '*Nelson*' on the mizzen and the ensign on the spanker.

They were rewarded later that morning when, through a long white cloud that lingered in front of them, they saw Taiaroa Head and the entrance to the Otago Harbour. This was not far from Port Chalmers, near Dunedin, where they would come ashore. There was cheering and shouting from those who gazed towards this unfamiliar green land. The younger Harcus daughter, Ann, also piped up with "and we didn't sink even once," which made everyone laugh heartily. Jane was very excited and happy, Margaret was overjoyed this day had come and would never forget the date: New Year's Eve, 31 December 1874. Tomorrow was a new beginning but they would have to wait and see what it would bring.

The *Nelson* signalled her presence and that 'All was well on board.' Captain Anderson now awaited a pilot to come from Port Chalmers and guide the ship to an anchorage close to the port.

The excitement grew as the minutes ticked away, but when they heard the *Nelson* was to be inspected by the Otago health commissioners, everyone went silent as it could mean quarantine and further delays before disembarkation was possible.

Margaret and Robert remained calm as there had been no infectious diseases on board as far as they knew. They could only think about how resilient the clipper had been to withstand the storms and force of the perilous seas on their long journey. The *Nelson* was more than a ship to them now, it had become a symbol of hope and strength. They both confessed they would be sorry to leave her. Jane, who was standing close to them, said that she would miss the *Nelson* and was sad to part from her.

On the crowded deck Robert managed to spot his trusted companion Archie and walked over to greet him. He was pleased to see him for two reasons; the first was to congratulate him on winning their wager as Archie had predicted that the *Nelson* would arrive by the end of the year and Robert had just missed the mark. The second reason was to bid him a fond farewell and a successful future in Otago, New Zealand. They had become good friends and Robert would miss him. Archie summed up their journey and said. "It was a pity the *Nelson* lost time on the first leg to the Cape of Good Hope due to bad weather, as it took 64 days. She sailed from there to Otago Harbour in just 27 days, she was such a fast goer."

Robert had to agree that the *Nelson*'s maiden voyage had been completed in a very respectable 91 days, considering a slow start she had proved herself a grand ship. They shook hands firmly before Archie said, "Lang may yer lum reek." He had wished Robert a long and healthy life.

Whilst the Harcus family waited patiently on deck, Margaret could see that the children had grown and needed new clothing, but knew this would be the least of their worries. She suddenly remembered to ask Robert to check how much spare money they had and when he searched deep into his pockets, he only found 2 shillings and 6 pence.

Feelings of dread and despair returned: emotions they hadn't felt since before they left Eday, Orkney when food was so scarce. They looked intensely at each other and knew a small miracle was now needed so Robert could find work to support his family.

Part Four

4.

A New Beginning in Dunedin, New Zealand

Upon her hill, Dunedin
How beautiful she stands!
The ocean wafting to her feet
The wealth of distant lands.
Round promontories bending,
Far as the eye can reach,
On every side extending,
Her rising suburbs stretch ...
Dugald Ferguson

Arrival in Otago Harbour

31 December 1874

When the *Nelson* reached the entrance of Otago Harbour, between Heyward Point and Taiaroa Head, those on deck gazed at the stretch of water which separated a finger-like, hilly peninsula on the left from the mainland. On the inner rim of the harbour there were many small inlets and Port Chalmers could just be seen on the right-hand side, about five nautical miles away. Straight ahead, in the distance, they could see the harbour was divided by two small islands beyond which the sea flowed all the way to the city of Dunedin. Since the first European settlers arrived via Port Chalmers in 1848 on the sailing ships, *John Wickliffe* and *Philip Laing,* Dunedin had become the thriving city of the new Edinburgh settlement in Otago.

In clear weather most passengers on board ship would have been struck by the beauty and mystique of what lay before them; the pure blue expanse and calm of the sea, the huge sky above and intense rays of sunlight that pierced through soft low cloud to bathe this new green land, the surrounding rugged hills which seemed to offer protection. The first sight of Dunedin and Port Chalmers would have appeared like the 'promised land,' just as they had been told.

On the *Nelson,* the Harcus family were standing close to Dr Macaffer, who was also admiring the spectacular view from the main deck. They could see the gleam in his eye and his genuine excitement at their pending arrival. He would not go back to Scotland on the ship's return passage but begin a new life practising medicine in New Zealand. Other passengers with trades such as stone masons, carpenters, farmers or those with domestic servant and labouring skills were also eagerly waiting to leave the ship and begin new employment in this foreign land.

All of a sudden there was a loud cheer from a group of immigrants on the main deck, who were first to see a small vessel heading directly for the *Nelson.* It meant Port Chalmers had received the ship's earlier 'signals' and sent a tug and pilot for her. They all watched the vessel draw closer and soon the steam tug, *Geelong,* was alongside. Once the pilot had climbed on board it was not long before the *Nelson* proudly glided off, as if by magic, to finally rest in a snug anchorage off Port Chalmers to await inspection.

Health Inspection

Due to fears that infectious diseases carried by passengers would run rampant in the province of Otago, all immigrant ships were inspected. Many ships were forced to go into quarantine and sometimes passengers were held on *Kamua Taurua*, the largest island in Otago Harbour. The *Margaret Galbraith* from London, which had arrived earlier in the month, was forced to quarantine due to a single case of scarlet fever on board.

The health Inspectors took no chances once they boarded the *Nelson*. They carefully inspected all the emigrant compartments with Dr Macaffer but found no trace of any disease and that cleanliness prevailed. Captain Anderson and Dr Macaffer also confirmed those on board were a good class of people as there had been little trouble on the voyage. They told the inspectors there had been four deaths and two births, the total number of souls being 367, two less than when they left Greenock. The inspectors knew that so light a death rate meant conditions on the ship had been favourable.

Margaret was so grateful the ship was free from disease and that her four children had survived. They were all in remarkably good health which was a blessing as they would be leaving the ship, their home for the last three months, before this day was over.

Captain Anderson had told passengers that Port Chalmers, about ten miles northeast along the coast from the city of Dunedin, was chosen as the seaport town of the province as it had a natural deep-water harbour. "Frederick Tuckett," he explained, "of the New Zealand Company, surveyed this area and inland Otago in 1844 on behalf of the British Government and decided it would make the best harbour for the purposed new Edinburgh settlement. The lower harbour, closest to Dunedin, was shallow which prevented the large clippers reaching the wharf and meant 'lighters,' a flat-bottomed barge, had to be used to transfer all the heavy cargo and passengers from Port Chalmers to the city." When Robert Harcus heard this he worried it would be a slow and laborious way to finally reach Dunedin after months at sea.

In the 1870s, the decade the Harcus family arrived, thousands of immigrants arrived at Port Chalmers due to free passages offered by New Zealand local and provincial governments. Agents looking to recruit immigrants back in Great Britain used advertising and propaganda to suggest New Zealand was the 'land of plenty.' For many, who were so poor and lacking prospects, this offered a fresh start, new jobs and a better life for themselves and their children.

Coming ashore at Port Chalmers

Those on board the *Nelson* were fortunate on New Year's Eve in 1874 as they were spared isolation on Quarantine Island *(Kamua Taurua)* prior to landing. The health inspectors were satisfied and had returned to port which meant everyone was free to leave once the ship docked at Port Chalmers.

Margaret and Robert would soon discover a bustling port which had been transformed due to the Otago Gold Rush in the 1860s when new shops and businesses had sprung up to service the ships and eager prospectors who passed through. As they waited patiently on the *Nelson's* main deck to come ashore, before the last leg of the journey to Dunedin, there were many tearful scenes as immigrants clung to each other to say final goodbyes to friends they had made on the voyage. They had all been through so much together on the sea but now they must make their own way on land.

Slowly the disembarkation of all souls began from the *Nelson*. Cabin class always went first and those still on board chuckled as they watched these fine people in their fine clothes and hats begin to stagger once they left the ship to take their first steps on dry land. Many of the single girls who stumbled behind them were upset and weeping. They had been well looked after during the passage and also protected by Matron from the single men on board. But those days were over and they would have to fend for themselves in colonial life and try to find work and husbands.

Margaret would never forget the relief she felt when she stepped onto the pier at Port Chalmers. Her jubilation was tinged with apprehension however as she placed her right foot carefully down on the earth before slowly summoning her left foot to do the same. She kept her eyes lowered for a few moments in order to utter a prayer of thanks and then raised her head triumphantly to gaze at the view of the town and the green hills high above. Such strange, unfamiliar surroundings but they had been safely delivered and their new life could begin. She was still overcome by the beauty of New Zealand. Her first sight of Port Chalmers and Dunedin from on board ship was like a dream and that vision would remain indelible on her memory. She felt joy and found herself secretly restored and glad to be far away from the cold, grey winter in Scotland.

From the pier she could see the customhouse near the harbour, some shops and Dobson's Provincial Hotel down a muddy street that led towards the town. The bush was like a luxurious canopy that extended as far as the shore in places but in the distance she could see a clearing with a church and small spire which someone close by said was Iona church, built only two years before in 1872. The trees and bush around and above the town were a deep velvet green which reminded her vaguely of the landscape in parts of Caithness but the native plant life appeared to have the most unusual foliage she had ever seen. At the sea end of the pier she had seen a strange tree with sword like leaves clustered at the tips of the branches and was delighted when she found out later it was called a NZ cabbage tree. There were other streets and shops she could barely make out and hoped to discover more once they left the port.

Due to Jane's excitement and the other three children around her, Margaret's thoughts were quickly redirected to her family and she could see that Robert desperately needed assistance with their belongings. It was a scene of joyous chaos as passengers from the ship continued to congregate on the pier, unsure what to do next. The crowd was also swelled by relatives or friends, (already in the colony), who had sponsored people to come to New Zealand. They were waiting patiently for these new immigrants to disembark.

Shortly after coming ashore, Margaret and Robert heard the good news that immigrants from the *Nelson* would be allowed to stay in temporary barracks in Dunedin for a few days. Margaret thanked God as a huge weight immediately lifted from them. Jane was also quick to spot how happy this latest news had made her parents. They were told to make their own way into the city but had no idea how to get there, let alone find the location of The Barracks. They thought they were going by lighter to Dunedin, but this was not the case. Times had moved on, and it soon became clear after talking to other families, that they would be travelling by train to the Flats. So they slowly walked off and followed the crowd towards the Railway Pier. Robert quickly broke into a sweat however as he was not sure he had enough spare cash for their fares and hoped he would not be embarrassed or refused the ten-mile train ride to Dunedin.

The Flats they soon discovered, was a suburb not far from the centre of Dunedin, called Caversham where new barracks for immigrant arrivals had been recently completed. It could accommodate a lot more people than the previous building in the heart of the city. What a blessing, Robert thought. He also recalled the pledges made before they left Scotland by the NZ Agents offering passages to the colony that immigrants should expect new job opportunities, better food and experience a more classless society in New Zealand. He hoped he would find this to be true.

On the way to the Railway Pier the exuberant crowd of immigrants came to a sudden standstill which caused loud complaints from many of the women and incomprehensible swearing in Scottish Gaelic from some of the men. No one wanted to miss the next train and a further delay was not going to be tolerated. After several minutes, two solemn policemen appeared who it transpired were dealing with a male corpse lying near to the pier. The story of his demise spread quickly through the crowd. It appeared that he and a friend were returning to their immigrant ship after many hours drinking grog in a local pub in Port

Chalmers. Due to the man's gravely intoxicated state he tripped over a railway plate, stumbled and fell over the side of the pier into the watery depths below. A lifebelt was thrown in for him from a vessel at the pier, but he struggled to grasp it and was only dragged out of the water after a heroic seaman threw himself in and tied a rope around him. Unfortunately the man had too much water in his lungs and could not be saved.

The crowd were silenced and thought this accident was a horrifying end, rather than a new beginning, for the poor soul. They also counted themselves lucky that they had come ashore so quickly from the *Nelson* as they heard that other ships had to anchor in the bay and wait days before passengers could disembark if the port was too busy.

Many of those on board needed to search for work straight away and were forced to pay a shilling from their meagre savings to be taken to and from their ships. Others were tempted to visit the local hostelries while their ships lay at anchor, but could find themselves in trouble after too much drink and never make it back!

Josephine - the Steam Train from Port Chalmers to Dunedin

In the early days, after Dunedin was founded in 1848, there were no roads or railways to the city from Port Chalmers and the lightering service by sea was the only way to the Dunedin Wharf. In the 1860s, a road was carved out along the coast to Dunedin from Port Chalmers but a round trip could take 3-4 hours and was not ideal. Fortunately, another great improvement came when the Port Chalmers to Dunedin railway line was completed during 1872 which connected the port directly to the city. It was the first single gauge track in New Zealand. Eventually this line joined up with the South Island railway network to Christchurch and Invercargill which helped to open up the country.

The surging mass of people continued to walk towards the Railway Pier and Jane was astonished when she got close enough to see the huge, heavy steam train waiting to take them on the last leg of their journey to Dunedin. It had a lantern on the front and a funnel or smokestack on the engine section which was belching out a mixture of steam and smoke although the train did not move an inch and sat as if glued to the track. "It has a name," Jane said excitedly and slowly tried to read out the word *Josephine*. She squealed with delight as did some of the other children and they hopped up and down waiting for a sign that something was about to happen, but the train continued to remain perfectly still.

There was a man in a soot-stained boiler suit watching the children and when he got closer, he said that he was a stoker and had just finished loading more coal for their journey. He proudly told anyone who cared to listen that, "*Josephine* was an E class, double Fairlie steam locomotive; the first to run on this line which opened on the 1st of January 1873 and the first locomotive to operate in New Zealand on the 3-foot 6-inch gauge railway line." That makes her very special thought Jane, who looked at her father, Robert for approval. "We are indeed fortunate on all accounts," said Robert who was intrigued and grateful that this track to Dunedin had been opened as it meant the journey time to the city from Port Chalmers was significantly less than by horse and wagon.

They would have to be patient and queue for *Josephine* however as there were so many people waiting but hoped to board the train soon and reach The Barracks before the day was over. Josephines's sister train, *Rose,* had already left the station totally packed with immigrants, so they had a good chance.

When the time came, boarding the train seemed more difficult than trying to embark on the *Nelson,* as immigrants and families were pushing and shoving to try and be first to find seats when the doors finally opened. *Josephine* was belching out more smoke and steam in anticipation of the journey commencing, but this only excited the crowds further. Eventually Robert asserted himself, rushed forward up the steps with their bags and secured enough space for his family who scrambled up the steps after him. Jane immediately dived into a window seat on the harbour side and Margaret quickly sat beside her with baby Robert on her lap. Robert senior sat opposite and looked after Ann and William.

There was a riot of noise from the passengers in the carriage but eventually, when everyone heard the screech of the brakes unlocking and felt a lurch they fell briefly silent as the locomotive prepared to leave the station. The whistle blasted, a loud 'toot' roared from the smokestack and then slowly the 'chuff chuff' sound took over as *Josephine* began to inch forward. "The coal is really starting to burn now," said Robert as he knew how steam engines worked. Some of the passengers had their heads out the windows to see the white trail of smoke and steam behind them, others just closed their eyes to enjoy the thrill of such a new experience.

When they had just begun to settle and relax, Robert, through heavy eyelids, spied the train conductor walking towards him. He was checking tickets and weaving his way down the carriage. Robert began to perspire profusely as he had not bought tickets and was worried he didn't have enough money. Eventually, he was confronted by the conductor who looked him straight in the eyes. "Tickets," he said loudly. He paused while Robert squirmed and dug deep into his pockets to produce his meagre cash. Sensing his fear, the conductor took some coins from Robert's hand and politely said, "nae problem," with a Scottish accent. "Welcome to Dunedin." Suppressing his surprise, Robert nodded politely, then breathed a huge shy of relief once the conductor moved on to his next customer. "Aye, that was lucky," he murmured to Margaret and she reached for his hand in quiet jubilation.

Jane fell in love with *Josephine*. She loved the sounds it made, the gentle rocking motion and the warm cosiness inside the passenger compartment. She also loved the view of the harbour and gazed at the small sandy bays with green vegetation coming down to the shore and other unfamiliar sights as they slowly made their way along the coastal railway track towards Dunedin. "New Zealand is not like Eday at all," Jane remarked to her mother who nodded in agreement.

When she looked across to her father, Jane suddenly became aware of an old man sitting near him with deep brown skin, a squashed nose and beautiful coloured feathers in a top-knot formed from his pulled back hair. He also had a green stone suspended on a plaited cord around his neck which intrigued her. She could not help but stare at him and became transfixed by the swirling dark lines on his chin and face. When he looked up she was taken aback by how ferocious he looked - his bulging brown eyes glared, piercing deep into her soul. In response, Jane's pupils dilated, her heart began to race and she wanted to run, but quickly realised there was no escape. Instead, she summoned all her courage and said to this man. "Do you come from here?" She was shocked, as he smiled at her baring a set of brilliant white teeth.

He slowly began to speak and said, "My child, I am not from *Koputai* which the *pakeha* (white man) renamed Port Chalmers. I am from *Otakou* or the *Kaik* as we call it, near Taiaroa Head by the harbour entrance. My people, the Māoris, have lived on the peninsula, the south side of the harbour for hundreds of years. After the *pakeha* came to settle, the name *Otakou* was changed to Otago which is used for the whole province now."

"Please tell us more." Jane said softly.

"Our Māori legends tell of a struggle with a dragon-like monster called a *taniwha* which ate out the Otago Harbour. Later, the *pakeha* believed it was the drowned remains of the Dunedin volcano which turned into a green valley. They say the tide slowly crept up the valley until the two small hills in the centre were surrounded by water. Māori calls these hills *Rakiriri* (Goat Island) and *Kamau Taurua* (Quarantine Island)." He raised his arm and pointed a long bony finger at the window and those near him tried to catch a closer view of these islands which separate the Upper and Lower Harbour of Otago.

Jane and now the whole Harcus family were under his spell. His story was entrancing and also explained the view they had seen at the entrance of the harbour from the Pacific Ocean.

He then said. "You must try and see the special sea creatures we have around the peninsula and harbour such as the yellow eyed penguins, NZ fur seals and sea lions as well as bottlenose and dusky dolphins." Jane was fascinated and hoped her father would take her to find them one day as she loved sea animals and birds.

"Please don't stop," said Jane and willed him to continue.

"Very well," he nodded. "Long ago the first Māori settlement in *Otakou* became the place where runaway convicts from Australia and other hunters came for the seals and to harpoon the many sperm and giant humpback whales for their oil and whale bone. Māori and white man helped these hunters to survive but eventually the whales were not seen and the ships left."

"But our land and sea had become known to others. The New Zealand Company asked to buy our land to form the *Otakou* Block and we sold it to them. They also bought land at the lower harbour end to begin the Dunedin settlement. Our chief, Potiki, was one of the Māori chiefs who signed the deed for the sale of *Otakou* land on condition we could keep some for our future but they will not honour this promise. We must still fight for it.

"That is so unfair," said Margaret.

"Potiki, our chief, may be old, but he is wise and speaks for us in the courtroom. He is also well known and was present when your important Governor, Sir George Grey, came on his special visit to *Koputai* a few years ago."

Everyone was impressed and as Jane wanted him to keep talking, she quickly asked another question.

"What are those patterned lines on your face, Mr Māori."

"Call me Rawiri," he said, holding back a smile. And while pointing to his chin, he continued speaking.

"This is my *moko*. It is a message about my identity and tells the story of my family and social standing in my tribe, the Ngai Tahu."

"How did you get it?"

"I had to sit very still while a chisel made from shark's tooth was used to mark my skin and then pigment was rubbed in."

Jane gulped then quietly asked. "Did it hurt?"

"Yes it did and my face swelled, but as it reflects my *whakapapa*, (ancestry and history), I did not mind."

Jane thought he was so brave and hoped he would carry on talking but *Josephine* interrupted all conversation with whistles, juddering and hissing noises. "Something on the track," they could hear in the distance from the conductor and the train began to slow. Fortunately it did not come to a complete stop and within minutes *Josephine* regained her speed and she chuntered on.

Rawiri looked up and silently rubbed the green stone object hanging around his neck with his fingers before he continued. "This is my *pounamu*. It is made of NZ greenstone and was passed down to me by my parents. I wear it for protection and good luck - it also links my past, present and future."

Jane's eyes widened and she sat enthralled. She had never met such an interesting person, ever.

Rawiri had become tired so Jane decided to let him rest and resumed gazing out of the window. Across the harbour, on the Otago Peninsula and beyond the two small islands Rawiri had already mentioned, she could see the small settlement of Portobello. Further along and higher up a volcanic mountain called Harbour Cone was visible, one of the highest points on the peninsula. Other small, picturesque bays on the opposite rim of the harbour from the train included Broad Bay, Company Bay and Macandrew Bay. As the end of the train journey drew closer, Jane could just see a tower high up on a ridge of the peninsula overlooking the harbour. She later discovered it was part of Larnach Castle which was not yet finished. Another passenger in the carriage had also spotted it and loudly said. "It will be the first castle in New Zealand but it won't be a real castle like those we have in Scotland." Jane remained quiet but thought it was exciting that her new city Dunedin would be the first to have one.

They had all become weary as they neared the end of their journey to Dunedin but had been fortunate to enjoy good visibility and see the sights. Now, on this last day of December, it was late afternoon and the mild summer weather was beginning to change. When Jane looked back towards the harbour entrance Taiaroa Head was barely visible and sea fret was slowly creeping in like a grey mythical serpent. In the opposite direction, foaming mist was accumulating high above the hills of Dunedin.

Josephine reduced speed as she approached the end of the railway line at Dunedin Wharf and eventually came to a halt with hissing and screeching noises. Jane was fighting back the need to close her eyes but didn't want to miss anything. Her younger brothers and sisters had all fallen asleep due to the warm compartment and gentle motion of the steam train.

They slowly clambered down the steps of the carriage and could see their new friend Rawiri was speaking to a small light skinned man, with narrow eyes, a shaven head and a long pigtail running down his back. He was holding his hat, and Jane waited for them to finish their conversation before she went up to the Māori to say goodbye. He looked at her and replied, "kia ora little one. This is my friend, John Chinaman." Jane stood rigid as he didn't look particularly trustworthy. "We met in *Koputai*," Rawiri continued, "he comes from China and is going to Macraes Flat, north of Dunedin, to try and find gold." "Really" said Jane excitedly. "I would like to go there one day."

Margaret then stepped forward and took Jane by the hand. "We must go now," she interrupted. "We have been asked by another family to share a wagon to take us to Caversham which will save us pennies."

They were spared a long wait as a wagon large enough for the two families soon came racing towards them. The driver pulled up the horses and yelled. "The Barracks" and they all piled in, grateful for the fact he had probably done the trip a hundred times already. Their luggage was bundled in behind them but most of it was still stowed away on the ship and they were not sure when it would materialise. For now, they were pleased to be on dry land and to have a roof over their heads for a few days.

The Immigration Barracks, Dunedin

On the way they found out they were going to the new site of The Barracks in Caversham, a suburb of 'the Flats,' which was about a mile and a half from Dunedin city centre. The previous barracks in Princes Street in the heart of Dunedin had to be abandoned as it couldn't cope with the number of new immigrants from the ships and easily became overcrowded and disgustingly dirty. If it rained, the new arrivals and their children could become knee deep in mud if they ventured out into the yard and the government became worried they would become ill or pick up diseases. It was a step up from when the first settlers arrived in Otago back in 1848 however. All they had to shelter in were 20 metre huts built near the shore of the harbour which were made from flax-bound posts with grassy walls and thatch on the roof. They were cold, damp, primitive shelters and cooking had to be done outside. Women with children particularly suffered in those miserable conditions.

The fresh air and rattling of the wagon helped to keep everyone awake but Jane was bright eyed with excitement and fascinated by their new city, the long muddy streets and where they would be staying. The driver said that they were lucky to be going to the new barracks as it could hold over 400 people and should be a lot more comfortable than the ship they had just left or the older barracks in town. They carried on and soon the horses began labouring up the hilly incline of the main road in Caversham. The wagon eventually slowed and the horses' breathing quietened as they approached a large wooden building on a slope in front of them. It was The Barracks and on the opposite side of the road stood a large imposing building, with pointed arches and a pitched roof, called the Benevolent Asylum. When their driver said that it had been there for about ten years and was used to house destitute men, homeless or deserted women and children, they all felt so sad for those who were incarcerated behind such walls. This night was New Year's Eve and the beginning of a new life, of new hope and opportunities for those who arrived on the *Nelson*. But one thing was for sure, they would never let themselves end up in that building. Jane looked at her mother and knew she would protect her from such a fate. Margaret looked at Robert who quickly clasped her hand and said. "We will make our own destiny and good fortune, you have my word, we will not end up there."

At the door of The Barracks in Elbe Street, they were greeted by The Barracks' Master, Mr Duke, who said that they would meet the Matron, his wife, Mrs Elizabeth Duke, later during their meal. He quickly explained how The Barracks was organised and told them some of the rules as he could see a queue developing due to many others arriving from the *Nelson*.

"Think of the points of a compass," he said. "There are four separate two storied wings with the kitchen in the centre. The east wing, nearest the road is accommodation for married couples and their families and the lower floor can take 130 people at the dining tables. There are lavatories, baths and a good supply of water for all. The west wing is also for married couples and their children but is kept for emergencies in case two ships arrive at the same time. The north and south wings are for single men and women. You are kept apart," he shouted, "just like on your ship. The bachelors and spinsters will sleep in bunks and there are 96 on each upper floor. The warders also have rooms in the north and south wings. They are there to enforce the regulations and ensure, in particular, that the 'young bloods' don't exceed the bounds of propriety.

You may also like to know that the grounds around the building are divided into four yards, which are used for drying clothes and recreation. Each class of immigrant is therefore not able to mix." Mr Duke stopped speaking abruptly and then signalled for families to head in the direction of the east wing.

They had all got the message that the chances of single men and women speaking to each other or to anyone who was married was not likely whilst they remained in The Barracks. It had the air of a large, well-managed institution which was spacious and spotlessly clean.

"They should call our wing Timbuctoo," said one of the young men jokingly which made many of the new arrivals begin to chuckle about the 'no mixing' rules. "This is worse than on board the *Nelson*," another single guy remarked and those around him all nodded in agreement. Jane didn't really understand why they were laughing but loved to see everyone smiling - it was such a change.

The Harcus family made their way to the upper floor of the east wing to find their new temporary quarters. After the trudge up the stairs Margaret was delighted with their room. It was light and spacious, clean and well ventilated. Jane remembered they had seen a hotel near the wharf on the way to The Barracks and had to ask her mother. "Would that hotel be even nicer inside?" Margaret smiled at her and replied. "One day, when you are older, you may just find out my bonnie girl?"

Margaret attempted to settle her youngest children, Robert and William and then began to unpack their belongings. Their clothes looked ragged and everything felt damp. Fortunately, she had discovered whilst downstairs, that The Barracks had washhouses and she intended to find one the following day. She couldn't wait to wash the smell of the sea and salt from their clothing while she had the opportunity. Once their clothes were clean and dried she would also mend and darn the rips and holes where she could as they had no spare money to buy anything new.

Soon it was time for their evening meal. They were ravenous. It was New Year's Eve after all and everyone seemed relieved and happy and most were in good health after their sea journey. They did not delay going downstairs to the large dining room - Jane skipped down beside her parents. They were greeted very favourably by the staff who had set out a feast for them. They sat down to large quantities of mutton and beef, potatoes and a selection of vegetables, some of which they had never seen before but tasted delicious. Jane loved a sweet potato called a *kumara* which had been roasted and the staff said that it was special as the Māoris had brought this to New Zealand in their canoes. There was freshly baked bread and copious amounts of tea. It was the best meal they had had in months and they gorged until they could not eat another morsel.

They felt they had been treated well so far due to plentiful food and spacious temporary accommodation. It was part of the plan by the New Zealand provincial government to make a good impression as they wanted contented immigrants who would write favourable letters home about the new colony so their friends and families would follow in their footsteps.

During their meal, the Matron, Elizabeth Duke was introduced. She offered help to any of the families if she was able. She also said that she would be keeping a close eye on the single, young women and their welfare but was available to help mothers and particularly those with young children. The Dukes were an English couple from Carshalton and had been living in Sawyers Bay before her husband, Charles, had been appointed superintendent on Quarantine Island. He still held a temporary position there but in 1874 they had both been asked to work in the Elbe Street barracks and accepted their new roles for the time the free immigration programme would last.

Margaret and Robert found out during their meal that there were 'engaging offices' on the ground floor near Mr Duke's office and Robert would be informed when employers were calling at The Barracks to offer work. They were overjoyed with this news and Robert hoped he would be one of the lucky ones and find work quickly. As a result of the Julius Vogel scheme which, currently, offered free passages to immigrants, in exchange the New Zealand Government wanted tradesmen such as shoemakers, tailors, stonemasons, agricultural labourers who could work on farms or join public works schemes to build new roads and railway lines. There was also demand for domestic servants and farm servants – all types of work force were needed to help make the new colony and provinces thrive.

The government wanted to help local NZ employers to find new workers and allowed them to use the immigration barracks as a recruiting ground. It was a clever and organised approach. Robert Harcus noticed, after their meal, that some of the men got up and went directly to the engaging office as the Immigration Officer was already overseeing contracts of engagement. He could not believe it and thought that these men might have known their employers before they left Scotland.

It was well before midnight but with food weighing heavy in their bellies and comfortable beds to fall into, most people began to leave the dining tables to make their way slowly back to the first floor sleeping accommodation. Some had a wee dram stashed to toast the New Year when the clock struck 12 o'clock but others were destined to see in the New Year when the sun rose the following morning.

Young Jane closed her eyes immediately her head had touched the pillow. She felt the most beautiful sensation as the pillow surrounded her like a soft, velvet cloud, allowing her whole body to float and feel weightless. She loved her new life and country so far or was this just a dream? She did not stir until she felt her mother gently rocking her the next morning. "Jane, time for breakfast and then you can help me with the washing."

Although she had enjoyed their steerage quarters on the *Nelson*, Jane admitted that she had had the best sleep since they left their small cottage in Eday. Margaret and Robert were not so fortunate as they had been awoken by raucous, drunken young men outside. Their room was on the street side of The Barracks and these fellows were returning from the hostelries in Caversham after celebrating the New Year. When Mr Duke finally unlocked the doors to let them in, they heard him reprimand the men for their bad behaviour and tell them how lucky they were not to be arrested by the local constable for disturbing the peace!

After a hearty breakfast Margaret had the washing to do and Robert decided to go down to the engaging office to ask about job opportunities. It was already crowded as many single men were waiting in an orderly queue to meet the employers who had come to The Barracks. He saw a young man walking out of the office with a smile who said he had just accepted a six-month hire, at £20, working for an Otago farmer. Single women would be next to meet employers for domestic servant vacancies and they could expect an average wage of about £30 per annual hire. Ploughmen, shepherds and farm servants could earn upwards of £50.

Robert met some of the single men he knew from the ship while he was waiting near the engaging office who said that the office was closing early as it was New Year's Day. Those who had accepted new employment wanted to celebrate and asked if he would like to join them at a local hotel in Caversham that night after their meal. Robert had little spare cash but agreed to go as he thought it might be useful to hear what they had to say about finding jobs in Otago. He left them feeling disheartened, as he could see it was quicker and easier for single men and women to find work as they could be more flexible. He had to prepare himself for the fact it could take much longer for a married man with children to find a suitable employer.

This was not the news he wanted to tell Margaret, but he was assured other employers involved in public works schemes were coming in to The Barracks the following day and he would be notified when to return to the office for interviews. It was possible therefore that something may turn up he could lend his hand to that would pay enough to support his growing family. All he could do now was wait.

Most men he had talked to were desperate to find work but a small number of the younger men from the *Nelson* were missing from the queue. Some had completely forgotten the routine of a working week and were happy to accept the charity of the New Zealand Government for as long as possible. They would soon find out, however, that anyone reluctant to find a 'situation' in the province would be immediately exiled from The Barracks.

The Harcus's venture into the city of Dunedin

That afternoon, another couple with children in the east wing, asked if the Harcus family would like to take a ride into town as they couldn't go. Ned Ross, a friend of a relative in Scotland was coming to collect them in his wagon, but as Flora's husband now had the opportunity to meet an employer in The Barracks, he did not want to miss the chance of an interview to find work. They hoped they could go on another occasion but it was too late to stop Ned's arrival.

Margaret thought it would be an ideal opportunity to get to know Dunedin and Jane was ecstatic at an opportunity to explore her first southern city. Robert was reluctant at first, but, as he was twiddling his thumbs, awaiting further information about employers he eventually agreed on the outing as it could also be a chance to find a local newspaper and look for job advertisements.

They kindly accepted the offer and the wagon arrived early afternoon as arranged. "All on board," said the wagon driver Ned, whilst gently pulling on the reins to keep the two horses still. They slowly made their way downhill, turning left at the junction to join the South Road which merged into Princes Street. This was the main road leading to the city and would take them all the way to the Octagon in the heart of Dunedin. It was only about a mile and a half but in a horse drawn wagon this would take some time as they hoped to make stops along the way. The weather was fair, they had the rest of the afternoon to see the sights and couldn't wait.

"Did you know?" said Ned a red faced, jovial, older man. "The name Dunedin comes from Dùn Èideann, the Scottish Gaelic for Edinburgh. It was originally called New Edinburgh after the Scottish capital, but this was replaced. Many suggested 'Mud-edin' would have been a good name, due to the many steep roads in the city and the fact it rained frequently, the streets often became brown and filthy very quickly. There is still a good trade in boots here!" he chuckled.

They had just passed the Southern Cemetery which began in 1858 and could see rows of graves and headstones. "Many folks died too young back in the 1860s," Ned muttered. "Typhoid and cholera got some of the poor souls including children who lived in the filthy slums of the city. We had those who made fortunes and built their grand houses in places like Heriot Row, but others were forced to stay in areas not fit for animals. Dunedin was only a village but the gold rush in 1861 soon turned it into a town and it became a city within five years in 1865. Trouble was, everything was chaotic as there was no time to plan housing properly and some people were forced to live in overcrowded hovels. Oh, the smell if you got near was almost unbearable as they had poor sanitation, ventilation and a lack of clean water. It was no surprise there was epidemic after epidemic and many lives were taken."

Margaret and Robert cringed at the thought of such suffering and, in silence, turned away to enjoy the views of the harbour and the coast of the Otago Peninsula. It was a contrast Margaret thought to the cemetery side of the road with the many long streets and wooden houses. "The Māoris," Ned informed them, "could often be seen arriving in their wakas (canoes) at the harbour in Dunedin and they would camp on the flat land nearby but this caused a great debate. Many people wanted the area to remain public land but others in the wealthy, business area of the city had other ideas."

"Do you like sports?" he bellowed, changing the subject. "Well, Dunedin has a special area called Carisbrook at the bottom of the Glen where sports are now played and just near here, pointing across to the right-hand side of the road, there is the Kensington Oval which had the first, first-class cricket match ever held in New Zealand. It was in the summer of 1864, about ten years ago." Robert and Margaret were particularly impressed Dunedin had managed to achieve this.

Margaret was still intrigued about the gold rush days and couldn't resist asking Ned if he could tell them a bit more about it. "Well," he said. "It all started when gold was discovered in Gabriel's Gully in Otago, in 1861. It literally made Dunedin the most prosperous place in New Zealand overnight and was the reason it expanded so fast. Gold miners flooded in as it was the gateway to the goldfields. All the supplies came from here, some via Port Chalmers and all the gold that was found was escorted back to the city by armed men riding alongside the Cobb and Co. red coaches. A sight to behold, I can tell you," he said beaming with pride. "The Provincial Hotel in the city became the depot and booking office for Cobb and Co. coach journeys to the Otago gold fields. I can point the building out to you on our way."

Jane was dreaming of the cavalcade and the noise of teams of horses thundering through the city when Ned began to speak again.

"Many people came here in search of gold. The miners journeyed from places like Ireland, Italy, France, even Germany. Some came from California, America,

Victoria in Australia and Chinese gold miners, already in Aussie, due to the NSW strikes, crossed the Tasman Sea or were brought in from Guangdong province (Canton) in south China. Some of the Chinese also got their ticket here by 'chain migration,' due to help from family already in New Zealand. They all hoped they would make their fortunes and strike it rich but, most of the time, it was not to be.

Many of these original Cantonese people seemed to have a hard life as our government favoured British immigrants and, during the gold rush in the 1860s, those worse off lived in a 'tent town,' near the business area in Dunedin known as the *Devil's Half Acre*. Even now, in the 1870s they are still not liked and keep together in mainly wooden hovels in this evil slum area.

We will be approaching this area soon and I warn you, it is not a place I would recommend you ever go" Ned pointed to the corner of Walker Street on their left and said that the *Devil's Half Acre* extended up to Maitland Street and then down to the lower end of Stafford Street which intersected with Princes Street. "This area forms a triangle of vice where among the Chinese hovels, no better than dog kennels, vagabonds, thieves and prostitutes can often be found lurking on corners." The fear of God ran down Margaret's spine. She found this hard to believe in a city with such a beautiful harbour and surrounding land. She told herself to be vigilant and to watch over the children as they continued on their way north towards the Octagon.

The main road they were travelling on was wide but in places rough and muddy with pot holes, so their ride was occasionally bumpy and bruising. They noticed improvements were being made such as limestone blocks being laid on the surface and there were now footpaths on either side of the road as well as gas street lamps. Ned said that all these advances had changed the look of the city over recent years along with the old wooden buildings and shops being rebuilt in stone. The wealth created from the discovery of gold was becoming ever more visible in the grandness of some of the buildings and the fashionable, well-dressed people they saw. Jane couldn't help but smile at two smart looking men in fine cut suits standing outside a tobacconist shop.

In an area called the Exchange, near to High Street, a very long steep road leading away from Princes Street, they saw a magnificent stone structure called the Exchange building which also had a tall clock tower. Ned said that it was first used as the central post office and stock exchange for the city but was also now used by the University of Otago. Jane's eyes widened when she tried to take in the size and scale of it. There were other impressive establishments nearby such as the Customhouse, the three-storey banks of Otago and New South Wales and they could see the Empire Hotel. It was obvious they were in the heart of Dunedin's business and financial area. They were also struck by a tall ornate monument in the middle of a plaza. Ned said that this was built in honour of Captain Cargill, the founder of the Otago Settlement who arrived on the first ship to bring settlers, the *John Wickliffe*. "His monument was moved to this prominent place from the Octagon two years ago," he confirmed. "The area needed to be cleared due to the Bell Hill excavation."

Jane goes Missing in Downtown Dunedin

Suddenly their journey came to a halt and Ned only just managed to rein in the horses. There had been a coach accident on the corner of Stafford Street and the busy main road, Princes Street. A man was lying sprawled and motionless on the ground in front of two horses whose nostrils were flaring while their large hooves pawed at the ground. Steam was rising off them and the coach driver was doing everything he could to keep control. From behind Ned could see that one of the wheels of the coach had come off and it was stranded on the road. He immediately thrust the reigns into Robert's hands and told them all to remain seated and jumped out of the wagon to lend a hand.

Jane, however, had spotted a fascinating building further up Stafford Street and cried out to her parents.

"It's a theatre. Can we go and see?"

Margaret had to agree it would be amusing and, as she desperately needed to stretch her legs, saw no harm in taking a short walk with Jane and Ann. Robert grunted approval. Ned was too busy to notice as he was helping to lift the injured man towards the footpath.

Jane had never been so excited and skipped up Stafford Street holding her mother's hand. It was the first theatre she had ever set eyes on and she couldn't wait to get closer. As they approached this splendid building, they could see it was the Princes Theatre situated beside a hotel called the Provincial. They edged closer towards a poster on the door to check the advertised performances and Margaret scanned the list, then read the titles out for Jane.

"*The Lady of Lyons* was performed last month, as well as *Our American Cousin* and *The Toddles*." She paused then said. "*Genevieve*, an operetta is on at the moment. It's about the heroine of medieval legend, Genevieve of Brabant: the story of a virtuous wife falsely accused of infidelity …. A Pantomime is also playing which is fun for all the family and on the 7th of January there will be another operetta, *The Grand Duchess of Gerolstein:* a spoiled and tyrannical young Grand Duchess who learns that she cannot always get her way …." Jane drew in her breath sharply as though she had just uncovered a treasure-trove of favourite sweets, it all sounded so wonderful.

"Please mother, can we go to a play?" Jane pleaded, but Margaret told her they had no money for such entertainment and would have to save their pennies. Jane felt bereft as her imagination struggled to visualise the splendour of inside the theatre or understand the air of excitement before the curtain rose. She had to know what it was like.

At that moment the main door of the Princes Theatre opened and a charming gentleman asked if he could help them. He was checking the front of house and extended his hand to Margaret. She automatically offered hers and blushed when he drew her reluctant fingers towards his lips in order to elegantly kiss the top of her hand. As Margaret had let go of Jane's hand, Jane decided to run off and follow the sign to the dress circle entrance in the hope of sneaking a peep at what the theatre looked like inside and to see if any actors may be rehearsing.

Jane thought she was heading to the dress circle entrance but had taken a wrong turn down a narrow alley that led to the stage end of the house. She was lost and couldn't understand how she had ended up in this dimly lit area of small wooden shanties. Frantically she tried to find a way back but her path became blocked by the presence of an evil looking man who terrified her.

"What have we here," she heard him say.

As he came towards her she noticed he had rotten teeth, strange black eyes and a filthy shirt. He leaned to within an inch of her nose and when she tried to turn away he continued to breathe his foul breath all over her.

"Come with me my beauty," he said and pointed towards the hovel nearby. But Jane had never been more afraid and could not move.

"Leave me alone," she wailed. "I won't go with you." In fear, and with no other choice, she let out a piercing scream for help, but he quickly placed his mucky hand over her mouth to muffle the sound.

"You will come with me," he snarled, and forced her body in the direction of the shanty. "You will fetch a fine reward as someone will surely want to get you back."

Fortunately for Jane, a woman had heard her cries for help and appeared from around the corner. She yelled at the man.

"What do you think you are doing, you bastard," and rushed over to rescue her.

"I will deal with the child," she said.

He gave the woman a deadly look, but she didn't flinch. Reluctantly he released his hold on Jane who fled to shelter by the woman's skirts. Quickly she guided Jane away from the lane and they walked out into the light.

"There now child, you are safe. I will not harm you but I need to know how you got here?" Jane wiped back her tears and whispered she had come to see the theatre.

"Well in that case, let me take you back there." It took only a few minutes but when they arrived, there was no sign of anyone at the main door. "I have a thought, said the woman. "Let's go to the Provincial Hotel which is next door and see if anyone is there."

It was a wise decision and, sure enough, Margaret was standing talking to the owner, a Mr Jones. She flew over to Jane the second she set eyes on her eldest daughter. "Jane, whatever do you think you were doing running off on your own. Never do that again," she scolded her, before clutching her tightly in her arms. "The kind gentleman from the theatre we met is also out hunting for you and deserves an apology if we ever see him again."

Shadrach Jones, holding back a smile, looked straight over towards the bawdy but proud looking woman who had returned young Jane and said. "Thanks Caversham Liz, a good catch, well done! Makes a nice change from your normal clientele?" Margaret did not understand what he was saying but thanked them both.

"What were you doing little one?" Shadrach said as he gazed down at Jane. She tried to answer but couldn't bring herself to speak as a strange, ugly dog at his feet with heavy folded skin and a dripping tongue hanging out the side of its mouth, was staring at her. She was also transfixed by Shadrach's glittering jewellery, chequerboard waistcoat and the big fat cigar in his hand.

"I was hoping to see inside the theatre," Jane said, keeping her head down.

"Well, you should have come to me straight away," he bellowed, laughing. "It is my theatre!"

"Follow me." And off he went swinging his hips towards the main theatre entrance.

Jane and Margaret waited while he unlocked the door. Once inside, Jane could not believe it, and was instantly mesmerised by the plush interior, the beautiful colours, the endless rows of seats going all the way to the ceiling, the thick, dark red velvet curtains spanning the huge stage. There were one or two people tidying in readiness for the performance that night and some stagehands were moving large props around, but no one was rehearsing.

"It will come alive in a few hours when the orchestra begins to play and the operetta starts," Shadrach roared. The audience will cry for encores once again and the room will be filled with joy. There was no doubt Shadrach Jones had kick started the NZ theatre industry and Dunedin was enjoying remarkable entertainment.

Margaret and Jane thanked him profusely and said that they must go as their family would be worried. They hurried back towards the wagon to explain their long absence. When Margaret told their story - first the glimpse inside the theatre, then the part where Jane got lost and was nearly kidnapped, Robert was speechless. Ned immediately enlightened them that Caversham Liz was a notorious prostitute who sometimes frequented the Flinders Lane part of town, so they were lucky.

"I warned you." Ned continued. "You didn't listen to me and were blessed that no harm came to you in the *Devil's Half Acre*." Margaret only then realised that they had unwittingly walked right into this area. She cursed herself, it was a lesson she never wanted to repeat. Jane sat close to her mother as the wagon carried on towards the Octagon. They would have to cut their trip short now as they needed to be back at The Barracks in time for tea.

"The injured man will live," Ned said, breaking the silence.

"That's good news," said Robert. "And thank goodness for Caversham Liz. It proves these women of 'ill repute' can do some good in this world." Ned nodded and quietly told Robert to be aware that Dunedin had many prostitutes and houses of ill fame. The women often became outcasts and lived amongst the Chinese but some belonged to brothel houses or used the hotels in the city to look for customers. "They can pass on diseases like syphilis, where men go mad, so be careful!" Robert looked at Ned bewildered as he had no intention of ever needing the services of these harlots.

The Dunedin Tour Continues but Time is Running Out

They were nearing the Octagon, an unsightly eight-sided plaza where the main street, Princes Street connected to George Street which headed northeast. It would have taken them out of the central city to the Water of Leith, The Garden where native and exotic tree species were established back in 1863 and to North East Valley, but they had no time to go that far now.

Ned told them that there were two other roads that also bisected the Octagon - upper Stuart Street, which climbed steeply to the northwest leading to the Town Belt and other suburbs, and lower Stuart Street which headed southeast to main routes out of the city. Ned went on to tell them about Charles Kettle, the original surveyor and architect of the city. "He was asked to reproduce the characteristics of Edinburgh in Scotland and tried to create a romantic effect," he said, chuckling to himself. "The problem is, although the city sprawls amongst the hills in rugged terrain, the green Town Belt separates the city from its suburbs and the harbour forms its other boundary, Kettle produced some of the steepest streets I have ever known. They are so steep for horse-drawn carriages and wagons, that the poor beasts often come to a standstill and refuse to go on, which creates havoc. Everyone loves the views on the way down to town though - with the harbour and Otago Peninsula as the backdrop. It makes your heart sing …

Margaret let her thoughts drift back to her first sight of the harbour from the *Nelson* and thought how beautiful it was when the sun danced on the blue Pacific water to make it sparkle. She was brought back quickly from her dreamy recollections when Jane let out a loud exclamation saying she had just seen a huge spire.

"Ah ha," said Ned, "that will be First Church and immediately veered off Princes Street to turn right down Moray Place. I need to show you the famous First Presbyterian Church of Otago before we head back." In a few minutes he pulled up the horses just beyond the entrance gates which had two Edinburgh street lamps either side. It was thought these lamps would help the congregation and early settlers feel more connected to Scotland.

The Harcus family didn't say a word as they gazed towards the church. It was breathtakingly big and impressive with its Gothic style. They marvelled at its multi-pinnacled tower, adorned by a spire rising to 185 feet. "It is Dunedin's tallest building and can hold about a 1,000 people." Ned said. "Oamaru stone, found in a settlement further up the coast was used for its construction and much of the detailed carvings on the outside and in the interior were the work of Louis Godfrey."

"The designer was a very clever man," Margaret commented. "You're right," said Ned. "Robert Lawson, originally from Fife in Scotland, won a competition for the best design for the church you know? He helped to shape Victorian architecture in Dunedin and was involved in the design of many other buildings in the city, including Larnach Castle on the Otago Peninsula."

"We saw it from the train," Jane responded enthusiastically.

"Do you remember I mentioned Captain Cargill," Ned continued, "who was the leader of the Lay Association of the Free Church of Scotland who founded Dunedin. Well, he was Presbyterian and his followers were very high minded and set on an evangelical mission to defeat Popish ignorance in Otago and the world! The Rev. Thomas Burns, (nephew of the poet Robert), arrived on the *Philip Laing*, the month after Cargill, and Burns was the spiritual guide here. But they both treated other religious denominations woefully; Anglicans were the 'Little Enemy' and they frowned upon the first Jewish synagogue built in Moray place in 1863. It was surprising their stern, no nonsense puritanism still appealed to many of the Scots settlers.

Thomas Burns was the force behind First Church's construction which was eventually completed in 1873. He believed that faith could move mountains and remained resilient during the delays while the provincial government set about lowering Bell Hill by about 40 feet. This massive project between the Exchange and the Octagon which began in 1868, kept me and other men in work for nearly a decade. It meant the church did not have to teeter on the side of a mountain and also allowed a roadway to be made through the Octagon to connect both sides of the city."

Robert was stunned by Ned's story and couldn't believe the scale of the task that had been achieved. The gold rush had brought such prosperity and adventurous people to this city; he felt pleased he had chosen to bring his family to Otago.

Ned pulled on the reins but before the horses lifted their hooves and the wagon turned, he told them that although experts believed First Church was the finest building in the country, some of the Scotch Kirk members thought it too fancy and cost too much. "Most people think it is a remarkable building however and were sad when the Rev. Burns died before the church was finally completed," he said.

Return to The Barracks

"Best get going," Ned sighed as he swung the wagon back up Burlington Street to turn left at Moray Place. "We could have gone down lower Stuart Street which would take us to a main route out of the city but this way will be faster." Soon they returned to Princes Street and, as they neared the Exchange area, Robert saw a sign for the *Otago Daily Times* newspaper and suddenly remembered the other reason he agreed to come on this outing and asked Ned to pull up the horses.

Robert clambered out of the wagon and walked over to check the newspaper stand but his heart sank as all the papers had gone. "There will be more papers tomorrow," said Ned but Robert knew he would not be in a position to see one tomorrow and his doubts about finding a suitable job came flooding back. The visit to the city had completely taken his mind off this subject until now and Margaret felt his fear about their future.

"The *Otago Daily Times* was New Zealand's first daily newspaper you know," said Ned. We are very proud of it and have to thank Julius Vogel and Mr William Cutten as they got together to make it happen in 1861. Vogel first worked for the *Otago Witness*, a weekly paper, as editor, but as Dunedin was so prosperous and the population grew from about 2000 people to many thousands due to the gold rush, he thought Otago was ready for a daily paper as settlers loved to hear the news.

Eventually Vogel got himself sacked towards the end of the gold rush in 1868, when Dunedin started an economic downturn. He had become more involved in politics and had used the *Otago Daily Times* to campaign for the separation of the South and North Islands, so he got the heave ho."

"We have a lot to thank him for however," said Robert. "Without his policies including free immigration we wouldn't be here." "Very true." Ned replied. "He is Jewish, a clever politician and our current Premier who now wants to help the whole country, not just Otago."

The horses were becoming weary. The wagon rattled its way slowly on to merge with the Main South Road to take them back towards South Dunedin and Caversham. "If we just keep going, we will end up at St Clair and the beach," said Ned. Jane was particularly excited by this and craved a diversion to see waves crashing on the shore, rather than returning straight to The Barracks, but she was over ruled as it was nearly time for their evening meal.

Much of the area called The Flat where they were headed was marshy so the earliest settlement in Dunedin took place along the hill fringes of Caversham and St Clair. Ned knew so much as he was an early settler and told them it was William Valpy, probably the wealthiest man in New Zealand, who in 1849 had a road built from central Dunedin to his St Clair farm which helped South Dunedin to flourish.

Originally, the first settlers relied on the Māoris for food but some of the industrious Chinese, also early residents in the St Clair area, worked hard to drain the swampy land near the beach and converted it to market gardens. Dunedin's first vegetables were grown in their allotments.

Jane was still dreaming of the beautiful sandy beach of St Clair, only a stone's throw away as the horses began to lumber up the hill to The Barracks. It had been so long since she had walked on a beach, or played in the sand dunes. She longed for the space and freedom having always lived near the sea. Margaret assured her that they would be able to go to the beach as soon as they were settled and her father had found work.

They thanked Ned for his time and knowledge and hoped they might meet him again. He had made this a special day and one which they would always remember. Even at her young age, Jane knew how lucky she was to have escaped the clutches of that evil man in the *Devil's Half Acre.*

Time in The Barracks Extended

That night following their tea, the Manager, Mr Duke informed those who had no prospects as yet of employment that they had a further few days grace of temporary accommodation in The Barracks. This was comforting news to many of the married men and women who breathed a sigh of relief as their families would be fed and watered for a bit longer.

Due to this announcement and the fact that Jane was safe and everyone was accounted for, Robert decided he would go into Caversham with the other men that night after all and Margaret could cope alone with the children just for once. The children were worn out from their adventurous day and would, hopefully, fall asleep early.

A group of six men assembled and set off about 6.30 p.m. Two of the single, younger fellows didn't know the married men but they had all travelled on the *Nelson*. Robert enjoyed the light hearted banter between them, as it was a distraction from the ever-present worry of finding a job. They decided to head for the Crown Hotel - one of the single guys reckoned he knew how to find it. After a 20 minute walk he pointed to the hotel. "Crown ahoy," he yelled and there was a cheer from the group. They all began to drool about the taste of their first drink after such a long wait. Robert wanted whisky, others wanted to try the NZ beer. They charged in laughing and headed for the large wooden bar to order drinks. Robert also asked for water so he could rinse out his glass after he downed the whisky.

There were many local men in the hotel, some were leaning on the bar while others stood or sat round the sparse tables. Some spotted Robert's group were 'new immigrants' and immediately started up conversations. "You won't go far wrong to remain in this part of town, you know," said someone who called himself Jack. "The Flats has just about everything you need like grocers, local markets, schools, churches, boot-makers and the like. There could be some work going to help further the railway construction too?" Robert's eyes lit up and he asked a few more questions. He discovered that this area was one of the first to become established in Dunedin, so it was possible to live, work, buy food and socialise all within the radius of Caversham and South Dunedin. It was good to know in these uncertain times that this area was so self-sufficient. The conversations he had with locals, during the first hour, reassured him to have faith and be patient as some form of work would turn up for him soon.

"Our leader, Mr Vogel will make sure of it," Jack jested and everyone howled with laughter. "He has big plans for this country and needs the likes of you immigrants to help," he bellowed, before gulping down his beer. "When he was colonial treasurer back in 1870, he persuaded the government that a public works programme was needed and subsidised or free immigration would attract the right sort of settlers to achieve their aims. He is now our premier and still believes in this policy. Time will tell ...."

Suddenly, they were all distracted by the proprietor of the Crown yelling for help. He was trying to detain a man at the top of the stairs whom he had found trespassing in one of the bedrooms. When he'd tried to throw him out, the man had refused to go and proceeded to give the proprietor a horrible beating. Everyone could see his shirt was ripped and bloodstained and he was failing miserably to defend himself or control his assailant. Quickly a couple of locals leapt to his rescue and managed to armlock the intruder. Two other men helped to pin him face down on the floor until the police arrived. At that point, Robert thought it was time to leave. He could see law and order were not always observed in a new colony and they all needed to watch out. They concluded that the intruder was probably looking for money or items he could pawn for cash.

Trouble in The Barracks

Despite the incident at the Crown, Robert was so relaxed when he neared The Barracks that he felt like he could slide under the door. It was the first time he had been apart from Margaret and his family for months but the camaraderie of his fellow Scots had done him a power of good and given him a stronger belief he would be offered work.

When he attempted to knock on the main door to be let in, he found the door ajar which he thought odd. He signalled for the others to follow, pushed the door wide open and stepped inside. A drunken scene awaited them as a single, female barracks inmate was out of control: blaspheming and behaving in a disgusting manner as well as throwing herself over a number of sailors who had accompanied her from the wharf.

Mr Duke was in a rage as he had demanded she leave The Barracks on several other occasions. It appeared she had refused to go. Then, like an apparition,

Robert saw a large policeman standing in the doorway and had to quickly move aside to let him pass. Mr Duke had cleverly got word to Constable Rooney to come and arrest the woman. Within seconds she was handcuffed and marched out of The Barracks along with the sailors.

The Barracks' Master, Mr Duke, apologised, gave Robert and the other men a quick once over and abruptly said, "Goodnight gentlemen." Like startled possums, they scurried past him. The single men veered off to the North wing and the married men found their way to the East wing but were unsuccessful in walking quietly up the stairs. Somehow their commotion did not awaken those already asleep and all remained peaceful with only heavy breathing and the odd snore breaking the silence. Robert managed to slip into bed beside Margaret without causing her the slightest stir. He went out like a light.

Their second night in Elbe Street barracks was heaven. The family quarters were so much more comfortable than the ship: there was no pitching or creaking from the rigging, no smell from the closeness of bodies and the latrines, no lack of air and light. The light of the moon shone through the window of their room, they could taste the freshness of the air as it cleansed their lungs and the only smell was from the newly laundered linen sheets.

They all slept a long, beautiful sleep on that second night, apart from Jane. She had heard her father return but did not cry out for him. She couldn't sleep as she was haunted by the vivid memory of the evil man with cold, piercing, daggers for eyes who had nearly kidnapped her. She knew she had caused much trouble during their journey to the city and had been extremely lucky; the fear of being taken away against her will persisted, and she bore it alone. She tried again to close her eyes but they remained wide open; from her bed she could just see a sprinkling of stars in the night sky which was her only comfort.

An Offer of Work for Robert

The next day went by quietly in The Barracks. Margaret continued washing and mending and Robert tried to remain positive although no interview opportunities from prospective employers came his way. It was disheartening but he held on to the belief that something would turn up. It did. Towards the end of the week, he was asked to go to the engaging office after breakfast to meet an employer involved with a Public Works Scheme in Otago. They were looking for labourers to help build new roads, bridges and railway lines in the Central Otago province. Robert was strong and used to working on the land which gave him the skills they were looking for. He was also smart and of good character which meant he would get along with others in a gang.

He spoke about this opportunity with Margaret and explained that he would be working away from Dunedin for the majority of the time and she would have to cope with the children alone. They both agreed this job had drawbacks but it was a start and they desperately needed the wages to feed and clothe their growing family. Robert knew in his heart it would not be a long-term solution but it was a first step to a successful new life and he would make the most of it.

Robert returned to the engaging office in the afternoon as instructed and was offered the job. He accepted on the spot and signed the contract of engagement. He was to start work the following Monday. His new employer allowed him only a few days to find new accommodation and move out of The Barracks.

Margaret could not help but smile for the rest of the day and evening due to their good fortune. Robert also reminded Margaret it was Julius Vogel they should be thanking as the Public Works Scheme, which had created many new jobs was his idea.

The Harcus's Move to Andersons Bay

Their number one priority now was to find new lodgings for the family. Margaret's mind raced when she thought about all the things they needed but agreed they had to focus on finding somewhere to live first.

At tea that night, Mrs Duke overheard their excitement about Robert's success in securing a job and their need to find alternative accommodation. She told them that she knew of a family who were moving out of the city and that their lodgings in Andersons Bay, not far from The Barracks, might be available to them. She would find out and let them know. Margaret was excited with this prospect and Robert understood, after conversations he had had in the local hostelry, that it would be wise to live outside the centre of Dunedin and remain near to the relatively self-sufficient area of South Dunedin. Other people also suggested possible landlords to follow up in the area or to look in the newspapers and local shops in Caversham for advertisements. It was a stressful time as Margaret and Robert only found one nearby dwelling which was no more than a hovel and unfit to live in. But their luck changed when Mrs Duke confirmed that the property she had spoke of in Andersons Bay, would be available that coming weekend and suggested they make a special visit to meet the owner in the morning.

As it was not far, the Dukes, who were such caring and kind people, offered their wagon and directions in order for Margaret, Robert and children to see their potential new lodgings. In 45 minutes, they had arrived. It was half way up a hill with a part view of the peninsula and harbour and, although it was a small, wooden property with few windows or rooms, it had a corrugated iron roof and would do for now. They accepted the weekly rent amount and Robert paid a small deposit which left them penniless but guaranteed they could move in the next day, Sunday. It was a huge worry not to have a penny to spend until Robert received his first wages but their new life was underway and all would be well.

That night after tea they said their goodbyes to fellow immigrants from the *Nelson* and Mr and Mrs Duke. Everyone was pleased they were moving on and wished them good luck. They were shown such kindness and offered bedding and food from The Barracks' stores for the first few days in their new home. Margaret was overwhelmed as the married couples and children in the east wing had become like a large family and she felt she was leaving them behind. She had formed strong bonds with these people as they had endured so much together on their journey from Greenock. Jane was excited but would miss all the comforts of The Barracks and the friends she had made.

Before they left, Margaret asked Mr and Mrs Duke to forward the rest of their belongings from the *Nelson* to their new address. Their boxes should have arrived days ago and they urgently needed them now.

The following day after breakfast, they set off for Andersons Bay. The sun appeared through the cloud as they reached the path to their new dwelling. It was a warm, summer day with a gentle breeze from the west. Jane, Ann and William were unstoppable once the wagon came to a halt and scampered off as fast as they could towards the house. Wearily Margaret got down carrying Robert junior and walked towards the other children. She had to try and make this place a home but there was much cleaning and organising to do first. As she came closer, she saw to her surprise, that there were two glass bottles near the door step which she nearly knocked over. Someone had left milk, loaves of bread, tea and a small pile of dry wood. Margaret was once again overwhelmed by the kindness of the settlers in Dunedin and hoped she would discover who had been responsible as they had seen few neighbours on the road to the house. They were fortunate as, together with food they were given from The Barracks, she could make these supplies last for several days.

Robert caught up with his family who were all huddled at the door and produced the large key which he slowly turned in the lock. The door flew open and the children rushed inside. Margaret and Robert slowly followed and tried to work out what they should do first.

Robert Leaves for Central Otago

Early the next morning Margaret kissed Robert goodbye and wished him good luck. He was to join a gang of men who were being taken to Central Otago to assist in the building of roads and bridges to help open up the land for farming. They took the southern route out of Dunedin, used during the gold rush, which passed Caversham and Look Out Point then eventually turned inland. He could not believe the natural beauty of the Otago province and was astounded by deep river gorges and river basins as well as magnificent mountain ranges that climbed it seemed to infinity. He was also amazed by huge, jagged schist rocks that were scattered over the landscape and by the hardy tussock grass that provided anchorage for the dry soil. He was told that Central Otago was a land of extremes which he could now believe. The summers were hot and dry but it was the coldest part of New Zealand in the winter, often with cloudless days and freezing nights. The journey was uncomfortable and he felt battered and bruised due to the rugged terrain but he filled his lungs with the pure, fresh air and hoped the sun would recharge his aching body.

By the end of the day the men were provided with pickaxes and shovels and told where the road construction was required and what they needed to achieve by the end of the week. It was back breaking, tiring work in the heat of summer. By nightfall the gang was exhausted and could hardly manage to eat before sleep claimed them. It took Robert most of his first week to become acclimatised but there was no escape from the piercing southern hemisphere sun. He often thought its rays were stronger in this part of the world than in Orkney but his old life seemed a strange, distant memory now. He had never worked so far from the sea, or been away from his family for so long which he found disturbing.

When Robert returned to Dunedin, he was caked with dirt, had lost weight and his clothes hung on him like rags. His beard had also changed colour due to the clay-like dust from the dry Central Otago earth. However odd he looked Margaret, Jane and the children were ecstatic to see him. Margaret cried when she saw his first pay packet as they were desperate for more food, clothing and utensils. She was exhausted and Jane, who was only seven and a half years, also looked pale and tired as she had to help her mother with many of the chores.

A Family Day Out at St Clair

As a special treat, particularly for Jane who had always wanted to go to the beach, they decided to take the whole family and spend a day at St Clair which was not far. Jane could not have been happier and her eyes lit up when she was told the news. She felt so lucky as it was not her birthday until May. They waited until the weather improved the following day and set off on foot. Margaret had a basket and they would stop for more food on the way. Robert carried a blanket and Robert junior. Jane carried a small bucket they could use on the beach to build sand castles.

By lunchtime they had passed St Kilda and were soon approaching St Clair. After climbing up the sand dunes they were not prepared for the breathtaking view of the Pacific Ocean which stretched for miles in front of them. The force of the sea and the white capped breakers were a sight to behold. They crashed and foamed and their pounding could be heard above the screeching of seagulls, which were flying low looking for morsels to eat. Far out to sea they could just make out a small jagged, white island which seemed home to sea bird colonies and following the white sand of St Clair beach to their left, they could see it merged into the beautiful St Kilda beach in the distance.

Jane could not wait to discard her shoes and feel the warm white sand between her toes. She quickly glanced at her mother who nodded and then ran as fast as she could towards the sea. Everyone was laughing and smiling and quickly set off after her. The joy of feeling the wind on her face and in her hair and the smell of salt and seaweed immediately brought back memories of her home on Eday but it was somehow different on the coast of Dunedin. The white sandy beach was vast and the sea appeared more lively and powerful. It tried to tempt her in by tickling her toes but she resisted at first as her father had said there were vicious, great white sharks in these southern waters.

The rest of the family caught up with her and together, holding hands, they all paddled in the cool water. Afterwards they walked along the shore line and Jane stopped regularly to gather colourful shells. As everyone was famished they turned back. The wind helped blow them towards the sand dunes where Margaret laid out a blanket and some food. After Jane had eaten bread and delicious NZ apples she was determined to build a sand castle. Slowly with the help of her father and Ann it took shape and the rest of the family gazed in amazement. Margaret enjoyed every minute watching her contented children. It was the happiest family day out and no one wanted to leave but, as it was a long walk back to Andersons Bay, they packed up and set off in the late afternoon. Once home Margaret noticed the colour had returned to Jane's cheeks and the sparkle was back in her eyes - their day by the sea had done wonders for them all.

Extremes of Climate in Central Otago

Robert returned to the gang and the hard slog of road building. As the months passed, the golden days of summer turned to autumn, which was in Central Otago a spectacular time of year. Robert stole glimpses of snow-capped mountains reflected in blue lakes and watched the leaves of the trees turn to the most glorious vivid burnt orange and yellow colours before they turned crisp and floated to the ground. The winter months proved the most challenging, and although he had experienced bad weather at sea and in other parts of Scotland, he was not prepared for the sheeting rain and chill from the snow and ice when working outdoors. Sometimes the torrent of rain caused landslides in treacherous parts of their newly laid roads and the piles of earth and stones had to be removed which severely delayed progress. Often, due to the cold, their hands were so frozen that they couldn't grip the shovels which made the job impossible.

Robert was relieved when spring arrived as the temperature rose but water from melting snow high up in the mountains often caused flooding and parts of their roads or bridges were washed away or damaged. It was relentless toil and Christmas and the New Year could not come soon enough as the gang were to have much needed time off.

Back in Dunedin and reunited with his family, Robert decided he would take himself off to the local hotel as some of the men he knew were meeting up in Andersons Bay. It was a rare occurrence to go to a Dunedin tavern and he was glad of the opportunity to have a beer with a wee dram on the side. Robert met other locals at the bar who shared stories of their work and the problems facing Dunedin. Some were aware that the city was heading for a downturn as revenues from the gold fields had slowed and Otago needed another product to export. They all agreed this would most likely come from sheep farming as there were several breeds of sheep doing well on the high country as well as on the rolling hills of the Otago province.

1876 and the Harcus Family is Expanding

Early in January after Robert returned to work, Margaret noticed she was feeling nauseous and had lost her appetite which was odd. It did not take her long to identify the symptoms and she knew she had fallen pregnant. She could barely cope with four children on her own as it was and another addition to the family would be difficult without more help. She lay awake that night worrying about her own health and caring for a new bairn plus the other children. She needed Robert but he would not return for many weeks which upset her further. She craved the protection of his strong arms around her and the reassurance that all would be well.

By Easter, Margaret was coping better with her pregnancy and Robert made it clear they would manage. He would ask his bosses if he could work closer to Dunedin so he would be home more often, but knew there was little hope of succeeding. Jane was turning eight years old in May and was already proving to be an invaluable help to her mother. She was good at entertaining her younger brothers and sisters and helped with other household chores Margaret struggled with. She had little time for school or to play with other children but never complained. Margaret felt bad about this but hoped things would change once her eldest sons, William and Robert started at the Andersons Bay school. She read to Jane and the other children when there was time and noticed her eldest daughter loved stories and was quick to learn.

The one thing that always fascinated Jane, were the stars in the Dunedin night sky. She would sneak outdoors after sunset to search for the Southern Cross, which she had first seen from on board the *Nelson,* or to study the magical Milky Way. One night she was overwhelmed by an astonishing spectacle of colour high above the Otago Peninsula and rushed inside to tell her mother to come and see. It was a breathtakingly beautiful sight and they both stood speechless for several minutes as they gazed in awe at magnificent swirling waves of green, pink and purple light with dancing stars above. It wasn't until the next day when Margaret took the children to a nearby shop that she overheard other settlers talking about the Southern Lights and realised it was what they had witnessed the previous night. She also discovered that this phenomenon is also called the Aurora Australis which originates in the South Pole and as New Zealand is close to the South Pole it can be seen in certain parts of the country. Jane felt so lucky to have seen the light show and couldn't wait to tell her father.

Robert was coming home soon, hopefully in time for Margaret to give birth, but Jane was concerned there was no crib for the new addition to their family. They had left the crib in Eday and Jane needed to know where this new brother or sister was going to sleep. Her worries were short lived however because when Robert returned he went off to borrow a large woven basket from a family they knew in Caversham. It did not rock like the crib but they assured Jane it would do perfectly well for the new bairn.

The days passed quickly for Robert once he was back with his family and it was soon time for him to return to work. On this occasion, as Margaret was so close to giving birth, he refused to leave and wanted to throw in his job there and then. He had also begun to worry about Margaret's health as sometimes her breathing was not good and she coughed far too much these days. But as always, he was amazed at his wife's strength of character as she made him go and said that she would not forgive him if he stopped earning his wages. The time was not yet right for a change to their lives. They agreed, however, that he would contact a friend of Margaret's and ask her to visit in the following days in case she needed help or the midwife.

Robert had only just returned to work when Margaret began contractions and, after a long night, gave birth to John Harcus on 9 October 1876 at home in Andersons Bay. Her new son thrived but the demands of another child to care for were overwhelming and Margaret had to battle on as best she could. She felt like a ghost most days as the lack of sleep made every chore seem twice as difficult. Jane was an angel and tried to help as she hated to see her mother suffer in this way. It wasn't until Robert returned for Christmas that Margaret could take time to rest.

The family continued to exist on Robert's wage over the coming months and if Margaret did manage to stash any pennies aside for emergencies, she always had to dip into the money. It was a long hard year. They also realised their new life was not turning out the way they had hoped and that something had to change. There was also talk of a depression coming and Robert feared that he could lose his job in the Public Works scheme. When Margaret told Robert she was pregnant with their sixth child, in the summer of 1878, a dark cloud descended over them which felt similar to the dilemma they had faced in Eday before they decided to leave.

The Beginning of Economic Changes in Dunedin and Otago

Robert decided to go off to the tavern and meet his friends as the walk would help clear his head. After he arrived and sat down with his dram there was again talk about the signs of the Otago economy slowing. The Otago Gold Rush had waned with only Macraes Flat in East Otago still producing and other sources of gold on the West Coast, including Hokitika, had all but dried up.

One of his workmates from Scotland said that a long depression was inevitable. He had heard that the City Bank of Glasgow had closed which meant the New Zealand Government would have problems borrowing enough money to pay for the current Immigration and Public Works schemes. Fewer immigrants were now arriving and slowly more people were crossing the Tasman Sea to Australia. Many farmers were also struggling to keep their homes and lands.

Robert felt that his long-term future and that of his family looked grim if he was 'to do nothing' and silently looked into his empty whisky glass in the hope of an answer. When he looked up a settler called James Curle asked if he could join them and sat down opposite Robert. He said that he was celebrating the fact that he had just been granted a land lease on a section in the Moonlight area near Macraes Flat. He told them that the area had been recently surveyed for agricultural land subdivision and sections could now be leased by settlers. Robert recognised immediately that this could be the opportunity he had been waiting for as he could not deny he longed to get back to farming. He got up and asked James Curle to join him at the bar where he bought him a drink. As they stood together, Robert admitted he was interested in a section and asked if James would help him. "After all," said Robert. "In Eday, Orkney, where I am from, I was a part time fisherman but also worked on the land. That's why they call an Orkney man, a farmer with a boat!"

This made James Curle roar with laughter and from that moment they became firm friends. James said that he would help Robert and they agreed to meet again after Robert talked to Margaret.

Robert Considers a Return to Farming

That night, when he returned home, he sat down with Margaret at the table to discuss moving away from Dunedin to Moonlight, near Macraes Flat in East Otago. Margaret was excited about the idea but knew they had no savings to rely on and was concerned where she would live with the children while he toiled on the land. Robert said that he would figure this out and she was not to worry. Margaret had such faith in him and reached for his hand. They had made hard decisions in the past and were no strangers to taking risks. They knew they should go for this opportunity and do whatever was necessary to make a change in their lives.

At the end of the week, Robert met with James Curle in the tavern at Andersons Bay. James came bounding over smiling but could see his new friend looked downcast.

Robert spoke first. "Margaret and I would gladly go back to the land but we have little money and nowhere to live until I could become established," he explained. "I must find a way."

James looked at him, paused, then said. "Well, my friend, I shall help you apply for a section in Moonlight. I also have a proposition for you. As I am already a land owner I need help with my new land lease in Moonlight as there is much clearing of niggerheads to be done before I can start planting. Would you come and work for me? Your family would have to live close by until you were more settled but I am sure my wife and I could help you."

Robert had many questions but could not help but show his enthusiasm. "I am sure Margaret will be agreeable but I must discuss this offer with her." He gulped down his drink and rushed away smiling and light headed as it felt like the weight of the world was lifting from his shoulders.

When he told Margaret the latest news she was overjoyed as they both knew it was the chance they had been waiting for - their route out of Dunedin and back to the land. He told her that the money he earned while labouring for James would help pay for their own lease to farm in Moonlight. They would become settlers and work towards being self-sufficient. It was also one of the few places in Otago where gold was still being found and Robert could not deny he was interested in prospecting for this illusive mineral. They agreed, there were many good reasons to go to the Macraes Flat area.

Jane noticed that her mother suddenly had more energy and seemed happier and asked her if anything had happened? Margaret told her that soon they would be moving from Dunedin as her father was changing his job so they could all be together as a family. Jane liked this idea but could not imagine where they were going.

As planned, Robert met with James the next day and gave him his answer. He would accept his offer of work in Moonlight and leave Dunedin as soon as he heard about his section application. They smiled at each other and shook hands vigorously.

"That is great news," James said beaming. "You will not regret your decision my friend."

Land Lease in Moonlight Agreed

By September 1878, Robert was successful in his application for a land lease and had taken up a section on the road to Nenthorn in Moonlight, it was opposite James Curle's.

But while Robert began his new adventure as a pioneer settler and labourer about 60 miles away, Margaret remained in Dunedin with the children and gave birth to her fourth son, David Harcus at home in Andersons Bay, on 7 December 1878. She found that life with six children to look after on her own was desperately hard and exhausting. Her eldest daughter, Jane, now ten and a half years, Ann had just turned nine, William was seven, Robert junior was nearly five years and John only two years old. They were to leave Dunedin soon as James Curle was helping to find them somewhere to live but it would be difficult until Robert built them a house on their land. The older children were at Andersons Bay school for part of the day, but Margaret prayed every night to be reunited with Robert to share in their care.

Compared to other cities in New Zealand Dunedin was facing a slow decline and some settlers were drifting north to seek new opportunities. The city had relied so much on the Otago gold rush for its prosperity but now other new industries were needed for its future growth. Brick-making, pottery and printing were beginning but as the depression set in many people lost their livelihoods. The *Otago Daily Times* had more reports of poor, depressed people being admitted to Dunedin's lunatic asylum as there was no other place for them. Margaret swore this would not be her fate. She also remembered Robert's promise after they arrived that they would never end up seeking charity in the ominous Benevolent Asylum building opposite The Barracks. It made her more determined to create another life for their growing family. Soon it would be time to leave the city and join Robert to make a fresh start on the rugged land in East Otago.

Part Five

5.

Settlers in Moonlight, East Otago

"He who is not courageous enough to take risks will accomplish nothing in life."
Muhammad Ali

Moving to Moonlight

Circa 1880

Jane stood and stared at the small house made of sun-dried earth bricks with a thatched roof that her father had made with his own bare hands. He had toiled for weeks mixing and moulding the soil and clay into this sod hut and it was now time to all move in. It was the beginning of summer, the weather was mild and while he disappeared inside to do one last check, the rest of the family waited patiently by the horse, wagon and cow on the dry tussock grass outside. He was not gone long but startled them all when he bounded out of the hut and ran towards them. Jane loved her father as he was always trying to make things better and she could not help but notice how proud and happy he seemed on this day.

From about 20 yards away Jane thought the hut looked smaller than the first house she had known in the Orkney Isles and, as she had more brothers and sisters now, she was puzzled as to whether there would be enough room inside. Robert saw the worried look on her face and tried to reassure her by saying that he realised the hut was on the small side but hoped to move them to a larger house in the future when their fortunes improved. "If we all work hard on the farm and can hunt or trap other food such as rabbits, ducks and pigs, all will be well," he said. Laughing, he picked up his youngest son, David, and bellowed. "Let's go inside." Jane rushed to follow them but stopped abruptly at the doorway to let her eyes adjust to the dim interior.

It was a wee bit like their Eday cottage she thought to herself when the room came into focus, but a backward step she quickly decided. She found it impossible not to compare this humble dwelling to the light, spacious barracks in Dunedin which had left a lasting impression but, knowing that her father had put his heart and soul into building this hut, she was careful not to show her feelings. She just hoped the thatched roof would keep them dry and not leak and that the small window she could see, would not let in too much wind and rain. One thing she had noticed in this area was the force of the wind and rain at times. Her father had said it was due to the closeness of the mountains. Almighty gales could blow up anytime and last for days. The rain, which was normally light, could occasionally turn to heavy downpours which made the rivers swell and caused flooding on the flats. The sudden floods were also due to melting snow in the mountains which could quickly make the local roads and tracks impassable and many risked their lives to help others who were isolated.

Fresh water for drinking, cooking and daily chores was crucial however and Jane hoped there would be a source close to the house as they would all have to walk to fetch it. Her mother, Margaret, was also concerned but their worries were dissolved after Robert explained that this part of Otago had lots of water for drinking due to the number of creeks and streams nearby and he had dug a bore hole not far from the house to be on the safe side.

Inside the hut, the fireplace looked large compared to the size of the room but Janes's mother was pleased as it was the heart of their existence. She would cook their food by open hearth cooking using suspended heavy cast iron pots, boil the water in the big black kettle hung by the fire and dry their leather boots overnight. Jane always remembered her mother's dread of her boots not being dry by morning as it put her in a bad mood and she would refuse to go outside.

Jane had also noticed the white wash paint and some old newspaper stuck to the walls to help with the drafts but knew that the fire had to be kept burning to keep them warm. This meant they would all need to help search for wood, dried cow pats and peat which could be dried and used for fuel. Jane had already noticed there was a distinct lack of trees in the surrounding, rugged countryside and was intrigued as to how they were going to manage. No doubt her father would have a plan, she thought. He is so clever.

They were now living in Moonlight, east of the Rock and Pillar Mountain Range in the Straith Taieri and Macraes District on the fringe of Central Otago. Their closest township was Macraes Flat, several miles away. The Rock and Pillar mountains formed the western border and the Hummock Hills, the border to the east. The district extended as far as the Shag River in the north and the Deep Stream to the south. The landscape was unusual and dominated by native tussock grass and rocky outcrops but hidden below the surface were deposits of minerals such as gold and scheelite. The early prospectors first found gold in Murphy's Flat about two and a half miles from Macraes in 1862, then at Highlay Hill, followed by discoveries in the Macraes Flat area in 1865.

Townships like Macraes Flat, Hyde and small districts such as Moonlight and Nenthorn had sprung up due to the 'gold fever' as hundreds of prospectors flooded in to stake their claims. Jane found it exciting that gold was still being found not far from where they lived. Elsewhere in the South Island, the 'rush' had all but died out. However finding gold was not why they moved from Dunedin.

Her father told them that the district was prospering in other ways now as the land was slowly being divided up or leased for farming. "It was the main reason we chose to come here," he said. Some of the early settlers had already established large sheep or cattle runs such as the Shag Valley station and Deepdell Station, not far from Macraes. These runs attracted labourers and shepherds to settle in the area as they were desperately needed to look after livestock, grow crops and clear more land."

Jane thought how hard it must be working outdoors all day in the extremes of temperature they experienced. One day, in the summer, when it was said to be about 95°F in the shade she watched settlers wither like plants if they had stayed out in the sun for too long. The weather could be harsh and unpredictable and she remembered in early summer, on New Year's Eve, when the white flowers of the clover were blackened by a surprise late frost.

Over the first months she got more used to the climate and was beginning to except the extremes of temperature but still worried about sudden high winds or thick fog. She had always felt responsible for her younger brothers and sisters and tried to protect them as best she could, but the weather was totally out of her control. On a positive note, she reminded herself that there was a lot she needed to learn about Moonlight and the neighbouring township of Macraes Flat and couldn't wait to begin exploring. That night they ate rabbit stew with potatoes which Jane decided tasted much better than it looked and she fell asleep beside her sister Ann with brothers William and Robert at the other end of the bed.

Searching for Fuel

The next morning they awoke early and, after porridge for breakfast, her father said they must all help gather fuel for the fire. Jane loved to be outdoors when the sun was shining and was happy to lend a hand and find out more about this strange, parched land. The silver tussock, on the lower ridges near the hut, glistened in the sun but Jane could not see any trees or a forest close by.

Robert then spoke. "We are looking for matagouri, it can grow into a tall shrub, has tiny white flowers but has nasty long thorns, so be careful if you get close."

Jane was not amused and trudged on beside her father who was holding the reins of the horse. When they found some matagouri Robert used his axe to chop through the tangled branches and bundled a good quantity into thick sacks. He was pleased with the load as it would be a useful shrub to start the fire burning.

As they moved on a deep gully opened up in front of them. Robert was hoping to find some totara trees but there were none in sight. He pointed out a large native flax plant with long fluffy stems which Jane took a fancy to but it was not what they were looking for. At the bottom of the gully there was a creek and Robert decided this would be a good place to dig for peat. As he had found in Eday, the peat could be dried in the sun and kept for fuel during the winter.

Robert drove his shovel into the soft ground and was fortunate to dig up a quantity of the dark peat. It was their lucky day and the children helped to cart it up the gully to be loaded on to the horse. It was hot, heavy work and they all needed to find shade.

As they were leaving, they were startled by a large, wild duck which quacked and fluttered its wings right in front of them. Robert could see another small creek up ahead and wished he had his shotgun handy as there were many others milling around. Wild ducks were a tasty addition to the dinner table but he had lost this opportunity. Next time, I'll be ready he hoped.

At that moment Jane was suddenly distracted by a large, beautiful red beaked and red legged bird walking on the ground. She could not help herself and set off after it, but it was too quick for her and scuttled off. The rest of the family stood and chuckled when she reappeared breathless, and Robert said that he thought it was a native NZ pūkeko which likes to run or hide rather than fly. "There are other birds here too such as the NZ weka, partridges and bittern I have been told …" but the children looked bored and continued the trek home.

Robert's friend, James Curle, and other settlers he knew had helped him to learn about the plants and animal life in the area and where to look for the peat. Jane was pleased that her father was so knowledgeable as she had always loved trees, flowers and birdlife and was intrigued that New Zealand had different species from Orkney.

Robert made it clear that night when all the family were gathered round the table that there was much to be done to carve out their new life on the land, but he was confident they were going to succeed. He thanked Jane, Ann and William for their help gathering the fuel and Margaret also thanked the younger children who had helped her gather dry cow pats for the fire whilst the others were away. She looked at Robert and holding back a smile, said. "This quickly turned into a game however with lots of squealing, as some of the cow pats were not dry!"

Going Rabbiting

One day, Robert needed to check the rabbit traps he had set and said that the older children could accompany him. Jane jumped at the chance but Ann was more reluctant and preferred to stay and help her mother. William said he was too tired but would go next time.

It was the first time Jane had studied a dead rabbit. She normally saw them hopping around or running like the wind to find cover, so the sight of a stiff, fluffy creature with tearful bulbous eyes was a shock. She was not sure what to do and wanted to stroke it but the ring of blood around its neck, where the trap had slammed shut, stopped her. She watched her father gently release its body from the trap then stuff it headfirst into a sack before they moved on to check the next one. By the time they returned home they had collected four rabbits and Robert was pleased. He had learnt to carefully place and reload the traps in good positions in the scrub or tussock and was becoming a skilled rabbiter. The rabbit population was expanding too quickly and they were plentiful but settlers agreed that their numbers could become a problem if they were not hunted. They were also a welcome source of meat for the family. Other fare like wild duck was a regular food in the cooking pot but it was a rare occasion to have other meat such as mutton or wild pig.

Once home Jane was horrified when the four fluffy bunnies were skinned and gutted and laid out like pink, naked corpses. Her consolation for attending this horror was a small rabbit's foot which Robert said would bring her luck. Reluctantly she went off to clean and dry it in the sun and decided thereafter it would be stashed away in her small memory box and only removed in emergencies.

First Visit to Macraes Flat

As the end of the first week approached, Robert announced he was going to take them all into the township of Macraes Flat on Saturday. They needed supplies and it would be a good chance to see more of the area and find out what the town had to offer. Jane was eager to go as she had heard there was a school in Macraes Flat and wanted to know where it was. She was also eager to see what shops and hotels were still there. It had been a busy place during the Otago Gold Rush, in the previous decade, as prospectors needed to stock up on supplies before they went off to the diggings. The unfortunate ones, the duffers, often returned to the township, drank too many nobblers in the hotels or spent their last pennies in the local whore houses before they moved on.

The family left early in the morning. The horse laboured with the weight of them all in the wagon but they made steady progress on the rough track. Robert decided not to follow the more direct route on Nenthorn Road to Macraes and headed towards Moonlight Flat instead. On the way he pointed out Shark Hill to the left, the road to the township of Middlemarch and the Moonlight Creek.

They turned in a northeast direction on the Moonlight Flat until they reached an intersection with the main road to Hyde and Macraes Flat. Jane expected they would go right to Macraes but they went straight on towards Horse Flat so Robert could show them some of the alluvial gold mining fields in the area. After another right-hand turn he pointed out the Deepdell claims and the Round Hill and Duke of Edinburgh reef mines which were still operating and producing gold. Jane could not help but wonder how gold could be found in this dry, rocky land.

It was a miracle she thought to herself. They must have been lucky or very clever, she concluded. She closed her eyes to try and imagine 'gold fever' in Otago and Macraes Flat in the early 1860s when hordes of miners with their swags, tin dishes and shovels gathered on the plain.

Robert knew a short cut to Macraes Flat and abruptly pulled at the reins to veer off down a narrow track which would lead to the township. On the way a sudden, strong gust of wind spooked the horse and he had a job to steady it on the rocky ground. He immediately looked over his shoulder to the children and spoke.

"This reminds me that we must constantly be prepared for dangers. I always carry extra rope, a spade and an axe in case I need to offer help or the wagon wheels get stuck. Not far from here Hurricane Valley got its name due to the way fierce gales can be funnelled through it which sweep up and destroy anything in its path …"

Jane held her breath. Her vivid imagination saw the possibility of being captive to a cruel wind which would throw her body to an untimely, excruciating death. She was not alone in her fear of atrocious weather conditions that could arise in this part of the country. Ann, William and Robert were gripping the sides of the rattling wagon so tightly, their knuckles had turned white.

They were pleased to leave the track and join the long, dusty main road which would take them to the centre of Macraes. On the way Jane noticed there were piles of debris and areas of old worked ground as they rattled along. She wondered what had happened to create such an unsightly wasteland.

Robert had seen this before and told Jane and the children it was caused by the first methods the miners used such as ground sluicing and paddocking to find alluvial gold.

"They dug down using picks and shovels and used water-buckets, sluice boxes or cradles to sift the gold bearing wash as gold will settle to the bottom being heavier than small stones. Quartz or reef mining came later as it was more difficult to extract gold bearing quartz. The large mines used shaft sinking and tunnelling and blasted the quartz. The ore produced was crushed in water in stamping batteries and the gold liberated. It was a long process.

Prospectors risked their lives in these mines," Robert reluctantly had to tell them.

"There was nowhere to run underground if a tunnel caved in ... and after their toil, recovering the gold often eluded them.

I still fancy trying my luck when I get the chance," he said with a confident look on his face.

The children looked scared as they didn't want their precious father taking any risks. But within seconds they all started cheering as Margaret turned to Robert, her eyes sparkling, and said.

"You never know, we may strike it rich!"

The wagon lurched on. In the vicinity of Golden Point and Gifford Roads outside the township, Jane spotted an unusual house with strange signs above the door. It stood out as other dwellings looked shoddy and small in comparison. "That is probably the house of Louis Gay Tan, called the Chinese Palace," Robert told them. "He was a well known Chinese merchant who came to Macraes during the gold rush. He lived in luxury while most of the Chinese gold seekers sought out the grog shanties and gambling dens and lived in hovels."

Macraes Flat School

When Macraes was visible up ahead, Robert pointed to a building on a small hill up Hyde Street and said. "That's the Macraes Flat school. It's the second school and has been here a few years now. The teacher's quarters for the old school became unsuitable so it was decided to build a new larger, stone school." Jane was impressed with the school which had a bell in the centre of the building. She would have liked to see inside but remained silent as she couldn't go to this school, it was too far from Moonlight. Robert could sense her disappointment but he had a surprise for her later.

As Robert had visited the township before, he knew that the gold rush had made the town flourish. He told his family that some of the proprietors he knew said that originally, there was an upper and lower township due to the hundreds of prospectors who passed through. Many shops, businesses and hotels had opened to help the gold seekers but only a few lucky ones made Macraes Flat their home and built grand houses made of wood or dried sods and clay with a thatched roof. Other fortune seekers gave up due to hunger and hardship. Some carried on prospecting in new places with the unquenchable hope that they would find that mother lode of gold or another valuable mineral like scheelite.

"This makes Macraes a special place," Jane said.

"Aye, it does," Robert said. "And we mustn't forget the settlers who came to farm on the high country and the plains. They worked hard to grow crops, meat and wool despite the tough conditions and climate."

They carried on towards the lower part of town where all the main shops and businesses were located. Robert said he needed to go to the bootmakers, general store and the blacksmiths and Margaret wanted to go to the drapers, the bakery and post office. She had with her a letter for her sisters in Caithness letting them know that they were living in Moonlight. They decided to split up, Jane and William went off with their father, whilst Ann and the younger children stayed with their mother. They arranged to meet by the Universal Dining Rooms in an hour's time.

There were all sorts of people in town and Jane was fascinated by how busy it was as she trailed along behind her father looking into the shops. The baker surprised her as he rushed out carrying many fresh loaves on his tray. She longed to try one and hoped her mother had managed to buy bread as a treat for when they returned home. She was surprised that many of the stores and hotels were made of wood and wondered how they could withstand the wind, rain and snow.

She noticed Mr Fraser's house was made of stone but other houses were made from sods and clay and occasionally, very small houses had coarse cloth as a roof.

As her attention was elsewhere it was no wonder she couldn't step aside quickly enough when two inebriated prospectors stumbled out of the nearby hotel. This caused a knock-on effect as by the time she saw them and stepped back, she could not stop herself from crashing into a strange little man who was scurrying along with a bag of supplies. After they had both recovered Jane apologised and noticed that he had a long pigtail down his back and could not stop herself from asking -

"Do you know John Chinaman who came here to find gold? I met him in Dunedin?"

He moved his head from side to side and said, "no …, me not know him, sorry."

"Where are you going?" Jane asked him with childish curiosity.

"I go to my camp in the upper town now I have supplies, then go to my claim in China Flat. I must join others," he said and ran off up the dusty street.

Jane would learn later that some of the Chinese remained long after other prospectors departed, being content to make small returns in grim conditions. She discovered they survived the cold winter in sod huts with canvas roofs with only an occasional fire from snowgrass or peat.

Robert found Jane and sternly asked, "What were you doing talking to that Chinaman?"

Looking sheepish, she slowly replied, "I thought I knew him father?"

Robert looked confused and said, "We have lots to do. Please be careful in the township as there are all sorts of people who could lead you astray. Sergeant Rooney has had to chain up many a villain, thief or 'washed up digger' in his makeshift jail near the old school. Don't talk to strangers!"

Mail Coach Arrives

They were about to cross the road when, all of a sudden, the rumbling of an approaching team of horses and coach could be heard. "This must be the coach from Palmerston and Waihemo to Naseby," Robert said. "No wonder the town is busy today. It's the mail coach, the lifeline to the community and people have come to see if they have letters from home."

Jane had always loved the drama of the big coaches. She enjoyed watching the muscle power of the horses, their flaring nostrils and sharp ears and felt the sense of urgency as it approached. It reminded her of the Cobb and Co. coaches which carried the gold, under armed escort, back to Dunedin. Heads turned to watch the spectacle. Within seconds the large coach was visible and pulled up near them. The groom jumped off and secured the horses. The reinsman also jumped down and the mail bags were hauled out and taken to the post office. They could see that a queue was forming outside and Robert hoped that Margaret had already been in to post her letter to Scotland.

As arranged, the Harcus's met up by Donaldson Universal Dining Rooms. Before they left, Robert was tempted to go for a dram at one of the local hotels but decided against it as he could see that his young family were weary from the hustle and bustle of the township.

Margaret was grateful to be leaving and once their wagon was loaded with children and supplies they set off for Moonlight. Jane had loved the stimulation from all the new sights, sounds and smells of the township and hoped that her father would bring her again soon. On their return journey, Robert took the Nenthorn Road and as Macraes slowly faded behind them they began to think about their chores once they arrived home. The youngest children, John and David, had already fallen asleep. It had been a long day.

Robert still had a surprise in store for his family however and took a right-hand turn which perplexed Jane as she couldn't understand where they were going. He pulled up after a few minutes and pointed to a small wooden building under construction on the corner of Moonlight Flat and School Road.

"This is the new school in Moonlight which is opening soon and you will be pleased to know that I am on the School Committee." He knew that after the Abolition of the Provinces an Education Act had been passed in 1877 by the New Zealand Government to make education compulsory and free to all non Māori children. Funding was helping to establish many new schools and he was pleased that his children could now attend this small, rural school.

Jane was beside herself with delight and could not believe she would be able to walk to school as it was not too far from where they lived. "Father," she begged, "please, when can I go?" After a pause, Robert replied. "Your mother and I have agreed that you, Ann, William and Robert will be enrolled in due course when the new term starts." Jane was over the moon with anticipation and could not wait. It was the best news she had ever heard and could not stop smiling for the rest of the evening. She knew she would have to work hard on the farm as well but going to school was important to her as she loved learning and would have the chance to meet new friends.

They returned down School Road and were soon back on their farm. The children all knew what chores were expected and without hesitation went off to fetch water and feed for the animals. Jane helped her father with the horse. It was not a young animal and as it was their only means of transport and also used on the farm for cultivation, it was extremely important to them. Robert grew wheat and other vegetables but he had a special crop of oats for the horse and it would soon be time for harvest.

1880 - Moonlight School

Jane was now 12 years old and counting the days before she could start school in Moonlight. She had abandoned her dream of going to Otago Girls' High School in Dunedin which she had heard was the first girls' school in the Southern Hemisphere and accepted she had a new, rural life in east Otago. She still longed to see the huge breakers of the cold Pacific Ocean crashing on the beach at St Clair and the beautiful stone buildings and churches in the heart of the city. She would remain hopeful and told herself that one day she would return to Dunedin.

Robert accompanied her on the walk to school on her first day while Margaret remained on the farm. She was pregnant with her seventh child and tired quickly.

Her health was not improving. The new school was a small one roomed wooden building in the centre of Moonlight Flat. The teacher, Mr John Simpson, who lived in a house by the school, was welcoming and asked everyone at the beginning of class to say their name and where they lived. This helped Jane as she quickly singled out who she would like to become friends with. There were few girls as they were needed at home, so the majority of the 29 pupils were boys.

Inside the class room was dark because of the old wooden chairs and few windows but she didn't care as she wanted to learn and absorbed everything the teacher had to say. Mr Simpson told interesting stories about the history of the area that amused all the children of the class despite their different ages.

Jane learnt about the enormous flightless bird, called a Moa, which had roamed free hundreds of years before. She was shocked to learn that it was an easy target and hunted to extinction by the fearless Māori Moa hunters. They ate its flesh, used its feathers and skin for clothing and made fish hooks and pendants from its bones. She was also fascinated that the Moa was only found in New Zealand and that parts of its skeleton could still be found where it had been slain.

"The Māoris," Mr Simpson said, "explored the area by following the rivers, eventually all the way to the southern Lakes and, en route, they found a hard glassy rock which they made into long blades to butcher these birds and other large animals."

She would have liked to ask Rawiri, who she met on the train from Port Chalmers, about these Moa hunters, as he was such a wise man.

As well as reading, writing and arithmetic lessons, Mr Simpson also gave geography lessons and sometimes got carried away and went off the subject. One day he explained why the prospectors found gold in Central Otago and places like Macraes Flat. He told them it was more to do with the geology, of how the land was formed millions of years ago, which created the special schist rock containing gold and other minerals.

Jane was astonished by how greywacke rock rose up from the sea to form Otago and Macraes Flat before it was turned into schist by heat and that parts of Otago became folded and warped to form huge corrugations.

Looking directly at Jane, Mr Simpson said,

"The Moonlight Valley, where you live, followed the line of a crack in the land that appeared later." She held his gaze for a few seconds before turning away. She was pleased however that he had helped her understand why she lived in a special place.

Jane found school a relief as it took her away from child minding and other domestic chores at home. As time went on, she learnt more about this part of Otago. She admired the early sheep farmers or squatters in the 1850s as they found a way over the Snowy Mountains from Dunedin to Waikouaiti before coming inland, probably on an old Māori route over Yellow Hill.

"The farmers and shepherds were made of strong stuff," Mr Simpson said loudly.

"Did you know Macraes Flat was named after John MacRae during this time and he liked to call it Bonny Brook? He was a shepherd and a boundary rider. As there were no fences to keep in the animals, boundary riders were used to ensure that stock were fed and kept in designated areas.

But if it hadn't been for the bullockies, who drove the bullock sledges in the early days, the first sheep runs and backblog settlements may not have had supplies. The bullocks were steady pullers and guided only by commands as there were no reins. They proved their worth on the rough tracks and ridges as they had split hooves which meant they didn't slip easily and could be used where it wasn't safe to take a horse. The well-chosen tracks used by the bullockies often became the routes for our later roads.

The biggest worry the bullockies had was the poisonous NZ Tutu shrub. If the bullocks ate it, they would have convulsions and die. Other farm animals could also be poisoned as well as children if they ate the pretty dark berries."

Jane grimaced but thought that Mr Simpson was full of such interesting facts. He also loved to sing and made everyone join in on a daily basis at school. She enjoyed her lessons and it was no surprise she did well in her first exams in 1881.

Winter in Moonlight

Jane dreaded winter in Moonlight. Some mornings when she awoke it was so cold there was a thin layer of frost on the blanket covering the bed and icicles around the window. Outside, however, the harsh white frost had transformed all that it touched into a fairy tale. The silver tussock glistened, the fine branches of the bush sparkled, the grass became a white magical carpet and the snow-capped mountains in the distance pierced the pure blue of the sky. All was clean, fresh and frozen in time. But it was hard.

She had never been so cold. Despite wearing all the clothes she possessed her body remained chilled like the landscape outside, stiff, white and brittle. She could manage some of her indoor chores but when the snow came after the temperature warmed up a notch, life outdoors became a nightmare. The journey to and from school became impossible as the track to the Nenthorn Road from the farm was impassable due to snow drifts. Daily chores to get water and feed the animals were hindered due to the snow, ice and sub-zero temperatures. Luckily, they had some fuel set aside for the winter months for cooking so they did not starve. At night they huddled together under blankets round the fire for extra warmth. Some of the family tried to read by candlelight or played guessing games to pass the time. They slept fully clothed. It was a miserable existence but they remained positive in the hope that spring would arrive soon.

Slowly the days lengthened and the temperature increased so normal life could resume once again. The melting snow from the mountains flooded the plain on occasion but the farm escaped the rising waters and survived. The high country farmers were much worse off due to the melting snow and bursting streams in the mountains and lost many ewes and lambs.

Jane and the Taieri Pet

In springtime, Jane was on her way home from school later than usual as she had offered to help Mr Simpson prepare the classroom for the next day's lesson. She became aware that the wind was picking up speed and over the valley, a long cloud was forming and drifting closer. It did not worry her at first as she thought the Rock and Pillar mountains would protect her but this was a mistake - the mountains acted as a spillway and within minutes she was in the path of a raging gale which covered her from head to foot with fine grit. She was blinded and forced to the ground to cower in the tussock. After what seemed hours, the gale had reduced sufficiently to allow her to stand but it was dark and starless and she didn't know how to get home. The fear she had felt when she was nearly kidnapped in the backstreets of Dunedin suddenly returned and her heart raced.

Her instincts made her cry out into the darkness. "Help, someone, please help me." But the only sound she heard was that of a fleeing bird in the wind. She dragged herself slowly forward unsure in which direction she was moving but soon fell to the ground from exhaustion. Tears began to flow down her cheeks but they helped her to focus as she managed to wipe dust and water from her eyes on the inside of her coat. She thought she recognised where she might be and, with no other options, slowly dragged her body forward into the wind.

After half an hour her prayers were answered as she saw a faint light in the distance and heard a voice calling her name .... It was her father, Robert. He had become so concerned for her safety, he had risked his own life in the gales, known locally as the Taieri Pet, to try and find her. Jane could not have been more pleased to see him and hugged him so hard he could not move. "Come now my bonnie girl," he said, "let's get you home and to safety."

Jane had learnt a horrible lesson of how quickly the weather can change in this rugged new world in which she lived. She made sure she walked with other children and did not delay her journey home from school ever again.

The following Saturday, Robert asked her to accompany him to Macraes township to collect supplies and to see if there was mail for them. He knew she loved to watch the coach arrive from Palmerston and the town would be busy. He had also signed the petition, sent to the Chief Postmaster in Dunedin, that an additional mail coach service per week to Macraes, Hyde and Naseby was desperately needed due to increasing demand from settlers in the district. The petition pointed out the injustice local residents suffered, as a smaller population of settlers served by the Pigroot – Palmerston line already had two services per week.

Robert was going to attend a meeting whilst he was in town with other early settlers to the area, including the Peddies, who felt as strongly as he did about the inconvenience of mail collections and deliveries.

Jane looked forward to time with her father as she knew her mother would be giving birth again soon and there would be much to do in the house. They set off early in the morning. When they reached Macraes she queued at the post office after the mail coach arrived but was disappointed there was no mail from Scotland. While her father was at the meeting, as instructed, she collected supplies from the store including flour, sugar, tea, butter, onions and candles and enjoyed the chance to be on her own in the town for an hour. She would have loved to take tea at the Dining Rooms and would ask her father if it would be possible next time, but knew her chances were slim.

She had proved a huge help to him as the supplies were on the wagon so they could leave as soon as he returned. Robert was extremely proud of his eldest daughter. She had always handled extra responsibilities well and he was grateful. She was growing into a capable and charming young lady. On their return journey to Moonlight, Robert told Jane he had heard that George Stanley was to buy an existing hotel and rebuild it in local schist stone. "The problem is, he has appointed a mason, called Budge, who is to be paid in gallons of beer, so nobody is sure when it will open." They both laughed as the wagon rattled its way down the Nenthorn Road.

The Harcus Family Continues to Expand

On 9 December 1880, Jane's mother gave birth to a daughter, who she called Margaret, after her own mother who had died young. When the time came to have the child she went to Waihemo where her friend Mary Curle helped her whilst Robert remained on the farm. Jane was pleased as it did spare the rest of the family from hearing their mother suffer during the hours of her labour. It made Jane miss school for a few days as she was too busy looking after her brothers and sisters. With another addition to the family she also became concerned about where her new sister would sleep and could only assume that she would use the crib and her youngest brother, David, now two years old, would join the others in the bed.

There was always a good community spirit amongst the settlers and when Jane's mother returned with baby Margaret the local farming community offered help. They had always looked out for each other in many ways and, as it was soon to be Christmas, some brought spare food or baking to their house in Moonlight. Other families offered second hand clothing or help on the farm until Margaret had regained her strength.

They all worked hard on the farm in the hope of a good harvest in the autumn. Jane's new sister thrived although her mother did not fare so well. Her poor health and the energy required to bring up her ever increasing family was taking its toll. The children loved to play outside when the weather permitted and the older boys, Robert and William often liked to surprise their big sister. One day they took her to see their latest find. They made her close her eyes then lifted a rock to show her Otago Skinks. It was their favourite small lizard, only found near Macraes and was black with distinctive grey and yellow blotches to provide camouflage. Jane gasped when she saw these unusual creatures but smiled as she watched her brothers having fun catching them as they were too slippery and fast and got away. The boys also found NZ geckos under the schist which gave them endless amusement.

During summer the settlers in Moonlight Flat met up for picnics or sports days which brought the community together. If a concert or soiree was organised, the event was always enjoyable due to the variety of local talent. Settlers loved to play their violins, concertinas and flutes; some took delight singing or reciting stories and poems. At the last concert, the singing of 'Scotland Yet' received an encore and Jane's teacher, Mr Simpson, proved a most popular performer with his rendition of 'The Sailors Grave.'

Letter from Scotland

Early in the new year of 1882, Margaret received a letter from her sister in Caithness, Scotland. Jane watched her mother slowly read it and could see that it was not good news. Her father, David Stephen had died in Tain on Christmas Eve 1881. Jane sensed this had deeply upset her mother as she would have wanted to say goodbye to him. She reflected on how hard it must have been for

Margaret to leave her family for the Orkney Isles to be with Robert, all those years ago, and how difficult it must have been when they all set off for New Zealand.

The thought of never seeing family left behind ever again must be the hardest thing to bear, Jane concluded. I would have liked to have known my grandfather, she said to herself. We have no other family in New Zealand apart from ourselves.

Robert was making good progress growing crops and was also considering planting pine trees that he could sell to other farmers. He had not given up hope of prospecting for gold, but the time was not yet right, he was too busy on the farm. Settlers were also talking about the first frozen meat shipment that had left for Britain from Port Chalmers on the *Dunedin* clipper in February 1882. This gave farmers more incentive to increase their herds of sheep and cattle as the export trade was expanding.

The four oldest Harcus children including Jane's sister Ann and brothers Robert and William, continued to attend the Moonlight school until they were eventually withdrawn to help with domestic chores or to work on the farm with their father.

Jane was rapidly growing up into a lovely young woman. She started to become interested in the dances held at Macraes and wanted her sister Ann to go with her, but Ann didn't have the same enthusiasm. There was no way however that Jane would be able to go at such a young age as her parents would never allow it. They were struggling to look after their growing family as they had nine mouths to feed and Margaret had fallen pregnant again.

Jane began to wonder if she was destined to have a life the same as her mother's which involved finding a husband and being a good wife. She knew her mother loved her father dearly but the reality was relentless chores in a harsh environment and having babies every other year. She was 14 years old and thinking about her future. Was she to remain in Moonlight or follow her dream and return to Dunedin. Her sister Ann was close in age and as they had been through a lot together Jane often confided in her which helped during her teenage years.

Birth of Another Sister for Jane

On 12 December 1882, Jane had been doing the washing with her mother outdoors when Margaret went into labour. Her contractions came quickly and there was little time to prepare. Robert was not around so Margaret asked Jane to go and fetch Mrs Ferguson as there was no doctor for miles. She was a lovely woman who baked beautiful cakes and scones but also offered her services if anyone needed help with childbirth or got sick.

Before she left, Jane took her mother inside and tried to make her more comfortable on the bed, told Ann to watch over the younger children, hung the kettle over the fire, then rushed off to find the woman. Within an hour they returned. Mrs Ferguson told Margaret not to push until she checked her progress. Margaret squeezed Jane's hand so tightly, it went blue and Jane couldn't withdraw it from her vice-like grip. Luckily William had found his father in a field. He appeared in the doorway and rushed over to comfort Margaret but Mrs Ferguson soon told everyone to leave apart from Jane. She became her helper and mopped her mother's brow and told her she was so strong and 'nearly there'…. Her mother screamed, Jane winced and after 20 minutes, which seemed like hours, and a final push, Margaret gave birth to a daughter. Jane cried, Margaret smiled and Mrs Ferguson stood with her hands on her hips and a large grin on her face. "There," she said. "It's all over, well done lassie."

Jane's new sister was called Mary. It would be her turn to sleep in the crib and Margaret, also born in December, two years previously, would sleep in the bed.

1883 Spare Rabbits for the Factory

Jane and her sister Ann were busy with domestic chores as their mother was preoccupied with the new baby. Robert was out shooting and trapping food whenever he could and announced one evening that he could do with some help the next day, Saturday, as he had excess rabbits he wanted to take to the rabbit wagon at Macraes. The carcasses were transported to the canning factory near Waihemo. He would receive a cash payment which was a welcome source of income. His rabbit trapping sideline had generated many rabbits of late and as they could only eat a small number, he needed to get rid of the surplus quickly.

Jane was 15 years old and eager to spend more time in the township, so she volunteered to help. Robert accepted gratefully. He knew she enjoyed visiting Macraes and hadn't been for some time. Margaret was happy for her to go as Ann agreed to stay and help with the other children.

The first thing Jane noticed after they arrived in Macraes Flat was that Stanley's Hotel had opened. It had been completed the previous year and looked distinctive, as it was a stone building unlike the other wooden shacks. "The mason did a fine job, despite being paid in beer," Robert bellowed. "He must have been paid the full amount," Jane replied laughing.

They tethered the horse near the rabbit wagon and set about hanging the carcasses onto the racks as the wagon driver was anxious to leave as soon as possible. Jane found the smell disgusting but did not complain and held her breath for as long as she could. Robert was pleased she had helped and gave her some money to go to the bakery to buy bread and buns. He decided to buy a copy of the *Otago Witness* as it had been some time since he had caught up on news about Dunedin and the province.

As Jane was returning from the bakery and crossing the main road, she noticed that the mail coach had just thundered into town amidst a cloud of dust. Through the haze she was startled by a tall, slim man who was suddenly in her way. She danced a side step but so did he and they both came to a halt. He was very apologetic and as the dust settled around them, Jane became transfixed by his dark eyes and curved moustache. She hardly noticed she was standing in the road and without hesitation, let him steer her by the elbow to safety.

"Thank you," she spluttered.

He then introduced himself as Frederick Davis and said that he worked as a groom at Deepdell Station but had been asked to ride the mail coach as far as Hyde as one of the horses in the team was having problems.

"What's your name?" He asked politely.

She hesitated and replied,

"Jane Harcus. Do you know my father, Robert Harcus? We live in Moonlight."

"No, sorry, I don't, I haven't been to Moonlight but I know Thomas Peddie has started a coach service from Macraes to Moonlight and I sometimes ride out near there."

"We have a farm and my father is a good rabbiter, that's why we came here today."

She wanted to learn more about him but was struggling to find the words. She had noticed he wasn't Scottish and spoke more like an Englishman.

"Well .., I must be going as my father will wonder where I am," she stuttered.

"Do you have to rush?" he replied.

"Yes, yes I do," Jane said.

"Very well, it's been good to meet you, I hope we will meet again."

Jane looked down toward the ground, then lifted her head to return his gaze once again. Her eyes sparkled and her lips parted, but she did not say goodbye as she gently shook his hand.

She slowly walked away and when she reached the wagon, her father was holding the reins and ready to leave. She jumped up beside him but did not recall much of their journey back to Moonlight as, thankfully, Robert did most of the talking. She only managed to nod her head at appropriate times.

He told her about the money they had made due to the large number of rabbit carcasses they had sold and that he hoped she could help him to take another load soon. He was also excited about some interesting news he had read in the provincial papers, The *Otago Daily Times* and *Otago Witness*, whilst he was waiting for her.

"The government have awarded a contract to the New Zealand Shipping Company and Shaw Savill for a monthly mail service with Britain by steamship. This is grand news for everyone as it will halve the journey time for our letters and other mail. Remember it took us nearly three months at sea. Can you believe it lassie?

There will also be the first tour by the New Zealand Rugby Union Team to New South Wales, Australia next year, whatever next!"

That night she had a dream about Frederick Davis, the groom, and woke up in a hot sweat before dawn, unsure how it ended. This man she hardly knew was constantly in her thoughts and not a day would go by without her recalling the first time they had met in Macraes. Her sister Ann was also beginning to notice that Jane seemed preoccupied and wondered why.

Frederick Makes an Appearance

There was more work to be done due to the arrival of her new sister Mary and Jane, as always, was a huge help to her mother. One day, while she was out walking to fetch more water, she saw someone on a horse in the distance who continued to ride in her direction. She thought it was odd but as the rider came closer she realised it was Frederick.

Within minutes, he splashed through a small nearby creek, pulled up the horse and expertly slid off the saddle to stand in front of her. His horse remained close, its ears pricked and ready for the next command but it soon lost interest to graze on the tussock.

"I wanted to see you again Jane," Frederick said. "I've been thinking about you."

She looked away. She was not prepared for this encounter.

"Oh really," she said, not wishing to mention her dreams.

They walked over by the water and sat down. The small brown lobsters in the creek amused them as they would suddenly pop out from their hiding places under the stones.

"They are a little bit like you and me," Frederick said, "we pop up unexpected!"

"Yes," Jane laughed, "you do …"

"How long have you been in New Zealand?" he asked.

"We arrived in Port Chalmers on New Year's Eve in 1874 and spent time in Dunedin before coming here."

His eyes flashed and he turned towards her. "That's a coincidence," he replied.

"My older brother, George and I got assisted passages from London on the *James Nicol Fleming* and arrived at Port Chalmers the same year as you, in May 1874. We decided to leave Finmere in Oxfordshire and seek our fortunes in the new world. We knew it was a risk but we had nothing to lose as times were tough in England, there was little work for us farm labourers."

"Back then it was also tough for my parents in Orkney," said Jane.

"Brother George left me in New Zealand and tried his luck across the Tasman in Australia, so I have no family here now. He says he is becoming wealthy but I am not sure whether to believe him."

Jane could see Frederick's eyes had turned glassy but did not remark on it.

"It must have been hard to leave your family and, in your case, have them leave you once you were here," Jane said.

"No one knew what life would be like in the New World," Frederick admitted. "It was difficult in the beginning and it's not easy now but food is more plentiful and settlers have worked hard to create a good community spirit wherever they have ended up.

I would like my own children and family in New Zealand one day. It would make me the happiest man alive."

Jane could see he was sincere and understood his emotions. Instinctively, she looked at him and her eyes told him that things would work out.

"Can we meet again soon?" Frederick asked as he got up. "I can come back again next month?"

"Yes, I would like that," Jane replied.

Before he mounted his horse he drew Jane towards him and kissed her cheek.

"Until we meet again," he whispered in her ear.

Jane smiled and her gaze lingered on his handsome face.

She skipped back to the house dreaming of their next encounter. At the last minute she remembered she had forgotten the water and had to go back and fetch it. When she came inside with the water, she failed to notice that her mother found her behaviour odd and asked her to sit down for a cup of tea.

"Is there something you would like to share with me?" Margaret asked.

Jane couldn't believe her mother's intuition and found herself blushing and unable to look her in the eye.

"What is it Jane, please tell me ..."

Slowly Jane summoned the courage to speak the truth.

"Mother, I have met someone special ... his name is Frederick and he has just come to see me."

"I like him mother and want to meet him again."

"Oh, my bonnie girl, I can remember when I first met your father. I think I fell in love with him as soon as I saw him."

Jane found this hard to believe as she had never spoken with her mother about such things before.

"Your father will not want you to meet him again as he will always try to protect you, so I suggest we keep this a secret for now until you are sure about your feelings for Frederick. But be very careful he does not take advantage of you. Do you understand me?"

"Yes mother, of course I will."

Jane was pleased her mother had such faith in her and would allow her to see Frederick again.

Frederick was true to his word and he returned within a month. Jane was walking on the road to Moonlight this time, so he stopped, quickly scooped her up onto his horse and cantered off so they could be alone. He didn't go far and they stopped to rest beside a rocky outcrop within half a mile of the Harcus farm.

Jane longed to be in his company and had been unable to think of little else so she was overjoyed that he had found her and they were together once again.

When they sat down, Frederick leaned over and swept aside a strand of hair from Jane's face before he kissed her forehead, her nose and then her mouth. She had never felt such emotion before and closed her eyes to savour his touch. Within a minute however, she regained control of herself and drew way. She wasn't sure what was happening and needed time to think, so she straightened her clothing and hugged her bent knees.

"I'm sorry if I surprised you," Frederick said.

"No, no, it's fine. It's just that I'm not used to this … " Jane replied.

"Well, I suppose as I am older, I am bound to have had more experience," Frederick acknowledged. "How old are you, Jane?" She did not want to admit her age on her next birthday but told him she would be 16 in May.

"I am surprised," he said. "You seem mature for your years."

"Perhaps because I am the eldest child in our large family and used to coping with things changing," Jane replied.

"Yes," said Frederick. "You have been through a great deal in your life so far."

"Tell me more about what you did when you first came here" Jane requested.

"Very well," Frederick agreed. "I tried farm labouring to begin with but I loved working with horses the best. I drove the mail coach from Palmerston via Macraes before I came to Deepdell Station. That was cold and dangerous work, particularly in the winter. We didn't have covered coaches because if the wind got up, it could blow the coach over. We often narrowly escaped accidents due to landslides, floods and broken wagon wheels on the rocky tracks. We trained the horses well to pull the coach but it was down to luck sometimes that we made it.

A friend told me that the king bolt snapped when he was driving a coach and the horses galloped on with the forecarriage, while the back wheels and body of the coach came to a halt. The passengers were scared out of their wits and were left stranded. Deep snow drifts and slushy mud were also a problem in winter and male passengers often had to get out and push. Occasionally, the coach driver had to stay in stables overnight with the horses and hope that the journey could continue the next morning. Due to flooding which is so unpredictable in the spring and winter, another driver I met parted company with his coach and made one of the horses swim with him across a deep ford in order to get the mail delivered on time.

So you can see why I took the job at Deepdell Station - I look after horses for the coaching teams and for farming and I am not in constant danger so often or have to risk my life anymore.

I also think that the railways will eventually take over bringing passengers and supplies once there is more track to open up the countryside. They are talking about trains from Dunedin to Middlemarch, Palmerston and beyond, so it won't be long. I'm happier looking after the horses for now."

Jane found this conversation interesting and would have liked to discuss it with her father but decided she couldn't as he would ask her where she had got her information from. He read the papers and would find out in his own way she thought. Frederick was her secret and she needed to keep him that way.

It was time for her to return to the farm so they walked back to the horse. Frederick skilfully climbed into the saddle and gave Jane a stirrup to climb on behind him. She loved being so close and put her arms round his waist and rested her head on his shoulders as the horse trotted off. When she closed her eyes, she felt safe and did not want to let go of him but reluctantly had to dismount when the Harcus farm came into view. Frederick was already on the ground and took her in his arms when she landed. He kissed her softly, then said, "Goodbye Jeannie." She liked her new nickname; it made her feel special.

Before he left, Jane said that she was going to Macraes Flat with her father to take rabbit carcasses to the rabbit wagon and could they meet on Saturday. Frederick said that he would try his best to be there.

Every time they met, the bond between them strengthened and Jane could not imagine her life without him. After a few months, it was becoming noticeable that Jane would disappear for periods of time. Her mother and sister Ann knew as Jane had confided in them but no one else had any idea. Eventually Jane told her father she had met Frederick Davis and agreed to bring him home so all the family could meet him.

They were both nervous after a date had been agreed but need not have worried. Her father liked him, her mother thought he was charming and her brothers and sisters enjoyed his company as he told good stories about England and his new life in New Zealand.

Frederick visited the farm on other occasions when time allowed. He gained the trust of Margaret and Robert to take Jane to her first dance at Macraes, the following Saturday, as he swore to take the utmost care of her. Jane had longed to go dancing from a young age and was thrilled at the prospect of a special night out with Frederick and could not have been happier.

Frederick Proposes

They were fortunate, it was a cool, clear evening and riding back under the stars to Moonlight was magical and a night she would never forget. Frederick pulled up the horse about a mile from the farm by a huge, grey schist rock which glistened in the rays of the moon. Once he was on the ground, he spun Jane round so he was looking directly into her eyes. She was totally besotted with him and returned the intensity of his gaze.

"Jane, I love you and want to be with you always ….

Will you marry me?" Reaching for her hand, he placed it over his heart and waited for her response. Time stood still for several precious seconds before she whispered …

"Yes, yes I will. I want to be your wife."

From that moment their hearts became as one - their love was shared - their fate sealed.

They looked up to see the canopy of Southern Hemisphere stars sparkling above them and noticed constellations such as the Southern Cross, the Plough and the spectacular star-studded Milky Way galaxy. They knew they were blessed on this night, nowhere on earth could have been more beautiful.

Jane wanted to linger forever by the schist rock with Frederick by her side but he reminded her they had promised to be back by midnight so she agreed they must go.

In late autumn 1885, Frederick made a special visit to the farm to speak to Robert and asked for Jane's hand in marriage. Robert was hesitant at first as his daughter was only 17 years old but gave his consent after Frederick swore to always protect and look after her with his life. It was agreed they would marry in the spring in Palmerston.

No one could deny the love these two had for each other. They had never seen Jane so happy. Margaret could not hold back her tears however when she heard her eldest daughter talking about marriage plans with her new fiancé. They were tears of joy, but it meant Jane would be leaving her soon and making a new life of her own. She also became concerned when she overheard Jane telling Frederick about Eday, the place where she was born along with her sister Ann and brothers William and Robert. It suddenly dawned on her that the time had come to tell Jane more about her past as she could not go to her grave without passing on important information.

Winter came, the temperature plummeted and the wind, rain and ice returned. For most it was a miserable time of year but not for Jane - she was preoccupied preparing for her wedding in the spring and hardly noticed the cold. She was so cheerful, her sister Ann was becoming tired of her chattering and questions. She was also amazed by the kindness other settlers had shown to Jane and Frederick as they visited with presents, supplies and utensils that might come in useful for a newly married couple.

Margaret Speaks to Jane Before her Wedding

Jane was trying to work out where to put all the gifts when her mother asked her to come and sit with her by the fire. The younger members of the family were all asleep and the hut was quiet. Margaret had consumption and had difficulty breathing so she needed to rest. It was always made worse by the damp and cold but on this night, she was stressed about a secret Jane was about to discover.

"Yes mother, what would you like to talk about?" Jane said with a smile.

"I have decided to give you some of my treasured possessions while I am still on this earth." Margaret replied with her head lowered as she was focusing on some items in her lap. The first thing she gave Jane was a beautifully embroidered linen handkerchief.

"This belonged to my mother which I kept with me on my wedding day. I would like you to have it."

"Thank you mother, I will treasure it."

Margaret also handed Jane some dried Caithness flowers. "I picked these myself for my wedding bouquet and would like you to have them as a reminder of where you are from." Jane looked puzzled but let her mother continue.

"I also want you to have this ..." and passed her a crumpled envelope.

Jane slowly pulled out the piece of paper inside and began to read. It appeared to be a birth certificate but she didn't recognise the name of the child and could see the word 'Illegitimate' written below. When she looked closer, there was no name given for the father, but she recognised the name of the mother; it was her mother's maiden name, Margaret Stephen. In small writing, she also noticed a 'name alteration' in May 1869 on the side of the certificate, it was her name!

Tears filled her eyes and she looked at her mother with confusion and shame running through her mind. "How could you do this to me and take all these years to tell me the truth?"

Jane had discovered that she was not born in Eday, Orkney. She was an illegitimate child, originally called Robertina, born in the Parish of Olrig, Caithness on 6 May 1868.

After her initial shock at discovering this news, she was overcome by sadness and bowed her head in disbelief.

"Please let me explain further," Margaret pleaded. "In Scotland, if a female child is born out of wedlock, it is common to use a feminine version of the father's name. Hence my father and I used Robertina to register your birth. Robert and I had your name officially changed to Jane Harcus six months after we were married in Barrock, Caithness and went to live in Eday. I was happy to call you Jane after Robert's mother, Jane Reid, as she had passed away just before you were born."

Margaret told Jane that she had fallen in love with Robert when he came to Caithness for the herring and did not know she was with child until well into her pregnancy. She would never forget the shame, the hopelessness and how her father, David Stephen had saved her life after she gave birth on Olrig Hill.

"You could have been taken from me as I had no husband and no future prospects but after I admitted to my father that Robert was responsible, he wrote to him in Eday to tell him he had fathered a child and would he do the honourable thing and marry me. It took time, but Robert agreed as long as you and I went to live with him in the Orkney Isles."

Margaret told Jane she wanted to be with Robert but was unsure about a new life on the small island of Eday. "Your father was a fisherman and a farmer. It was always hard to make ends meet and became much more difficult when we had four children to feed and clothe. As we struggled to provide enough food and wanted a better life for our family, we decided on a fresh start and applied for subsidised passages to New Zealand. Many from Scotland, Ireland and England were taking up opportunities to leave the United Kingdom back then."

Tears were falling down Jane's cheeks as she listened to her mother's story. She could not believe it after all this time and was also upset for the pain and grief her mother had suffered all those years ago. She was saddened her mother had not shared this painful piece of her past until now, but was beginning to understand why. Eventually, Jane dried her eyes and looked at her mother.

"I may have been born out of wedlock but I was born out of love and here, in this place, we all deserve a new start."

Margaret took Jane in her arms and held on to her tightly. "Please forgive me," she said quietly.

Afterwards, they talked about Caithness until the candles burnt low as Jane had many questions. Margaret told her of the view from Olrig Hill, her favourite place, of the wild Caithness flowers, of the legend where St Coomb's church and manse disappeared forever in the sand on the Links of Old Tain.

Jane was to go to Palmerston the following day to spend time there before her wedding, so they agreed to try and sleep. Margaret would miss her eldest daughter and before she kissed her goodnight, she looked at her as only a proud mother could and said, "My special child, I want you to be happy and to know love as there is no greater thing. May God always keep you safe."

Part Six

6.

Jane Harcus Finds Love

*There is only one happiness in this life,
to love and be loved.*
George Sand

The Wedding

Palmerston 1885

It was the happiest day of her life when Jane Harcus married Frederick Herbert Davis. They were gathered in the house of Mr Benston on Monday, the 7th of September and recited their vows in front of the Presbyterian Rev. James Clarke. Jane was only 17 but her father had given his written consent for the marriage to take place. Frederick was 32 years old, now a labourer and living in Waihemo, about 15 miles away from Palmerston.

Jane thought she was going to faint, she was so nervous. Her heart was pounding and her mouth so parched she was afraid she couldn't speak. But, when she looked into Frederick's eyes, he gave her the confidence she needed and she did not falter or miss a word of her wedding vows. It felt so special to be married in the house rather than the unfamiliar St James' Presbyterian church in Palmerston and they were grateful to Rev. Clarke as they wanted a small, intimate ceremony.

Ann, Jane's sister, now 16, was a witness and beamed with happiness for the new bride and groom after Frederick placed the wedding ring on Jane's finger. They had been through so much together and she would miss her. Ann envied her sister's new life but she was enjoying her freedom and secretly knew there would be plenty of time to become a wife and mother in the future. She had only just become interested in boys and found most of them loud and annoying.

Early that night as Jane turned the wedding band on her finger and felt the smooth warmth of the gold, she repeated her wedding vows over and over in her head as they were the most beautiful words, apart from: 'until death us do part.'

"We will have unending love," she said softly, as she looked over to Frederick. "And this ring is our symbol."

"Yes, my dearest, always," he answered, smiling at her.

Jane adored the ring and did not know how Frederick could possibly have afforded it but did not like to ask. Frederck was watching his new wife and seemed to understand what she was thinking. He finally spoke using his special name for her.

"Jeannie, would you like to know where the gold came from for your ring?"

She nodded and moved closer to him.

"I have to thank your father and brothers as they were a great help." Jane looked confused as she knew they had not been prospecting for gold as they were too busy on the farm.

"Go on," she said and poked him in the ribs with her finger. "How did they help?"

"Well, they helped to shoot and collect the ducks in the Macraes Flat area and extracted the gold from their gizzards! It would have taken a long time for me to do it all. Ducks ingest pebbles to help digest their food and small nuggets of gold were among the pebbles. Once I had the gold, I had to sell the ducks, rabbit carcasses, in fact anything I could, to pay for the ring to be made. I wanted your wedding band to be special and to come from Macraes Flat gold."

Jane sat amazed as tears of joy ran down her cheeks. She had not known that gold could be found in this way and thought it such a clever method. The mystery of how Frederick had managed to give her such a beautiful ring was now solved and she loved him more for it. She would never part with this ring and never take it off. She still couldn't believe her father and family had helped Frederick without her knowing and would thank them all when she next saw them.

Wedding Night

After her first night with Frederick Jane felt she had touched heaven as she had never known the pleasure of love making. She had heard it was an act women had to endure with their husbands but Frederick had shown her this was not true.

He had aroused such strong emotions in her as he explored her body. She had savoured his touch, his taste, and every second they shared on their first night together. As she lay in his arms the next morning she reminded herself she had totally committed to her wedding vows, and given her body and all that she possessed to Frederick, her love, her heart.

Somehow, they untangled their limbs and Frederick slid off his side of the bed but Jane did not want to get up and rolled over pretending to be asleep.

"We must get going Jeannie," he said anxiously, trying to wake her. "We will miss today's coach to Waihemo."

She knew they must return and reluctantly sat up, swung her feet onto the floor and unruffled her hair with her fingers as she stretched backwards. Frederick had dressed quickly but Jane couldn't remember putting her clothes on and only managed with her husband's help. He also tied her boot laces as he didn't want her tripping over and once he checked they had all their possessions, they scurried out of the house towards the departure point for the coach.

From previous experience he knew the coach would leave on time and, sure enough, the horse team was harnessed and the coachman eager for the journey to begin. They were the last passengers to climb on board but were grateful they had made it.

Jane spent the first part of the journey asleep on Frederick's shoulder and when she awoke, enjoyed the view of the Shag River valley they were following. He told her that the river started high in the Kakanui mountain range which borders the Maniototo, about 30 miles away, and flowed all the way to the Pacific Ocean near Palmerston. She also learnt that the early whalers named the river after a black sea bird found in the area. As she had spent the last five years in and around Macraes Flat the landscape on the journey became more familiar with rocky outcrops and snow grass tussock as they ventured inland.

Frederick's predictions about the railways opening up the countryside were proving correct as he told Jane that a new branch to Waihemo had been completed the previous month from the Main South Line in Palmerston. "This will make it easier to reach the lime deposits in the Inch Valley and the train will carry passengers and freight," he said.

After what seemed hours, the coach came to a halt by the large Junction Hotel in Waihemo. It had been built from local schist and limestone about 20 years ago and was used as a place to rest between Palmerston and Ranfurly to the north on the Pigroot and Middlemarch via Macraes Flat to the west. Passengers could take refreshments while the horses were changed so a fresh team could keep up the speed and distance required of the coach on the next leg of the journey. Frederick was expert with the horses and could immediately spot any problems or whether their hooves needed attention.

They stepped down from the coach and retrieved their bags. Jane loved to get her feet on the ground after the hard ride and rocking of the coach. Frederick suggested that as they had skipped breakfast they should have something to eat in the hotel before the long walk to where he lived. Jane was not accustomed to hotels and enjoyed being escorted inside by Frederick and shown a seat. She found the interior dark and could smell beer, but the barman and waitress were smiling and jovial which made for a good atmosphere. Other passengers were also laughing and enjoying the break in their journeys. She wondered what it might be like inside Stanley's Hotel at Macraes Flat and hoped her husband would take her as she had always wanted to go there after it was rebuilt in local stone.

They left the Junction Hotel within an hour as it looked like a thunderstorm was brewing and Frederick wanted to get going. They walked briskly along the dusty streets of the small town, passing wooden buildings and a few shops. Jane saw nothing remarkable she could use as a landmark and just hoped Waihemo would have a good community spirit like Moonlight and Macraes Flat where settlers looked out for each other. With each step she became more excited about being in charge of their household but it filled her with some trepidation as her mother and father were no longer close by to offer help and support. It would be up to her and Frederick to make ends meet, but she knew she was lucky to have her husband, a good man, who she totally believed in.

Married Life Begins in Waihemo, Otago

The rain clouds had gathered but the storm had blown over and they reached the door of the house, her new home, with dry boots. To Jane's surprise, Frederick opened the door and carried her over the threshold. She squealed with delight and hung on to him tightly. She had never been so happy and could not believe how lucky she was. Gone were thoughts of the unforgiving environment in which they must survive with few home comforts, running water or electricity. Her thoughts focused on the fact she had a loving husband and they were beginning a new life together. It was spring, and the feeling of renewal, as new flowers blossomed, was ever present. They were determined to live the best life they could and be thankful they had found each other.

Jane could not help but smile as she took off her coat and looked around the room. It was small, it needed sweeping and cleaning, there was much to be done, but not tonight; Frederick had love in his eyes and reached for his new bride to follow him to the bed.

It was nearly dark and Jane knew her second priority, Frederick being the first, was to start the fire and keep it burning. She had learnt that from her mother.

"Always have the kettle at the ready for tea or for washing," she would say.

Jane smiled to herself as she would take pride in keeping the fire alight to have hot water in the house and would make sure Frederick knew it was his job to provide the wood and peat.

They managed to eat some warm soup and bread and washed it down with beer before falling asleep in each other's arms. In the morning, rays of sunlight streamed through the window and flickered on Jane's face. She felt blessed her new life had started so well and was full of energy and optimism about their future. They both felt invincible and able to handle any obstacle that came their way.

After New Year's Eve in 1885, Jane realised she was expecting their first child. Frederick was overjoyed he was soon to become a father but Jane, although excited with the prospect of becoming a mother, knew about the difficulties of giving birth. Her mother, Margaret, was not close by to reassure her and was understandably preoccupied bringing up her own children, ranging from 3 - 16 years of age in Moonlight. She was also pregnant again with her ninth child and Jane found this worrying due to her ill health. Every winter she seemed to deteriorate further and had more trouble breathing as the cold weather took its toll.

Her mother was an amazing woman in every way however and by mid-summer 1886 had given birth to her fifth son named James, in South Palmerston. When she felt strong enough, Margaret took him back to Moonlight to be with the rest of the Harcus family. Soon after she was home, Jane decided to make a special journey to Moonlight and felt better once she had met her new brother, James. She saw that her family were thriving and the children were enjoying school, working outdoors with their father and trapping rabbits. They also never failed to laugh about hunting ducks for the gold in their gizzards.

Jane missed her large family. Her father was such a character and was becoming well known in the area as he supported the school and was in favour of other changes like the subdivision of farming land and the future expansion of the railways. She had a deep love for him and great admiration for what he was achieving on the land. She also enjoyed spending time with her younger sister Ann which was such a tonic as she heard about all the new developments in Macraes and that there was a dance soon which her sister hoped to go to. Jane missed the stores in Macraes township and longed to go to the bootmakers, the post office and the dairy and see the familiar faces of the people she knew. As yet, she had not made any new female friends in Waihemo but hoped this would change soon with a baby on the way.

Her mother told her to keep strong, that she had a good husband who would look after her so she had no need to worry. But Jane was reluctant to return on the coach. She felt isolated living in Waihemo and although she loved Fred., the days were long and lonely without him. It was her first visit since their wedding and she hadn't realised it would stir up such emotion. She loved seeing her family and would count the days until the next time.

Doctor Calls to See Jane

Late in Jane's pregnancy, Frederick was fortunate to find out when the doctor was visiting Waihemo. Jane had been experiencing unexplained pains and needed medical attention. There was always a scarcity of qualified medical people and the rural doctor had a large area to cover which included Macraes Flat, Moonlight and Waihemo. The doctor came on horseback and would sometimes have to ride through driving rain and gales, cross flooded rivers or fords to reach the sick or dying. They risked their lives on many occasions, especially in winter, as the tracks became unrecognisable due to the snow.

The doctor arrived late in the day as he had made other calls to patients on the way. Frederick was pleased as he had made it back from work to be with Jane. After the doctor examined her he said that he was concerned she may have a difficult birth and recommended they go to Dunedin Hospital immediately as there were specialist doctors who could care for her if complications arose. They agreed to leave the next day and the doctor said that he would send word of their arrival. They were alarmed that Jane was so close to giving birth but grateful for the doctor's advice. He accepted only a small fee from them and said to put the rest of their pennies towards the cost of the journey as they would need to take the coach to Palmerston and train to Dunedin.

Perhaps it was the journey or the fact their child could not wait to enter the world, but Jane's labour began before she arrived at the hospital. She was petrified there would be problems giving birth and when Frederick was asked to leave her side, it only made matters worse as she did not see him again for hours.

The pain was unbearable and the doctor had to resort to forceps to pull the child out. Thankfully on 18 September 1886, Jane was delivered of a healthy son whom they named Frederick Herbert Davis. She was weak and had lost a lot of blood but after several days rest was well enough to return to Waihemo. Frederick senior was over the moon he had a son and heir and told Jane how proud he was of her. The painful experience of giving birth was now in the past but she could not stop thinking about her mother who had been through this test of endurance nine times.

"I must let her know about our son's arrival as soon as possible," Jane said to Frederick when he came to visit her in the ward.

"Do you realise that the arrival of Frederick Herbert and the birth of my youngest brother James, in the summer this year, makes James an uncle?"

"He must be the youngest uncle ever," Frederick replied grinning.

Once back in Waihemo they lived on love. Jane had never been so tired in her life but their new son was a joy to them both. Frederick would come home totally drained after a long day labouring but would still find the energy to help with his son and the chores around the house.

When he went off to work in the morning Jane hated the fact that she would be on her own with the child for the rest of the day. The feeding, washing and lack of sleep were taking their toll and she was becoming emotional at the slightest thing. She missed her mother and family and would have given anything to see them. They were not far away, about 15 miles, but they could not afford to travel over the rough tracks to Moonlight at that time. It depressed her, but she did not share her feelings with Frederick as she knew it would worry him. She prayed that in the New Year she would be reunited with her family in Moonlight, the place she had grown to love.

In the following months Jane's mothering instincts developed and she felt more in control. On her occasional trips to town she had met other women with young children who shared their stories of child rearing which helped her.

In late summer of 1888 Jane realised she was 'with child' again. A second pregnancy concerned her at first but Frederick reassured her all would be well and they would manage. He decided, however, that he would look for work as a groom. If he found the right employer, it could involve being both a groom and coachman and the wages would be better. A groom in charge of breeding the draft horses, such as the Clydesdales or other horse breeds also interested him, as he could earn even better wages, however, he knew he was short on experience. By the time their new son, Robert Harcus Davis, arrived on 28 December 1888, Frederick was working as a groom and made journeys to Macraes Flat for supplies for his boss with a Clydesdale and dray.

Jane had her 21st birthday in May the following year and Frederick surprised her with a visit to Moonlight to see her family as he knew how much this meant to her. It was a happy day as they celebrated with a birthday cake and watched all the children laugh and play together.

A Death in the Family

In early December 1889, when the weather was starting to feel warmer, Jane was informed of the saddest news. Her brother David, only 11 years old, had died of diphtheria. He had been complaining of a stiff neck, sore throat and difficulty swallowing but his symptoms were not diagnosed in time and the nasty infectious slime spread quickly from his tonsils to other organs and he died of exhaustion and suffocation. There had been outbreaks in the district and elsewhere in the South Island for some time and as it was such a dangerous, contagious disease, the Harcus family were distraught when they discovered the cause of David's death. They were also worried they could still catch diphtheria as there were reports where people became infected 11 months after the contagion was known to be in the same room. To reduce their risk they cleaned and disinfected their hut as best they could. Robert senior also checked their drinking water supply to make sure it was not polluted and looked for stagnant waste nearby that could lead to spread of the disease. Kissing was thought to be dangerous, so they refrained but they still embraced each other at this time of great sadness.

When Margaret realised Jane was pregnant, she advised her not to come to the funeral due to the potential risk of infection, although she knew it was minor. This did not deter Jane as she desperately wanted to support her grieving family. Frederick accompanied her and was able to borrow a wagon for the journey.

They set off early with the children and headed directly for the Macraes Flat cemetery. It was the saddest day she could recall as never in her wildest dreams did she think she would be present at her younger brother's burial. She watched from a distance and clung to Frederick and their children. Her eyes filled with tears as her father and brothers, William and Robert, slowly carried the small coffin toward its final resting place. The minister, who had ridden to Macraes on horseback to give the service, was standing by the graveside holding the Bible. Her mother and the rest of the family walked behind the coffin, then gathered in a circle around the deep grave.

Jane walked closer so she could hear the prayers and committal from the Rev. Robert also paid tribute to his brave boy who fought to his last breath. Macraes earth was sprinkled on the coffin and Margaret threw in a wild flower. It was over, they could go and try to resume a normal life.

Margaret and Robert could see Jane and Frederick and came to within a few yards of them. Jane saw the pain on their faces and thought that her mother looked ill. It would be weeks before Jane would return to Moonlight and she wished she could offer more help to her family but she did not live close enough. Her sister Ann was still at home, which was a blessing, but she was worried for her mother's ailing health which would be weakened further by David's passing.

Jane and Frederick hardly spoke on their return journey to Waihemo. He knew Jane had a lot on her mind and needed time to process her thoughts and feelings. After a long silence and with her head still lowered, Jane spoke,

"Life can be so cruel and unfair."

"Yes," said Frederick. "It has been a painful day but now we have our own children, we must be thankful they are safe and well."

"I will protect them with my life," Jane replied.

"And I will always protect you and our children, while there is strength in my body."

Frederick placed his arm firmly around her shoulder and Jane knew he meant every word.

With a new son, Robert, and Frederick junior only two years three months, she had little time to dwell on the loss of her brother David as she was permanently tired. Fear of her own children catching diphtheria or other diseases haunted her but she knew it was something all mothers had to live with.

Frederick was away more than he was home due to his new employment and that meant all the domestic chores fell heavily on her shoulders. But her love for him never faltered. He was trying to improve their livelihood, she understood.

They soldiered on but in late summer of 1891 Jane fell pregnant again and gave birth to another son, George William Davis in Waihemo on 9 November. With three children, the eldest just over five years old, her domestic chores had increased yet again and her energy and fortitude were stretched to the limit. She needed to see her mother and longed to talk to her.

After spending another day on her own, Jane was waiting for Fred. to return from Macraes. It was gone 10.00 p.m. and he had still not arrived. She was fretting as she knew the dangers of driving a coach or a dray on the rough road between Macraes Flat and Waihemo. Outside, it was dark, there was a chill in the air due to the high altitude, and the wind had whipped up into a fierce gale.

Coach Accident by Cranky Jim's Creek

Frederick was returning to Waihemo and close to Cranky Jim's Creek on a bend in the road. He had been struggling to control the big Clydesdale which was pulling the dray as the wind had changed and a sudden gust spooked the horse which turned violently and swung the dray around so the back wheels slid down a shallow gully. With not a second to waste, Frederick jumped off the wagon and took hold of the horse's bridle. He had to use all his strength to steady the animal and, very slowly, it was able to pull the dray back up to the road. After he removed the mud, he found the rear wheels were not damaged and set off again towards Waihemo, thanking God he had come to no harm.

The gale was still relentless. As he rounded the next bend he was shocked to find that the mail coach had been blown off track and a man was lying on the ground under one of the wheels. His heart raced as an accident such as this, on a remote road, had always been his worst fear when he drove coaches from Palmerston.

He pulled up his horse, led it to an old hut near the side of the road, and tied the reins to a post. He then rushed over to the man on the ground who was not moving. There was no one else around so he assumed he must be the reinsman. Frederick tried to lift up the wheel a few inches but it was a dead weight and he decided he needed the horses to help. Carefully he approached them and grasped the reins of the front two mares. They were shaking their heads in the wind and pawing the ground with their hooves so he had a job to steady them. Once the front horses had calmed down, the two at the rear quietened and, very slowly, he urged them to walk on a few feet which was enough to pull the wheel from on top of the coach driver.

There was still no movement or sound from the man once he was free and Frederick feared for his life. He managed to carry him inside the hut and was startled when a preacher came out from the shadows. He had been the only passenger and was saying prayers and clutching his Bible. Frederick placed the bleeding man on the crude bed but his body was lifeless, his eyes had rolled upwards and there was no sign of him breathing. They concluded he was most probably dead. The preacher began saying more prayers and was visibly shaken that he had survived this nasty mishap as he had been thrown clear. He was in no fit state to make decisions so Frederick decided the best thing to do was head back to Macraes to find Constable Rooney who would deal with the matter. The preacher would have to remain alone with the dead man until help arrived. Frederick left the Clydesdale and dray secured and rode one of the coach horses back to Macraes as it was faster. His other main concern was the fact he could not get a message to Jane to tell her of the delay and knew she would be worried sick.

He arrived back in Waihemo at dawn the next day. Jane had sat up all night waiting for him.

"Never do this to me again," she pleaded. "I thought you were dead."

Frederick could only apologise for the unfortunate series of events and, after he told her the story, she held on to him tightly and did not want to let him go.

The Move Back to Macraes

Jane had always missed her family. Her mother was a source of inspiration to her and she now realised she needed to live closer to the Harcus farm at Moonlight. She was concerned for her mother's health which had deteriorated further after the tragic loss of her young brother, David, and being closer would mean she could keep an eye on her.

One night, after Frederick returned home, Jane had a long talk with him so she could explain why she no longer wanted to remain in Waihemo. He had a reasonable job grooming horses for the coaches that stopped at the Junction

Hotel but agreed to look for other work in the Macraes area. He wanted Jane to be happy and understood it would better all round if they lived closer to her family. He also never wanted to put her through the agony of thinking he had died in a coach accident ever again. She was overjoyed at the prospect of moving which lifted her mood and gave her more energy.

Frederick knew, before they got married, that New Zealand was suffering from a depression and there were fewer jobs. Free immigration had slowed dramatically and now there were more settlers leaving the country to go to places such as Australia, than there were arriving. There was also a poll tax on Chinese immigrants and the number of Chinese settlers had nearly halved. He did not feel that confident about finding another job but knew he was fit and strong for his age, experienced at working on the land and remained hopeful something would turn up.

After a few weeks he was fortunate, and found work as a farm labourer in the Macraes area. The wages were not good and there would be less work in the winter months but they could survive for now. The farmer also knew of a hut that was available for Frederick and his family to live in. He couldn't wait to let Jane know they could plan their move back to Macraes and tell their eldest sons they would be enrolled in the Moonlight school.

Women Get the Right to Vote, 1893

Jane had little spare time for herself or to read the newspapers but there was a woman she loved to hear about as people were debating her cause. Her name was Kate Sheppard and she was striving to help women get a voice and vote in society. It was a male dominated world and on the whole, men were not in favour of women getting the vote and having more freedoms. Women had been denied freedom of speech and the vote due to male dominated parliaments for too long and wanted things to change. Kate Sheppard and her colleagues felt so strongly that they had organised massive suffrage petitions for women over 21 to sign so they could lobby parliament to change the law.

Jane loved her words. "Do not think your single vote does not matter much. The rain that refreshes the parched ground is made up of single drops."

Jane's sister Ann, had moved to find work in Dunedin and she hoped she had signed the current suffrage petition. Jane was 24 years old and would have signed it herself if she was able, but she lived too far from the city. She was aware many things needed to change for women and having a vote was a huge first step.

On 19 September 1893, Kate Sheppard, the figurehead of the suffragette movement in New Zealand, succeeded in winning the right for women to vote in parliamentary elections as Governor, Lord Glasgow, signed a new Electoral Act into law. Other countries followed but the UK parliament resisted giving all woman a vote until 1928.

Jane was thrilled when she heard this news and was interested to know what her father thought. Frederick said that it was only fair that women could vote but he was the younger generation, the older men were more against the decision.

Between winning the right for woman, including Māori women, to vote in September 1893 and the General Election in November when the Liberal Party's, Richard Seddon became Prime Minister, Jane gave birth to another son on 31 October at Macraes. They called him Thomas Makepeace Davis.

Thomas's middle name was the surname of Frederick's mother, Ellen Makepeace. She married Frederick's father in 1834 in Westbury, Buckinghamshire and went to live in Finmere, Oxfordshire. Jane and Frederick never wanted their children to forget that their roots came from England and Scotland.

Now with four sons, Jane got some relief during the day when the older boys, Frederick junior and Robert were enrolled in the Moonlight school. She loved to share her memories of the school with them and often asked if they had learnt about the Moa hunters as she had always been fascinated by their stories.

As Jane had hoped she was able to see her mother and family more often. It gave her great comfort as she had a special bond with her mother and loved being in her company. Her father took delight in seeing his eldest daughter and growing horde of grandchildren who he never failed to amuse.

Early in 1895 Jane realised she was pregnant once more. The thought of another child to feed and clothe worried her deeply but Frederick and her mother told her she would manage. The grim reminder of the pain during childbirth returned. If only there was a way of preventing more pregnancies, Jane often said to herself. But she knew the only way was abstinence and this was impossible, as she could not stop her husband making love to her. It was the most precious thing, it meant too much to them both.

On 18 October 1895 Margaret Harcus Davis was born in Macraes. She was named after Jane's mother. A bonnie girl, Jane fell in love with her from the moment she arrived. Her older brothers were infatuated by their tiny sister whose turn it now was to occupy the crib.

Gold still being Discovered in Straith Taieri, Otago

Around about the time of the New Zealand and South Seas Exhibition in Dunedin, in 1889-1890 which commemorated the 50th anniversary of British sovereignty in the colony, gold was found in the Nenthorn valley. New Zealand was in a depression and news of the Nenthorn gold rush, not far from Moonlight, caused great excitement in the city and Otago. Companies quickly invested in the area to uncover the gold-bearing quartz reefs but the returns were disappointing in relation to the time and effort of sinking shafts below ground. Within a short period of time companies found themselves in liquidation, mines were abandoned and the rush petered out.

In the 1890s, Frederick continued to follow reports in the *Mount Ida Chronicle* about new gold mines and claims in the area. He could not deny that the quest to find the illusive mineral, gold, was a temptation. He was living too far away in Waihemo during the Nenthorn rush but, now they had moved, he was interested to learn there were still other reef mining opportunities in the Macraes area. With a wife and five children to support, he needed to earn more money. So when he heard that miners were needed to work the Mount Highlay reef which had been discovered in the Mareburn Creek some time ago, he put himself forward.

Within a few days he was offered a contract to work at the Mount Highlay mine. His next step was to talk to Jane and convince her of his plan. She had not been aware that he was considering changing his job and was taken by surprise when he sat her down to tell her the news. He told her it would be hard work but, as the mine was close to Hyde, he would be home regularly. He also said that it would be constant work, not seasonal as was sometimes the case with farm labouring. Jane knew it meant moving to Hyde and was not in favour as she would be further away from her family in Moonlight. She had also heard that Hyde could be difficult to get to when the nearby Taieri River flooded as the tracks became dangerous and often impassable. She hated the thought of being alone again and isolated in a place she didn't know.

Frederick understood her fears but insisted it was an opportunity not to be missed. In the end, she had little choice but to go along with his plan. He was the sole provider for the family and could earn more money. She had her doubts but admired his optimistic spirit as, like her father, he was trying to make things better and improve their prospects.

The Move to Hyde, Otago circa 1897

Frederick found a place to live and they moved to Hyde. The older Davis boys, who had taken exams at the end of 1896, were sad to leave the Moonlight School and their friends, but their faces lit up when they heard they could go to the school in Hyde. Originally the school was in an iron church and freezing in winter but a wooden school had now been built which had two classrooms. They could attend as soon as the family settled in.

Jane and her family were now living about 12 miles to the west of Macraes Flat. It was a small town at the end of the Hyde - Macraes main road and at the northern end of the Rock and Pillar mountain range. She never had a desire to go there in the past and could only think of the problems caused by snow and flooding which delayed supplies and the mail coach reaching Hyde on its way to Naseby.

Frederick, trying to humour Jane, told her more about the town's history.
"It was originally called Eight Mile as years ago it was close to eight miles from the Hamilton's gold field. During the Eight Mile rush in the 1860s, when gold was found in the Hyde gully, an early settlement sprang up including shops and hotels

built of only canvas. It was renamed Hyde in 1864 and became a lively place with frequent horse racing balls and suppers."

"Did the gold run out?" Jane asked. "It's not like that now?"

Frederick went on to say that the easy pickings for gold got harder to find and many prospectors left to chase gold nearer Macraes or elsewhere. The richest finds were deeper underground and needed shafts to be dug or water to sluice the large amount of soil. Some of the miners got together to develop water races from the Rock and Pillars, but it wasn't until mining companies were formed, who could use more land for sluicing and build longer water races for their mining operations, that yields improved. The population of Hyde reduced dramatically but some remained to take steady work at the mining companies and settled in the area.

"Those people who still thought there was plenty of gold to be found had to work for the companies who could raise the money for the equipment to crush the quartz and extract the gold. I am grateful these companies still exist," Frederick said. "It has given me this new opportunity."

Mount Highlay Mine

The Mareburn or Mount Highlay reef was discovered some years before, in 1887, and Frederick now had the chance to work at the mine, an established operation, which extracted gold and scheelite.

He had never worked in a reef mine before so the dust from blasting and erecting wooden shafts underground in dim light was daunting and claustrophobic. Sometimes they had to bail out underground water and it was cold and damp work. His clothes were always covered in dust or sodden with sweat and water. It was difficult to breath at times and the most physically challenging toil he had ever experienced. Occasionally he got to load the schist onto the Tramway above ground. It took the rock to the Battery which meant he would be in the fresh air for at least a few minutes.

Despite everyone's efforts, they extracted low grade gold and scheelite but at least the mine was still working as it had changed ownership many times since the Mount Highlay Consolidated Quartz Mining Company formed in 1888.

Frederick Becomes Unwell

Jane was at home with the youngest children when she heard loud rapping on the door. She was startled by the urgency of the knocking and shocked when the door flew open to see her husband slumped between two miners who were holding him up. It was a bitterly cold afternoon and the men brought him in quickly along with the chilling wind. She ran to help and guided them to the bed where they laid him down. They told her that Fred. had been having trouble breathing when working below ground in the mine and they had been asked by the boss to take him home.

"Better get the doctor to take a look at him," one of the men said.

Jane knew how difficult it was to get the doctor as he covered such a wide area but would make enquiries in the town.

"We better get going," the other man said. "The boss needs us back at the mine."

Jane tried to make Frederick comfortable but he was in too much discomfort to notice. She took off his dusty jacket and boots, gave him water which he could barely swallow, and propped him up with a pillow. He was in pain but she could not understand what was wrong with him. She had to find a doctor urgently.

The older boys were still at school, so she took the younger children to the town to find help. She was unsure how to find a doctor as they had not lived in Hyde very long and thankfully had not needed medical assistance until now. She was about to ask a stranger for help on the dusty main road but saw the post office and rushed inside. She found out the name of the doctor was Dr Shields and was advised by the postmaster to send him a telegram. All she could do was wait and hope that he would arrive soon.

She lay awake listening to the rain lash their small house and to Frederick's laboured breathing beside her. It was a long distressing night. She was relieved when Dr Shields arrived the next morning. He looked exhausted however, as he had battled his way through the night in the chilling wind and rain from St Bathans which was over 50 miles away. There was also a sprinkling of snow on the nearby Rock and Pillar range, so they were still in the grip of winter with few signs of spring.

Dr Shields immediately went over to examine Frederick who was on the bed. He got out his stethoscope and Jane watched him use it on her husband's chest and back. Frederick was having problems speaking but the doctor ascertained he had become ill at the mine and now his chest was so painful it was becoming increasingly more difficult for him to breathe.

As the doctor turned towards Jane, she handed him a cup of tea which he accepted. He welcomed the hot liquid and took a long sip to help warm himself. Then with a grave look on his face he slowly spoke.

"I have done all I can for your husband. I fear he has a problem with his lungs which cannot be treated."

Jane looked at him bewildered, "but there must be something you can do?"

"I am very sorry, my dear. I can give him something for the pain, but that is all."

Jane stood rivetted to the floor in disbelief.

"I must be going," Dr Shields said with his eyes lowered. "I have another patient to attend."

He left a powder for Frederick's pain and handed her the cup.

When he opened the door on his way out, a bird suddenly fluttered into the room. The children immediately leapt up to try and catch it but it was too quick and acrobatic for them. Dr Shields paused and looked back towards the children.

"I have seen this NZ bird with white eyebrows and a long black and white tail before. The Māoris call it a *piwakawaka* but it is otherwise known as a fantail due to its beautiful tail." The children smiled and carried on trying to catch it.

He stopped himself telling the rest of the story as he had been told the *piwakawaka* was a messenger of death in Māori mythology.

Jane thought Dr Shields was a polite, genial man but she did not believe what he told her about Frederick's condition. She carried on nursing him as best she could and prayed for his recovery. But he would not eat or drink and every day became weaker. He was slowly fading away before her.

After seven days, his breathing became increasingly more erratic and Jane was helpless to offer him any further remedy. She knew he needed laudanum to ease his suffering but she had no means of acquiring the opium tincture.

Frederick's cheeks were now hollow, his eyes had sunk into their sockets and his body was thin and emaciated. Early in the morning on the 29 August 1897, when she returned with a damp cloth to moisten his face, she noticed that the rattling from his windpipe had ceased and his eyes were wide open, staring at the wall. She waited for his chest to rise and clung to his limp hand willing him to live, but he had taken his last breath. His soul had left him, he was now a corpse.

"Don't leave me," she wailed. And the children, who were huddled in the corner, were distraught as they watched their mother crumble and sink to the floor.

Dr Shields was recalled and was accompanied by Dr Fletcher. They pronounced Frederick Davis, aged 44 years, had died from inflammation of the lungs.

Jane could not remember how she survived the day of Frederick's burial in the Hyde Cemetery, 48 hours after his death. Her family came from Moonlight to support her as did many of the people from Hyde but she was in shock and denial that her husband had left her. When the coffin was slowly lowered into the ground she was drawn into this dark, cold space as she could only see a life of uncertainty and suffering ahead of her. Soon she would be destitute. The fear about the future of her five children consumed her as she had no way to provide for them.

Jane returns to the Hyde Cemetery

Within days of Frederick's death Jane returned to the Hyde Cemetery and stumbled through the ornate iron gates towards the graves, which were nestled in front of high trees on the cemetery boundary. Dr Shields, who had come to help her husband, had died. On his way overnight from St Bathans to be at Frederick's side he had caught a chill when battling through the extreme weather. The retired doctor of the area, Dr Fletcher, came from Middlemarch to help save his colleague but he was beyond medical help. There were no antibiotics in 1897 and he died from the same cause as Frederick - inflammation of the lungs.

There was an outpouring of grief from the town's people for Dr Shields as he was a young man of 36 years, was well liked and respected and had only been practising in Hyde for about two years.

Jane stood at the graveside holding Margaret, nearly two years old, in her arms whilst her other children, aged three, five, eight and ten years, hovered round her skirt. She was trembling and her head was bowed as Rev. Griffiths recited the final committal prayers. She was unable to look at Dr Sheild's widow, Mary, on the opposite side of the grave as she felt so guilty. It was because her selfless husband came to try and save Frederick that he lost his own life. Now they had both lost the most important person in their worlds. It was like a double wound to Jane - the knife had been torn out of her heart to stab her again.

Jane Struggles to Provide for her Children in Hyde

The people of Hyde did not blame Jane for the death of Dr Shields but she was inconsolable. They were concerned for her welfare and during the interval at a local concert for the Hyde Cemetery the town had a collection for her and the children and raised £3.

Jane would never forget the kindness and generosity from the Hyde community and spent every penny she was given carefully. She still desperately needed a regular income as Frederick had been the family's sole means of support. But whenever she tried to find suitable employment it became impossible due to the young age of her children. Margaret, her only daughter, was not yet two years and needed her constantly as did her other young children. Jane despaired as everyday was a struggle to feed them and keep a roof over their heads. She prayed for more help from her mother but she was unwell, and the rest of her large family had their own problems.

As a last resort, she applied to the Benevolent Institution in Dunedin for help. She was grateful when her application was successful and thereafter received 7s 6d per week. With five growing children to provide for, plus rent, it was not enough to survive on. She knew of someone who had fostered a young boy and they had received 7 shillings a week for just one child. Her situation did not improve, and towards the end of March 1898, she was forced to apply for an increase to her weekly amount. To her surprise, her request was granted, allowing her an extra 2s a week. She could still not make ends meet on this level of subsidy and, with no other choices left to her, she made the hardest decision of her life. Jane asked for help from Constable O'Brien of the Hyde Police to have her children committed to the Caversham Industrial School in Dunedin for their safe-keeping. The school had a good reputation for helping orphaned or neglected children and she hoped they would have a better future there. Based on Jane's circumstances the Maniototo County Council recommended that the Davis children be sent to the orphanage.

Jane Returns to Dunedin

Jane realised she must go to Dunedin but the thought of giving up her children became unbearable once she arrived and she could not bring herself to part with them. They were her world, all she had left, and to not have them near her or touch their soft skin was inconceivable. She could hardly breathe at times during the day, her anguish became so intense. Her dearest mother Margaret was also in Dunedin for hospital treatment but unfortunately could not help her as she was slowly dying of consumption.

Jane struggled on and became weaker as she would often sacrifice her own food for the sake of the children. Her heart still ached for Frederick. She missed him more as each day passed and could not fathom how the love she had shared with her husband had turned to dust so quickly. She remembered her mother's words and wanted to tell her of the love she had known with Frederick, pure, true love which she found impossible to live without.

During the day if she heard the song of the NZ Bellbird or Tui in the trees nearby it always appeared louder when she walked past as if Frederick was calling her. Sometimes at night, when the children where fast asleep, she would creep out and search for him in the shadows around Great King Street where she lived, but he always eluded her. One night she followed a shadow and found herself in a dingy, pungent opium den. She was tempted to numb her grief but when asked to trade her wedding ring for a pipe, she refused vehemently and a woman called Opium Mag let her out as she saw the pain in her eyes. She had sworn to never take off her wedding band, made from Macraes Flat gold, and could never pawn it. It was too precious to her.

As the days and weeks went by Jane became more unwell and unable to cope. She could not accept she was nearly destitute and that life had been so cruel as to take her Frederick so young. Throughout her life she had always been strong and able to handle changing circumstances but to have the most precious thing in her life, the love of Frederick, taken so suddenly, was an inconsolable burden. She also knew the only way to save her children from further suffering was to have them committed to the Caversham Industrial School but the agony of losing them was too great.

A Lonely Christmas in 1898

Christmas Day had passed in Dunedin but Jane had hardly noticed. Her little Margaret had turned three years on the 18th of October and Robert would be 11 years on the 28th of December but her thoughts were elsewhere. It was late and all five children were fast asleep. As she watched their innocent, beautiful faces she said a quiet prayer.

"Have a long and happy life, my angels.

Keep reaching for the stars and do not be afraid of the dark.

I hope you find love one day when you grow up, it is a gift, hold on to it for as long as you can."

She kissed each child on the forehead then slowly crawled to her bed on the other side of the room. Normally she fought sleep as every night a black cloud of fear descended on her when she closed her eyes. It was a frightening dark world, like a room with no way of escape. On the 27th of December 1898 however, Jane could not stop her eyelids from closing after she lay down. She became aware this night was different, as there appeared to be a way out of the dark room. Slowly she was drawn to a bright opening in the distance and could see someone, a man, standing there waiting. She reached out for his hand.

Frederick junior, who was 12 years old, awoke first and went over to see his mother who lay motionless on the bed. He was soon joined by his brothers Robert, George and Thomas. When his sister Margaret woke up, Frederick junior picked her up and went back to his mother. They all tried to rouse her. They shook her gently, said they were sorry for the bad things they had done, but she did not wake. She lay still with a faint smile on her lips.

Explanatory Notes

The verdict of the jury was death from natural causes and Coroner Carey ruled that Jane died from failure of the heart. Others in her family believed she had died from a broken heart. Her unfortunate death was 16 months after her husband Frederick passed away - he was the love of her life.

Jane (Robertina) Davis (nee Harcus) was my Great Grandmother. She died aged 30 years and is buried in the Northern Cemetery, Dunedin. Block 54. Plot 54. Her tragedy continued even in death, as when I visited the cemetery, I could not find her grave, (a joint plot with 3 others) and I discovered, with sadness, that another plot had been placed on top of hers due to a lack of space in the cemetery at that time.

Frederick's death – It is thought by some in the family that he was killed in a coach accident but I have not found any evidence to support this story. He worked as a groom at times in his life however. His death in Hyde was reported in several newspapers including the *Otago Daily Times*, *Otago Witness, Mount Ida Chronicle,* stating that he worked at the Mount Highlay Mine where he contracted an illness which developed into inflammation of the lungs (today we call it pneumonia), and he was sent home where he died eight days later. Dr Shields and Dr Fletcher certified his death before he was buried in the Hyde cemetery.

Although his wife, Jane, received aid from the Benevolent Institution, it was not sufficient to support her family. In the late 19th century, it was extremely difficult for a widow to find work and care for five children at the same time. When Jane died, she left her children destitute as there was no one who could look after them as their parents were dead and Jane's mother, Margaret, was slowly dying of consumption, (tuberculosis) and unable to help. She lost her battle in 1900.

The Police took the Davis children and they were committed to the Caversham Industrial School in Lookout Point, Dunedin, on 5 January 1899. Frederick junior was 12 years, Robert was 10, George was 7 and Thomas 5 years. Jane's daughter Margaret, my Grandmother, was just 3 years old.

The Industrial School opened in 1869. Few inmates were orphaned children, the majority had been neglected or removed from their parents by the courts due to the child's criminal activity. Many came from families with difficulties, such as parents in prison or with alcohol problems. Some had been removed from 'immoral' situations such as living with prostitutes. Others were illegitimate - their mothers could not work and also look after them.

At the time the Davis children were committed to the school government policy had shifted to a 'boarding out' (fostering) policy and they were split up. Frederick remained in the school in Dunedin and did well being voted most popular boy at the end of 1899 for which he received a prize. The other children were quickly entrusted to guardians (boarded out) and attended other schools. George, Thomas, and Maggie ended up staying in the Oamaru area. Frederick junior and Robert went to the North Island.

The Industrial school provided a good grounding for children and helped them to take up trade apprenticeships if they were over 12 years. At 14 years old they became eligible for farm or domestic work and their foster parents could also help them find suitable work.

New Zealand's fortunes changed in the new 20th century. From 1900 and after the long depression, the country prospered again. Refrigeration in ships opened up overseas markets for meat and butter, dairy farming expanded and other industries and services grew. With jobs on offer, the flow of immigration returned.

Years later in 1914, George and Thomas Davis enlisted in WW1. Their brother Robert followed in 1915 and although wounded in action, he was the only one to return.

George was killed in action in Egypt Canal Zone on 9 August 1916 and has a grave in Kantara War Memorial Cemetery, Egypt. His name also appears on the WW1 Memorial in Pleasant Point, Canterbury, New Zealand.

Thomas was killed on the battlefield on 12 October 1917 in Ypres, Belgium also known as the Battle of Passchendaele. He is remembered on the Tyne Cot Memorial, Tyne Cot Cemetery, West – Vlaanderen, Belgium.

Robert fought in Egypt and returned to New Zealand to be discharged on 5 September 1919 after nearly four years war service. He died in New Plymouth on 5 September 1970 but had previously lived in Auroa, Taranaki.

Frederick junior worked in the Whanganui Fire Service and died in Whanganui on 25 October 1963. He married Elizabeth Perrett in Manawatu, Whanganui in 1909.

My Grandmother Margaret Davis, (Jane's only daughter) married James McBeath in Weston, near Oamaru on 23 April 1919 before they came to live in Dunedin. She had 3 children. Margaret South (nee McBeath), Jean Law (nee McBeath) and Thomas Lennox McBeath.

My mother, Jean Law, was named after Jane (Robertina) as Jane's husband Frederick Davis liked to call her Jean or Jeannie.

Jane's wedding ring made from Macraes Flat gold is now in my possession and was passed down from my mother in 2014 after she died. She had always treasured it as I do.

Otago Girls' High School, Dunedin is said to be the oldest girls' school in the southern hemisphere. In the 1970s, one hundred years after Jane arrived, I attended this secondary school and achieved an education my Great Grandmother was denied. I also tried to attend the 150th Anniversary of OGHS, 1871 – 2021, but it was cancelled due to the COVID-19 pandemic restrictions in New Zealand.

Finally, in honour of Jane's childhood dream of one day reaching the crow's nest on a sailing ship, I achieved this for her by climbing to the crow's nest on a five masted clipper sailing ship on my 62nd birthday in 2018. I quickly overcame my fear and once I had squeezed through onto the small platform, I was spellbound by the panoramic view from high above the ship. I thought of Olrig Hill, Caithness, of Eday Orkney, of the storms in the Southern Ocean. I felt free, and with the wind in my face, I looked towards the horizon and thought what's next ….

Acknowledgements

I would like to thank my husband, writer Jago Harris, for his help and comments and to colleagues, friends and family who provided feedback.

A special thanks to Teresa Scott on behalf of the South Canterbury Genealogy Society, previously the South Canterbury Branch of the New Zealand Society of Genealogists, NZSG, for her research on Frederick Davis and the plight of the Davis children, David Frame from Invercargill, New Zealand for sharing precious information about the Harcus family after his extensive research and to H. M. Thomson for compiling the most excellent account of life East of the Rock and Pillar, *A History of the Straith Taieri and Macraes District*.

Printed in Great Britain
by Amazon